CINNAMON BAY

CINNAMON BAY

A SUN KISSED ROMANCE

BEATRIX EATON

Starfish Publishing

PO BOX 2753

Kennebunkport, Maine 04046

First Starfish Paperback Edition September 2024

ISBN   979-8-9900853-1-2

ISBN   979-8-9900853-0-5 (ebook)

Written in the U.S.A.

For my husband,
who only likes islands he can drive to.

Author note:

Writing Isa's story was a dream come true for me. I hope you enjoy her story as much as I do. St. John is a real place, with real people, and I hope I've portrayed them well.

Bright skies and warm beaches have their bad days, however, and Isa has gone through her fair share of them. She experiences an unexpected pregnancy, and she's a survivor of domestic violence, some of which is shown on the page. If you are a survivor, I wish you nothing but good days! Please take care of yourself, and be aware that physical and emotional abuse from Isa's ex-husband is portrayed on the page.

If you need help in the US, please reach out to the National Domestic Violence Hotline by calling 1-800-799-SAFE (7233) or visiting https://www.thehotline.org/.

PROLOGUE

February 10

Raindrops hit the roof, a continuous weeping that echoes the state of my soul. I've cried for hours—days—until my well is dry. My eyes sting and burn.

After tomorrow, I'll no longer be Mrs. Ben Cushing. After tomorrow, I'll no longer be a full-time mother to Luke and Cole.

I shift on the couch and put my feet on the coffee table to stretch my weary body. A pile of unopened mail falls onto the floor as I cross and uncross my feet. I can't find it in myself to care.

My husband of seven years is staying at his mother's house with our sons. I should have seen it coming. He never does anything nice for the boys, but he volunteered to drive when his mother called to invite them over to decorate gingerbread houses. Carol and I don't get along well—she's always saying Ben could've done better when picking a wife—so I used the time to finish wrapping the few gifts I had purchased for the boys.

When they didn't return in time for bedtime, I started to worry. Ben had never kept the boys out that late. When I called to ask Ben when they'd be home, he laughed at me and said they were already home.

"We'll be staying at Mom's until you can get your shit together and move out of my house," he said. "My sons won't be raised by a waste of space." He paused, then added, "Divorce papers will be served on Monday, and the house is going up for sale." The phone went dead, leaving me empty, lost, and mysti-fied. I stood there in the kitchen, staring into nothing, not coming back to earth until the dial tone kicked in.

Two months later, I still feel empty and lost. I'd done every-thing I could to be a good wife, but it wasn't enough. Our house had never looked like my dream, but it was our home. I used to take pride in keeping it neat. I kept everything perfect, making sure to tidy up the kids' toys before Ben got home from work every day, night, or whatever time he decided to show up.

A sudden heavy downpour startles me out of my trance and I shove the memories away, then bend over to pick up the mail. It's mostly bills, but I catch the flash of Kennebunk Library's return address as I flip through the pile.

The library has been my savior ever since the first time I visited, checking out *What to Expect When You're Expecting* after the first pregnancy test showed two pink lines six years ago. During the long days with an infant, I'd decided it was more enjoyable to pace in the library's reference room, looking at all the old portraits on the wall, than to stay confined in our tiny home. Some days, I'd even get a reprieve when other patrons would coo over Luke and offer to hold him.

When Cole came along two years after Luke, I took advan-tage of all the toddler classes, encouraging Luke to play with the other children while Cole slept in a front carrier. Eventually, I even talked to Ben about me getting a job at the library to earn household money, but he was angry. Said it would embarrass him—it would look like he didn't provide enough for our family.

Ben's anger is a fearsome thing, so I dropped the subject. Instead I became a volunteer, shelving books and helping patrons find titles while Luke and Cole play quietly in the children's section. Whenever I can, I give a few dollars here or there to the Friends of the Kennebunk Library, the fundraising arm, in gratitude for all the free programs we've attended and all the books we've borrowed over the years.

"Don't tell me I have an overdue book," I say with a sigh as I pull the envelope from the pile. Mine is the first human voice I've heard all day. The rest of the mail I put into a Hannaford's grocery bag. I'm way too nice to not give Ben all the bills that are due; I'll take them with me to the courthouse tomorrow. What they say is true: nice girls finish last.

After I slip my finger under the cream-colored flap and pull out the contents, the Friends logo in the letterhead grabs my attention. Huh. I don't think I've ever received a letter from them—at least not one on fancy paper.

January 20, the letter begins. I didn't realize I'd neglected the mail for so long.

Dear Isa,

Congratulations! You've won the grand prize in the Friends of the Kennebunk Library's annual New Year's "Start the Year off Write" raffle contest: a getaway to St. John, USVI! Your prize includes round trip airfare from Portland, Maine, and hotel accommodations at the Cinnamon Bay Villas for two people. You're scheduled to fly out on February 25. Please contact us as soon as possible to claim your prize.

Thank you for your support of literacy and our local library!

Martha Sullivan
Director, Friends of the Kennebunk Library

I've won? I've won a trip? I've never won anything. Even Ben, who I thought was such a prize when we met in college, had turned out to be fool's gold. He didn't even take me on a honeymoon, just borrowed a buddy's cabin and had a good ol' time drinking Natty Light and watching his teams on the eighty-five-inch TV until we left for home the next day.

Well, at least Martha seems excited for me. The trip is for two; it comes a little late for me and Ben. Who can I take with me?

I think about all the people I know, but none of them are close friends. Ben made sure of that. When I wasn't taking care of the house and the boys or sneaking away to the library for a few precious stolen hours a week, I worked in our garden. I'd resorted to growing our own produce to offset the meager amount Ben gave me for groceries each month. I don't know where his money went. He should've been earning a decent wage as a kitchen manager, but I never saw any evidence of it.

The library offered adult-oriented programs in the evening, and I might have made friends there, but Ben was never home consistently, so I couldn't plan to attend any of them. Also, Ben demanded that I have a hot meal waiting for him when he got home, and that could have been anytime. Long hours on his feet meant he never wanted to cook for himself.

I can't remember the last time I spent quality time with someone who wholeheartedly enjoyed my company. Yes, the library ladies dote on the boys and are appreciative of my help, but they're in their sixties and older. I don't *relate* to them.

Ben was my best friend in college—or at least, that's what I thought. When he proposed, I looked around and realized I didn't have anyone to share my happiness. All the girls I'd been friends with during my first two years had disappeared; Ben had thoroughly isolated me. And now I don't even have him. Before he moved out, he rarely touched me, except when he wanted to *relax*. After Cole was born, Ben insisted I get the birth control shot. Condoms were too restrictive, he said.

I chuckle ruefully. The honeymoon was over before it ever started.

Ben's typical thump at the door pulls me from my thoughts. I put the letter back in the envelope and tuck it under the sofa cushion. I don't want him to take my prize like he's taken everything else.

When I open the door, Ben stands there in the dark, wet from the rain. The cold damp air from the storm almost knocks me over.

I don't say anything, just look at him, trying to keep from shivering. Why is he here the night before our divorce is finalized? Has the house finally sold? Has he had a change of heart? Is he here to apologize? I'm willing to forgive him for everything and start fresh if it means I get my boys back. He's broken my trust, but I'm willing to give him one more chance for the kids' sake.

"Damn, it's cold out here. Let me in?" Ben smiles as he takes a step toward me.

I fold my arms and stay where I am. "Did you forget something?"

"No, I just wanted to talk. See how you're doing."

"Oh." Maybe I'm right and he's having second thoughts.

"I miss you." Ben shoulders his way past me and into the house. He grabs a towel from the linen closet and dries off his hair, then drapes it around his neck and unbuttons his sodden shirt. I slowly close the door, my belly twisting with nerves—whether they're from hope or despair, I don't know.

I fall back against the door when I realize Ben has toweled off his chest and is removing his pants. "What are you doing?" My voice rises at the end of my question.

"Isa." His voice is deep, an echo of the man who claimed my full attention between Psych 205 and Comms 212. Just as then, a shiver runs down my spine, but like the unidentified source of my nervousness, I can't tell whether I feel lust or revulsion.

He drops his pants and strips off his briefs in one quick movement, then wraps the towel around his waist. His handsome face is stretched into a big smile as he steps over the pile of wet shoes and clothes and saunters over to me. He runs his hands up my arms to my shoulders, then lifts my limp hair from around my neck and kisses me below my ear. I curse my body, which reacts to the first touch I've had in more than a month by flooding me with warmth.

"Please don't do this tonight. If you need something for the boys, I'll go get it for them, but I just don't have it in me to play games."

"No, Isa. I came to see you." Ben drops my hair and looks into my eyes, and I see hope. "I've had a lot of time to think, and I really miss you. I miss us." He steps back, then stoops and gathers up his clothing. "I'll just throw these in the dryer."

"You're staying?" My voice does its high-note trick again. This is not good. Why is my soon-to-be-ex-husband practically naked in my house?

"We had a good life, and I fucked it all up," Ben says as he makes his way back into the room. He wraps his hand around mine, a tenderness in the gesture that hasn't been there in too long. "I'm so sorry."

My heart races as I struggle to keep up my emotional shield. The adrenaline flooding my body has put me on edge.

"How can I believe you?" I move to show him the door, but

he pulls me into his embrace. He smells good, and even after being caught in the winter rain, his body is warm. With his arms around me, I convince myself that he does want us. He wants my support. He wants my love. He wants my forgiveness. Why else would he be here now?

But I don't hug him back immediately. My fear isn't quelled just because he's here. I don't trust him, but his apology is the first step in repairing our marriage. It feels good to be hugged, and I finally allow my exhausted body to melt into his arms. I forgot how safe he can make me feel.

Ben softly strokes my back, and we sway to the rhythm of the rain. He leans down and kisses my neck, hugging me tighter. My hands are on his hips, on top of the towel, so it quickly becomes obvious that he's aroused. The towel shifts even as I feel his hardness press against my leg. I never thought I'd experience this again.

I'm so weak from the pain of the last few months—no, the last few years—that my shields crumble and I give in to him.

This Ben—kind, gentle, apologetic Ben—this is the man I married. Perhaps the separation was good for him. Perhaps he realized he wants to live up to his vows to love, honor, and cherish me. Perhaps I just don't want him to stop.

"You did this to me," he says, pushing himself into my leg. "I've been thinking about you so much. I miss you; I want you."

Why is it easy for me to believe every word he says? We have a difficult past. Did we love each other? I certainly loved him, and early on, I thought he loved me. Were we attracted to each other? Definitely. Our relationship wasn't all bad.

Ben kisses me, and I kiss back, eager, because I need this right now. This is my last chance to keep our family together. With a low chuckle, he ends the kiss, and I realize I have my hands in his hair and I'm tugging him to me.

He leads me to our bedroom, our marital bed. It's unmade

and the sheets haven't been changed in a month. Piles of dirty laundry are all over the room, a reflection of how I've been feeling about life.

"Do you want me?" Ben asks, and I nod. He starts to undress me, kissing my collarbone sweetly. He's taking care of me first. He wants me to feel good first. He wants me. He wants us. He's never taken care of my needs before his. Never. I assumed he either didn't know how or my needs weren't important to him.

I untie his towel, and there he is. A familiar distant memory that has come back to me, but it's a memory of how I wanted our marriage to be. Not how our marriage actually was.

He sits me down on the unmade bed and guides me to lie back while he kneels in front of my dangling legs. With his big hands, he separates my thighs, holding my legs open so he has unimpeded access to my most private parts.

He kisses the insides of my thighs, making his way up to my folds. Expertly using his tongue to navigate, he drives his tongue inside me, and I moan. Oh. This is new. When—where —did he learn this? Some of his shirts smelled stronger of perfume than the restaurant's usual odor, but I thought he might have had to deal with complaints. The food isn't that good there.

Ben's tongue relentlessly circles and flicks my clit, interrupting the train of questions running through my mind. Somehow I come, but he doesn't relent, continuing to suck on my sensitive areas and extending my climax until I can't bear to be touched. I reach down and pull his head away. I have never known him to be this unselfish. During all the time we were married, he rarely brought me to orgasm, and the few times he did were early in our relationship. I always ended up taking care of myself when he wasn't around.

Sex with Ben always took place in a dark room—more a

marital chore, not a fun expression of love. After our non-honeymoon, he never acted affectionate or showed interest in foreplay. I thought he hated seeing my body and that made me hate it too.

At first I tried to get Ben interested in being the sweet, romantic man he was while we were dating. I hoped sex would get better between us, but it never did. The longer our marriage went on, the more impersonal the sex was. Tonight is the first time I've ever had an orgasm with him in the room and the light on. Why now? What does he want?

"Do you want me?" he asks again with a sharp slap to my hip.

"Yes," I say, trying to find the breath to produce the word. I rub my hip, wary now. He stands up, moves me farther up the bed before positioning himself as though he is doing a push-up over me. With one thrust, he shoves inside. His eyes are fixed on an unknown focal point above the walnut headboard. After a few, quick thrusts, he freezes and lets out a moan.

Grunting, he pulls out and rolls over, his stare now fixed on the ceiling.

Where once my body was heated with passion, it's now cold as ice. My stomach churns. That's it. He's done. He came and then there was nothing. No kisses, no hugs, no emotion.

I'm afraid to say anything. That slap could so easily become a bruise if I say the wrong thing. Ben's face is stone, and the distance grows like a chasm between us. All that sweetness and light from earlier was just a façade. Our marriage is really over. After all these years, he's choosing not to have a happy marriage. I trusted him; I thought he was here to keep our family together, but he was here to make sure I'm destroyed emotionally. One more dagger in my heart.

Ben sits up, then leaves the bed. Not even bothering to

clean himself off, he gets his clothing from the dryer and redresses.

I quickly pull on a robe and run out to the living room where he's toeing on his shoes.

"I'll see you tomorrow in court," Ben says as he pulls on his coat. The door shuts behind him with a *snick*.

ONE

February 25

THE TURBULENCE IS TERRIBLE. I've never flown before, so I should be a nervous wreck and afraid the plane will break apart, but I'm numb. Shortly after takeoff, the captain announced that in-flight service is suspended for the remainder of the flight. Looks like no Goose and cran to further dull my senses.

I scroll through the songs I downloaded to my pay-as-you-go phone. Ben canceled landline service at the house when he moved out. He had no reason to talk to me anymore. I'm glad I had enough money tucked away to buy this phone. I don't have anyone to call—Ben's family won't answer—but I want to be available in case my sons need me. A mother can always hope. At last, I pick the '70s playlist, shut my eyes, and enjoy the distraction of Crosby, Stills, and Nash's "Southern Cross."

I startle awake when the car hits a massive road bump at high speed, only to realize I'm on an airplane, not on the back roads in Maine. I was dreaming about Cole's birthday. After the judge ruled Ben gets full custody, Carol made a point of telling me she was hosting a party next week and I'm not invited. They're keeping me out of the boys' lives completely.

Wiping the tears that well in my eyes, I turn my gaze toward the window, where everything's a blur. When Ben moved out, his parents let me visit the boys every Wednesday and Saturday, but when I asked about Christmas, which was on a Thursday, they said I wasn't allowed to see the boys at all. I was too greedy. And then since I hadn't seen the boys in nearly two months, the judge said I'd abandoned them and gave full custody to Ben. I absently rub my chest to soften the pain. Do hearts literally break? I wish I had money for an attorney to fight for my boys.

The Cushings haven't let me talk to my sons either.

"Cole is running a fever today and won't be able to come to the phone."

"Luke has a playdate that can't be changed."

Or the worst excuse: "Isa, they don't want to talk to you."

I sold the furniture Ben didn't want and my dead mother's wedding bands, but that won't pay for an attorney's retaining fees. I'm glad Martha was able to convert the second ticket into cash so I can afford to buy meals during my trip. I'm hoping my appetite returns. I just haven't been hungry these past few months.

The seat belt sign has been on for nearly the entire flight, but now the captain announces we're making our approach to St. Thomas. I blink, and the beautiful aqua waters of St. John and St. Thomas come into focus.

This trip is perfectly timed. I'll be so far away I won't be tempted to show up at the Cushings' for the party. It's likely I would've been arrested for wishing my youngest son happy birthday. I rub at my sternum and wince. Even if I had the money for an attorney, what family court judge would grant even partial custody to a mother who had to be forcibly removed from her child's birthday party by the police?

I want Cole to have a wonderful day, even if it is without his mom. I hope someday he understands why I wasn't there when he turned three. I hope the Cushing clan says nice things about me—even if they don't believe those things—and hugs the boys when they're sad and missing me.

The huge bumps don't rattle me as we come in for our landing at STT, St. Thomas's airport. Despite the rocky approach, the landing is smooth and unremarkable. I gather my things from the overhead compartment and wait my turn to exit the plane. I make it through customs quickly, but I suppose that's because I'm an American. Now I need a ride to the ferry over to St. John.

Outside, taxi drivers with vans that would never pass an inspection in Maine are parked in a line. A look around shows these are my only options, so I walk over to the first van, and a driver meets me, reaching out to take my luggage.

"I'm Sebastian. I can drive you wherever you want to go on the island, ma'am," he says as he puts my bags, which contain everything I own, into the back of his van.

"I need to get to the St. John ferry." My face is too stiff to smile, so I try to at least look pleasant. The warm breezes feel good on my broken body.

"I will take you, ma'am. It's a short ride to Red Hook Ferry."

Once seated in the row behind the driver, I allow him to make eye contact with me in the rearview mirror. "Where are you visiting from?"

"I'm from Maine." I don't have a home or family left to be with.

"That's very north. We welcome many in from the cold!

You will enjoy the warm sunshine here, ma'am. It is a beautiful day on St. Thomas." Sebastian smiles, and it lights up his dark brown eyes.

I watch out the window the winding road takes us over hills and past tropical palms and flowers. The nutmeg scent is relaxing, and the intensity of my body's aches eases somewhat. The sun hits the island at a different angle than at home, and the change is a nice distraction.

At the ferry landing, I thank the driver and pay him, being sure to tip him as extravagantly as my meager budget will allow, mostly for being the first person in a long time who was genuinely kind to me.

"Enjoy your stay, ma'am, and you call Sebastian whenever you need a ride." He hands me his business card that says only "Sebastian" and a phone number written in neat blue ink.

"Of course. Thank you." I tuck the card into the pocket of my leggings as Sebastian gets into his van and drives off, beeping his horn with a happy beat.

I walk over to the small building to look at the ferry schedule and to exchange my voucher for a ticket to St. John. "The ferry is due in about fifteen minutes and departs every hour on the hour," the woman selling tickets dutifully says.

"Thank you." I accept my ticket and store it in the front pocket of my backpack, making sure to move Sebastian's card there too. "I'm thirsty from the plane."

"Then you want to go that way"—she points across the marina's parking lot—"and try an island slush. Made with fresh fruit grown right here on St. Tom."

I follow the ticket seller's directions and soon find myself with half a coconut in my hands. Its hollowed-out shell is filled with an icy concoction that a sign said contains pineapple, orange, coconut water, and ice. I take a big bite, then wince as brain freeze strikes. Ow! I rub my forehead, finding it somewhat sweaty. A low stone retaining wall borders the street, so I find a section out of the sun and sit down.

My surroundings full of sun and warmth are so different from the land I left behind this morning. I swing my feet idly as sedans, trucks, and motorcycles drive by. Some of the occupants wave as they pass; similarities do exist.

A marine horn sounds, and I look up to see the ferry maneuvering into its berth. I gather my luggage, swing my backpack onto my shoulder, and hop off the wall. The sun beats down on me, heating my head as I cross the asphalt. My fingers are sticky from the island slush, and I'm grateful my path passes a trash can. I dispose of the coconut shell—I'm tempted to hold onto it as a souvenir, but I don't have the space or a place to rinse it out. I don't know how far away my lodgings are from the ferry on St. John.

After boarding the ferry, I drop my bags next to my feet at the bow. Leaning against the safety rail, I look out across the most beautiful blue sea to my destination in the distance. This is enough to cheer anyone up, no matter how sad and broken they are.

The other ferry riders are loud, raising their voices to be heard over the boat's engines. A child screams. The woman next to me at the railing jostles me as the ferry cuts through a particularly rough wave, and I step away, only to bump into another traveler. Does no one know the meaning of personal space?

The ferry easily crosses the four miles between the islands, and we dock in no time. Once on shore, I swing my backpack around to my front so I can retrieve the folder of information from Martha Sullivan. I brush away the memory of the pitying look on her face when I claimed my prize and said I'd be going alone. I orient myself as I look at the map I found in the folder. A pink sticky note tells me I'm in villa eight at the Cinnamon Bay Villas; the key is in the conch shell on the step.

I drag my luggage toward the villas, my feet dragging too. Hot, sticky, and thirsty again, I'm miserable and ready to collapse. A cool shower will be even more impressive than the harbor views.

The key is indeed beneath the conch; how cute. I open the door and smile with relief. This is better than I dreamed of. The kids would love it, and my smile turns into tears at the thought of them.

Once through the door, I drop my backpack on a dining room chair. A bowl of local fruit sits on the table along with a note from the management company. "Please enjoy yourself and if you need anything at all, please call. Thank you, Sam."

I look around the small villa, marveling at the wooden cathedral ceiling that makes the space look larger than it is. The villa is wider than it is deep. To my right, beyond the dining table, is a tiny kitchenette. To my left is a rattan couch and matching easy chair. The couch acts as a partition, separating the bedroom area and a door that must lead to the bathroom from the rest of the space. French doors open onto a white-sand beach, and I decide to forget the shower. The ocean is calling my name.

I pull my suitcase to the bedroom and heft it onto the webbed stand put there for this purpose. The zipper protests at first, then slides smoothly along the track. I dig out the pieces of my suit and my flip-flops, slather on sunscreen, and grab a towel. I follow the sandy path a short distance to the beach and set my towel down on one of the lounge chairs. My flip-flops are quickly left behind as I dash to the water.

Warmth splashes over my toes, and I shudder with plea-sure. The Caribbean Sea is a stark contrast from the icy waves that jab into a person on Maine's shores. I wade out into the water and push off the bottom so I can float. My body feels good and warm and happy now that I've put distance between me and the craziness and lies from over the past few months. But I still miss my babies.

I allow my legs to drop so I turn upright and bob in the gentle surf. The water is crystal clear, and when I look down, I can see the bottom perfectly. My body feels weightless in the new red bikini that I bought for the trip.

Before now, I never owned a bikini. Buying a swimsuit in Maine in February meant I didn't have much of a selection. I wasn't sure about the skimpiness of this bikini, but whatever self-consciousness thoughts I may have had about wearing it are gone. Maybe because I have lost weight not eating while going through the custody battle and divorce, but more because the sun is able to touch most of my skin, its rays healing me from the inside out. I'm not here to turn heads anyway.

I lean back and resume floating; it's effortless. The water is saltier than in Maine, and I feel much more buoyant in this warm salty water. I'm enjoying the serenity until something hits me on the head, pulling my hair clip off. I let out a scream —was I bumped by a shark?—and flail toward shore as fast as I can. I've been afraid of sharks since childhood. Swimming in the ocean in Maine, whenever something touched me in the water, I automatically thought it was a shark.

"Hey! I'm sorry. I didn't see ya," a deep voice drawls behind me, and I stop fleeing. As I turn around, a small wave hits me and knocks me down in the shallow water. I try to get up, but more waves keep knocking me down again. How graceful. Finally getting myself to my feet, I smooth my wet, matted hair off my face so I can see who scared me.

"I didn't mean to startle ya." A blond man with an all-over tan easily jumps the waves as he heads toward me, his mirrored goggles reflecting the sun. As he nears, I notice how perfectly conditioned this shark's body is. Maybe he's an Olympic swimmer? He sure has the body of one. I wonder if he's in training.

He grabs my arm and steadies me as another wave almost takes me down. "Thank you," I say, coughing up a little seawater I swallowed when I was knocked down. Thank goodness no one is on the beach to have seen me make a fool of myself. No one other than this hot guy in goggles.

The man pushes his goggles up on his forehead, revealing the bluest eyes I have ever seen, along with a few crow's feet. He's close enough that I can see the liberal sprinkling of gray in his sun-bleached hair. He's older than the swimmers I've seen on TV, so if he is a competitive swimmer, he's probably retired. "I'm really sorry. I need to watch where I'm going."

"It's okay. I wasn't paying attention either." Coughing did nothing to clear the water in my nose, and my voice sounds nasally, like I have a cold. "I'm just glad you aren't a shark."

"No, not a shark today." He laughs and puts his goggles back over his eyes, and I catch a glimpse of myself in the mirrors. I look like a drowned rat. "Make sure ya wear plenty of sunscreen; you're a little pink."

I nod and watch as this gorgeous polite man turns away and dives back into the water. His strong arms slice through the surf, pulling him down the beach, parallel to the shoreline.

After being interrupted by that *hot* swimmer, I reapply sunscreen, then go back to my floating. I don't want to work hard at anything, and I can't allow that handsome swimmer to distract me from doing nothing.

When the tide starts to pull me away from the shore, I rouse from my semi-conscious state. The sun is no longer overhead, so I must have allowed the sea to cradle me for longer than I realized. A Jimmy Buffet song drifts my way as I climb from the water, and I look toward its source. A group of people wearing tropical shirts and khaki shorts are talking and laughing in front of what looks like a beach bar with a thatched roof a short walk away. I sniff the air, realizing that the fresh saltiness has been joined by the fragrance of frying fish. My stomach rumbles, reminding me I haven't eaten much at all today. That bar smells like a great place to have dinner.

After drying off, I wrap my towel around my waist like a skirt and gather my things, then follow my nose. I finger-comb my hair along the way so it looks somewhat presentable.

The man playing guitar and singing "Margaritaville" up-nods when I walk past the tropical shirts and through the doorway made by a retracted roll-up door. That side of the structure is open to the ocean, and I make a note to find out when sunset is. I think I'd enjoy a nightcap while watching the sun set into the sea.

Sand dragged in by customers crunches under my flip-flops as I make my way to the end of the bar farthest from the missing wall. My skin is starting to feel tender, and I want to stay out of the sun. The bartender comes over with a smile. "Welcome to We Be Jammin', where the tunes are as fresh as our fruit. What can I get you?" She looks about my age, but I feel ancient next to her youthful, easy-going self.

"I should drink some water first, but I really want to try a local specialty. Nothing too sweet."

"How about a sunburn?" she asks as she fills a glass with ice cubes and water and slides it in front of me. "It's local rum—made with our own bay grown on the island—and I make all the juice fresh from local fruit. I don't like supersweet drinks either, but I love this one."

"Sounds good."

As she makes my drink, I scan the bar. Not counting the tropical shirts loudly enjoying their drinks outside, there are probably about fifteen people here, including me. Seven couples and me. I sigh, and a wave of weariness sweeps over me. It's been so long since Ben and I went out together. Hell, it's been five years since I've even stepped foot in a place that didn't offer a children's menu. I guess this is my new normal—dining alone, without even the boys to keep me occupied.

"Here you go." The bartender sets my drink down in front of me. "My name's Sarah. Are you here by yourself?"

"Yup. I'm alone." I straighten my shoulders and decide to embrace my new status. By myself, I have no one to answer to, no one to determine my schedule. I can order a dish for myself, not plan to eat my children's leftovers. I beam. "I'm Isa." I move the skewer with slices of pineapple, mango, and lime to the other side of the tall glass and take a sip of my drink. "This tastes like sunshine!"

Sarah salutes, then pulls a damp rag from below the bar and starts cleaning the bar top. "Are you a guest here at the villas?"

"Yes." I take another sip. "It's beautiful here."

"How long are you down for?"

"A month, maybe more, if I can make my finances last." I take another sip of sunshine. "I have to figure some things out, and what better place to do that than on a tropical beach?" My newfound bravery seeps out of me, leaving behind a familiar emptiness.

"Well, if you get lonely and want a friend, I'm here." Sarah wipes crumbs into her hand and throws them into what I presume is a waste bin out of sight of her customers. Does she see a lot of lonely people like me? Alone and troubled?

"Thanks. I may take you up on that." Sarah's accent is distinctive, leading me to ask, "Are you from New England?"

"Boston. Born and raised." She laughs. "I'm so glad I'm out of there. Too much drama and people trying to take everything from you." The surface cleaning finished, she moves on to washing dirty glasses. "I came down about six years ago and never went back. Your accent reminds me of home."

"I'm from Kennebunk, Maine. Not far from Boston, just over an hour away."

"Ah-ha! See, I knew we were supposed to be friends." Sarah's glee is contagious, and I push aside the hollowness inside me, choosing instead to order another sunburn and a tropical salad that has oranges and coconut grilled shrimp on it.

This is just what I need to gain perspective—my tropical island escape. The sun lowers over the water and the man with the guitar continues to sing beach music. I send up a prayer of thanks to the raffle gods. Coming here was the break I needed.

"Thanks, Sarah. I really enjoyed talking with you," I say as I pay my bill. *More than you know.*

"See you tomorrow?" she asks, extending her hand to shake mine.

"I'll be here!" I exit through the open wall and head up the sand path to my villa. I discover a showerhead just outside my bedroom door, so I rinse off the salt and the sand. Inside, I take a longer shower, luxuriating in the coconut-scented shampoo and body wash. I face the mirror as I dry off and comb through my long brown hair. My cheeks and nose are red and tan lines are starting to show on my shoulders.

My body is exhausted from all the travel and the water and relaxed from the sun and the rum. Physically, I feel good.

My arms are heavy as I pull my oversized T-shirt over my head and crawl between the bed's white cotton sheets.

I pick up my phone and look at the picture of my boys that's set as my wallpaper. No texts or call notifications block their faces on my home screen.

I love you, sweet boys. Momma loves you always. I set my phone back down on the nightstand, and sleep drags me under in an instant.

TWO

February 28

THREE DAYS INTO MY VACATION, and I've never felt physically better. I've spent two long days on the beach and in the water, and I've visited the local library; it's air-conditioned and quiet, and for a tiny island, it's well-resourced. I've been poring through reference books, trying to make sense of what I'm reading about custody laws. When my brain begins to protest, I switch over to memoirs written by divorcées. I want to know how they survived. How did they start living again?

I feel healthier, stronger, and I'm gaining perspective on my life. I'm trying to figure out how to be reunited with my boys and what I need to do next.

When my body tells me it's time for dinner, I head to We Be Jammin'. I've become comfortable sitting at the end of the bar nearest the beach, where I'm reached by the breeze off the ocean. The salty air and the daily taste of fresh fruit and rum have become some of my favorite sensory memories. This afternoon, country music is playing quietly over the speakers, filling in until the band advertised on the sign out front arrives and gets set up. It's been the same routine every night I'm here. I tap my fingers to the beat.

The messy bun on top of my head is shaken and I jump, startled by the contact. I turn to look, and there he is—the retired Olympic swimmer.

"Hi, sunshine!" he says with a big smile.

Anxiety skitters down my spine to join the punch-in-the-gut sensation from being startled. I'm not used to being touched, least of all by strangers. Maybe I'm too sensitive, but the tap on the head reminds me of how this man hit me when I was floating in the ocean. But I'm new to the island, so maybe this is just how some people say hello. The social customs down here are a lot different from what I'm used to in the cold north.

"It's the shark," I say, making an effort to match his smile as he sits on the stool next to mine. I look over at Sarah for an out, but she's busy behind the bar, bouncing to the music's rhythm while slicing fruit for garnishes.

"I'd like to properly introduce myself. I'm Jack." I'm a bug caught under a microscope as he focuses on me. "Are ya enjoying your time on St. John?"

"I'm Isa, and yes, very much. It's a nice escape."

"What are ya escaping from?" He leans toward me, and I lean back.

My smile disappears immediately. "Maine."

"Now, what would a beautiful lady like you need to escape from in a place as beautiful as Maine?"

That's a personal question! Oh, why couldn't I have just said something inane in the first place? I don't want to think about my life when I'm trying to enjoy myself.

"The cold." ...my ex-husband, his family, the grief that I can't see my babies.

"When do ya head back to the cold?" Jack's smile is blinding against his tanned skin. The white around his eyes from his goggles makes his eyes appear brighter too. I look away, afraid he'll see too much. I crane my neck around; we're the only people in the bar. Sarah must have run to the stock room to get ready for tonight's crowd.

"I'm not sure? I don't have plans yet. My ticket's open-ended." Oh, why did I tell him that? Isa, you *have* to get better at keeping private information to yourself. Remember, you're a single woman on an island by yourself. Be strategic!

"Don't ya have a job to go back to? Family? Boyfriend?"

"No, I don't." I hold back the tears threatening to roll down my face.

Jack is blessedly silent, and thirty seconds pass in which neither of us speaks. My nascent tears are drying as I try not to squirm with awkwardness at having Jack stare right at me. I have to look away.

"Well, hey. I'm going out on the boat in the morning. Gonna do some snorkeling at one of my favorite reefs. Care to join me? It'll be a lot of fun, give ya something else to think about, and you'll see more of the island than this bar."

"Just you and me?" It's a sweet offer, but I can see the headline now: *Mainer missing at sea; tan stranger suspected of murder.* My stomach churns, and I take a sip of my drink to wet my suddenly dry mouth.

Jack chortles and lays a hand on my arm. "Oh, no. Some of my friends are coming too."

"Well, as long as other people are there. I've never snorkeled before." I pull away from Jack's grip, dislodging his hand, and not knowing what to do with my arms, wrap them around myself. Are all the folks on the island this touchy-feely?

"You'll look cute in a mask and snorkel." Jack is undeterred by my coldness.

I push my lips into a polite smile. All this attention from a man is unfamiliar. Why me?

"So, how are things in Maine?" My train of thought skids off the rails with his question.

"I just"—breathing deeply, I pick up my drink—"would rather not talk about it right now. Can I buy you one of these?"

"Oh, sure. No pressure. And I'm buying." He holds his hands up, fingertips toward the ceiling, then swings around to the bar and to Sarah, who's checking the stock in the well. "I'll have what Isa is having." She makes Jack a rumrunner too. "Thank ya." He raises his plastic cup with an umbrella and orange slices in my direction before downing nearly all of its contents in one swallow. From the speakers, Old Dominion sings advice about ending a relationship. I wish I would've thought to end things with Ben when he began to show his true colors, but then I wouldn't have had my boys.

I laugh bitterly to myself. I don't have my boys anyway.

Jack is back to looking at me when I peek at him from the corner of my eye. I'm on edge, afraid I've angered him by refusing to answer his question. I cast about for a change in subject to head off his negative emotions.

"Um, I noticed when you bumped into me that you have professional goggles, and um, you're really tan. Do you spend a lot of time swimming or something?" *Smooth, Isa. You scared little rabbit.* Ben's scorn-filled voice is loud in my head.

I'm out of practice at having conversations with people in my generation, let alone hot retired Olympic swimmers. I take a sip of my drink, and the rum makes my head dizzy.

"I have a place here. I'm from eastern Tennessee and back home is beautiful, but I prefer the island lifestyle. Much more laid back and happy and easy. No stress." He move his hand away from himself as if mimicking a surfer gliding in to shore.

"I've never been to Tennessee."

"I've been to Maine several times. I love the small fishing towns. Lobster and Damariscotta oysters..." His eyes go soft, and he absently rubs his hand across his abdomen, his surf-board-themed T-shirt covering those defined abs I'd seen when we met.

"Yeah, some of the towns are pretty, and lobster is good. I've never had the oysters." Lobster is cheap in Maine, but I never learned how to prepare oysters, and they're expensive in restaurants. The one time I went to try them early in our marriage, Ben said we couldn't afford them, making me miss my chance to see what all the fuss is about.

"The water is too cold for me there," I add. And the people aren't warm either—at least the ones I know.

We talk about our favorite things to do when we were young. I'm surprised when he tells me he learned how to play guitar. I thought he would tell me about all the medals he won on his swim team.

Sarah winks at me when she brings us new drinks, but otherwise she stays away. That wink—is she matchmaking by not interrupting us? What does she know about Jack? My breathing quickens as the panic rises. I'll have to pin her down and ask her later. I'm newly divorced; it's too soon to start a new relationship.

Jack's not picking up on my vibes, though. Instead, he's increased the frequency of his flirty questions, and I'm answering them between deliberately deep breaths. This is not like me at all. But then, the me of six months ago never imagined she'd be divorced, let alone temporarily living on a tropical island.

I'm relieved he's leaving out the hard questions. The ones I want to forget the answers to. I still don't understand what he sees in me. But it's nice having someone's full attention. And even nicer that he's good-looking. Although I once thought Ben was handsome.

I swivel around on my stool, putting my back to the bar. A few more people wander in, some obviously tourists, while others could be workers here for happy hour. They greet each other like long-lost pals. One woman's mesh beach bag catches on a chair in front of us, and Jack's quick to untangle it for her, his fingers deftly plucking at the crocheted strands. What a thoughtful guy.

Maybe it's the rum, maybe it's the loneliness, but I'm looking forward to going out on the boat tomorrow. It's time to get to know more people. Branch out. Make friends.

The canned music is nearly drowned out by the newcomers, but it's loud enough for Jack to sing harmony with Thomas Rhett about sometime in October. His voice is smooth and smoky, and when he hits a particularly low note, my insides get all squirmy and my face gets hot. At the part about the guy guessing the girl's middle name, he stops singing.

"Mary?" Jack asks me.

"What?" I rotate so I'm facing Jack.

"Mary? Is Mary your middle name?"

"Nope."

"Anne? Is it Anne? Anne is my momma's name."

"Not a chance." I laugh, knowing this could go on all night. My middle name is the one thing my parents left me with that I always wanted to change growing up, but now that they're gone, I'll keep it for always. I just won't ever use it.

"Lynn?"

"Getting closer."

"Can I have your last name? So I can use it for flow?"

"Flo is not my middle name."

He throws his head back and laughs. "She's got jokes! If I

had your last name, I could see how your middle name would flow with it."

If you had my last name, I wouldn't have a bastard of an ex-husband. My smile disappears.

"It's not Isa Flo Cushing," I force out between clenched teeth. The good time I was having at a bar on a beautiful beach far away from what I'm trying to forget has drained away. Jack puts his hands on my bare knees and holds them tight.

"Did I say something wrong?" Jack seems genuinely concerned, and the last thing I want to do is to start crying. *Stay strong, Isa. Stay strong.*

"No, I think I've had too much to drink."

Jack keeps holding on, absentmindedly stroking the insides of my knees. The calloused tips of his fingers scrape along my sensitive flesh, and I suppress a full-body shiver. "I'm not trying to pry or hurt you in any way. I come here to escape reality too. When I'm stateside, all people do is try to take from me. It's the nature of the business I'm in—I realize that. But here, I can relax and just enjoy my life."

"I'm sorry. I'm really not used to nice people. It's been a long time since someone has been kind to me, let alone taken the time to get to know me. I'm new at this." How can I enjoy life when my children, my life, were taken from me?

As my voice fades, Jack softly squeezes my knees. "I'm not going anywhere. I want to get to know you, and I swear I'm not mean to anyone." I look from his hands on my knees to his face and return his smile, although I'm sure it's more like a grimace.

"Thank you. I'm not sure I can be a good friend. I don't have a lot to give to anybody."

"I'm not asking for anything, and don't underestimate yourself. You're a lot of fun, and I'm bored." He looks sincere, and if his bleached-out T-shirt and swim trunks are evidence of the time he's spent lounging on the beach, he's not kidding.

"Besides, you need a tour guide. Did you rent a car to get around the island?" I shake my head. They drive on the left side of the road down here, so it's too dangerous for me. I have too much on my mind to have space to learn.

"You want to be my tour guide?" It feels good to laugh again. "You've already invited me to snorkel with your friends. You're doing a lot."

"You look like ya need a friend, and I just so happen to be looking for a friend. So, we're a good fit." Jack sobers. "And in case you're wondering, I'm not a stalker, a serial killer, a psychopath, or a thief. Ask Sarah."

Sarah looks up. "Nope, not a serial killer." She goes back to what she's doing.

"There ya have it—Sarah said I'm alright."

"Jack, listen, you're very nice, but I..." I try to find the right words. "I have a lot of things to figure out. I doubt I'll be good company."

The sun has started to sink over the water, creating a warming light that shows off our tans. The warm breeze blowing in from the beach is competing with the air moved by the large wooden ceiling fan above us. I'm in an alternate universe, and the past six months—no, the past five years—have never happened.

"Just be yourself."

I bite my lip and consider Jack's offer, then finally give in. If I'm honest, I'm getting bored too. I need to do more with my days than go to the library, and it would be fun to explore the huge national forest that takes up much of the island.

"Sure. You can be my tour guide." Jack's smile grows bigger when he hears my answer. I cover his hands, still on my knees, with my own. This time I'm the one who squeezes. "Thank you."

We pull away to toast on our agreement, then continue our

guessing game while we finish our drinks. It takes me a long time to guess his middle name is Avery.

"It's time to put ya to bed. You have a big day tomorrow."

Maybe it's the rum, maybe it's the warm night, but I feel renewed and optimistic about the future. Funny how after one night of talking with someone who isn't trying to cause you emotional pain can help you make it through a rough patch in life.

Jack stands up and takes my hand. "Let's go," he says, and leads me toward the water and my villa. Our feet splash in the warm returning tide as we make our way down the beach. I point out my villa and Jack accompanies me to my door.

"Thanks for hanging out with me tonight," he says with a chuckle.

"Oh no! I forgot to pay our tab." Worried, I want to run back to pay Sarah.

"It's all set; I have a house tab there. Please let me take care of it. It's the least I can do after scaring ya the other day." We turn so we are facing each other, like two teenagers on a first date. "You really made my night. I've had more fun tonight talking to ya than I've had in a long time."

"Me too." I put my hand on my door to steady myself as dizziness washes over me. Rum and hot men are a dangerous combination.

"I need your number so I can let ya know when I'm on my way."

I laugh, thinking that Jack, being older, should be smoother than that. I fish in my bag for my phone and look up the number; it's still new enough that I don't have it memorized. He pulls out his phone and enters my number as I read it to him.

"Get some rest. I have a fun day planned for ya." Jack leans forward and kisses my cheek, leaving his lips there longer than required. Long enough to mean something. "I'll see ya in the morning, Isa Jane."

The kiss on my cheek—that simple, tender gesture—is enough to break my heart and make it whole again. It's a revelation of kindness and generosity, and my arousal becomes more than I can bear.

"Jack, um, do you want to come in?" After being forced into bravery over the last few months, this time I make the choice myself.

He stills and looks into my eyes, as if he's checking to see whether I'm certain. Yes, I am. I'm certain I'll combust if I don't get this man into my bed.

"Yes, ma'am," he finally answers, his voice gravelly. "I do indeed."

THREE

March 1, past midnight

JACK LEFT last night after rocking my world. I never knew sex could feel like that. He was such a sweet, attentive guy. I'm so glad I chose him to be my first after Ben.

I have so many questions about Jack. I wonder what brought him to the island. Why did he leave Tennessee? What does he do to allow him to spend so much time on the island? Was he married? Did he break someone's heart? Or was his heart broken?

I don't know anything about him except that he's a great swimmer, he's really funny and makes me feel good, he has beautiful blue eyes, and he's great in bed.

I giggle. I haven't had time or energy to feel attraction to anyone, not for years.

My stomach rumbles, and I wonder if the villa staff stocked the kitchen with a few snacks yesterday like they said they would. Throwing the sheets off, I turn the light on and swing my legs onto the floor. It's too early to get up, but I'm wide awake. Perhaps a snack will help me sleep.

I wonder where Jack sleeps. Does he live in a tent? He seems to live a kind of "beach bum" lifestyle. His clothes last night were old and worn, and I bet he rides a motorbike like I've seen a lot of people using on my library commute. Well, I guess I'll ask him tomorrow morning when we go to breakfast.

In the kitchenette, I find a box of crackers and some small bags of chips. The small refrigerator contains bottled waters and sodas. *Thank you, whoever did this!* I take a ginger ale and a bag of chips and sit down at the table to eat my snack.

Sitting here by myself reminds me of sitting in my old kitchen and the many nights I stayed up late to wait for Ben to come home. I would call him, and he would say he was still at work and would call when he was on his way.

The call wouldn't come.

The following morning, the phone would ring from its place on the kitchen wall, and I'd have to scramble from the bed to answer it before the shrill tones woke up the boys. It was always Ben, saying he *fell asleep in the back room* or *it got too late and I didn't want to wake you.* I was so naive, I believed him when he told me he was working. After reading those books about divorce recovery, I've realized it's more likely that he was going out on the town after his shift and picking up women while I worried at home.

I pull the top of the chip bag apart and pop a few chips in my mouth. "Ben is such an ass," I declare between bites of the salty snack.

It feels good to say it aloud.

Several of the self-help books suggested journaling as a way of recovering. Now is as good a time as any to get started. I'm here to heal, right?

I kept a diary when I was younger and happy. Before Ben

whirled into my life and overwhelmed me. It seems the more unhappy I became, the less I wanted to journal. If I didn't write about what was happening with my marriage, it was like it never happened. I've always been grateful I didn't keep a record of those days. The five-inch scar along my hairline itches with phantom pain. At least, no written record.

The drawers of the desk provide a pen and a notepad that says Cinnamon Bay Villas across the top. I make myself comfortable at the table and stare at the pad's white expanse, suddenly unsure of what to write.

I've been out of Maine for only ten day, but everything I've been through doesn't seem real. I came prepared here to forget and to move on from my marriage to Ben, but now I realize I should be learning from my mistakes, not forgetting them. I feel like a different person than I was even a few days ago. A much stronger person. No matter how painful the memories, I need to write them down. My scar throbs again. Might as well start there.

MAY 25, *four years ago*

NOT A HAPPY MEMORIAL DAY. And not a happy birthday to me. I thought turning twenty-five would be a milestone in my life, A day to remember. As it turns out, it was a day I would like to forget.

Everything started out the same as any other holiday weekend. We woke up and had a quick breakfast with no mention of my birthday. I was pregnant with Cole, and Ben and I had planned to take Luke to the public beach. Ben was in a grumpy mood when we started packing the car up. I thought that once we got to the beach, he would enjoy himself. But I was wrong.

Ben used bungee cords to put Luke's wagon on the roof so there would be plenty of room in the cargo area for our cooler, towels, beach toys, and the umbrella before running back into the house. I packed lots of water and juice pouches so everyone would stay hydrated. I buckled two-year-old Luke into his car seat and took my place in the front seat of the car. We sat there with the air-conditioning blowing, waiting for Ben so we could leave.

When he came back out, he had a paper bag. He opened the back of the car and put the bag in. I had no idea what it was. Maybe it was a birthday gift? I smiled; I didn't want to ask and spoil a surprise.

We got to the beach and unloaded everything into the wagon. Ben pulled it, and Luke ran ahead of us. We looked like a cute, happy family about to enjoy a day at the beach. We found a nice spot on the sand away from other people who were laying on their towels. Ben set up the umbrella, and I set up the chairs, then Luke and I walked down to the water so I could see how cold it was and Luke could play in the tide pools.

I looked up to where we had set up and saw that Ben was sitting in his chair going through his phone, sipping from his insulated cup. I realized later that he was drinking Canadian whisky from the bottle in the paper bag. Within ten minutes, Ben was refilling his cup.

Apparently bored with only my company, Luke climbed the slight hill to his dad and begged him to play in the water. Ben snapped at Luke for dripping water on his phone and made a big deal of drying it off before carefully hiding it away.

When he and Luke joined me at the water's edge, I could smell the whisky on him. A feeling of doom crashed over me. I tried to distract Luke from his dad, but Ben grabbed him away from me. He put Luke on his shoulders and waded into the water.

Luke was laughing as the waves hit Ben and splashed up on Luke. Ben waded in way too far and then they were gone. Dragged under.

I screamed. People who heard me jumped up and ran down to me. A lifeguard came running and swam out with his rescue board and found them quickly. He paddled in with them, Ben and the guard holding on to the board and pushing Luke, who was riding on top.

It all happened so fast. They were OK but shaken. Luke was coughing. He had swallowed a lot of water.

Someone called the police; I guess it's protocol when there's a rescue. A policeman went over to Ben while I was carrying Luke to the umbrella. I wanted to get Luke wrapped up in a towel and warm him up.

Ben and the policeman walked up to us. I could see Ben was about to explode, but he refrained because there was an audience. An audience that included a policeman who introduced himself as Officer Chabot. He lectured Ben about how lucky he was and that it's very dangerous to be drinking and taking a young child into the water. He told us this could have turned out a lot differently if either of them had gotten caught in the undertow.

The lifeguard came up to check on Luke, who I was holding on to for dear life. "Thank you so much for saving my family," I said to the rescuer.

"How are you doing, buddy?" the lifeguard asked Luke and held his fist out for him to fist-bump. Luke thought that was great, and with a huge smile, untangled his arm from his towel and bumped his fist with his.

Officer Chabot made eye contact with me as he and the

lifeguard left. His face was full of sympathy as he saw me hugging my son, tears still falling from my eyes.

I thought it was a good idea to pack up and go home. We'd had enough excitement for one afternoon. Besides, if we stayed, Ben would drink the rest of his whisky. We repacked the wagon and headed back to the car.

I got Luke buckled in and helped put the wagon on top of the car. Ben and I were tying it down when he let go of the stretched bungee cord I had just fastened, and it came flying over the wagon into my face. He just let it go.

My reflexes must have been honed by raising a toddler and kicked in just in time. I turned my head so the hook end of the bungee hit my temple, not my teeth or eyes. The skin instantly split and blood sprayed the side of the car. I caught Ben smirking as I winced with pain and dripped with blood.

Officer Chabot was in the parking lot. I tried to hold back my sobs, but as he came over to me, I started crying. He had grabbed his first aid kit from his police car and used its contents to stop the bleeding. Ben stood there while the officer worked, explaining how the bungee slipped out of his hand and catapulted over and hit me.

Ben put on a show in front of Officer Chabot and apologized up and down, making up how this "accident" ad happened. But Ben and I knew this was not an accident. Officer Chabot said it looked like I needed stitches and told Ben to take me up to the ER in Biddeford to see a doctor. Ben said he would take me right then. I guess Officer Chabot thought Ben was sober enough to drive.

Ben took me to the emergency entrance at the hospital. He told me to call him when I was ready to get picked up. He wanted to get Luke home and changed. Now he wanted to be dad!

When the doctor was finished giving me fifteen stitches from my cheek across to my scalp, he said I might be in a lot of pain and he was going to prescribe me something to help with that. When the nurse came in with my discharge papers, she handed me a bottle of some pain pills. I had her call Ben to come pick me up. Ben didn't answer, so she left a message. She had me sit in the waiting room.

An hour and a half later, Ben walked into the waiting room and told me to hurry, Luke was in the car.

"Don't you look pretty." Ben laughed.

My hair was a mess, my clothes were damp, sandy, and bloody, and I had a large bandage across my bruised and swollen face. I looked down and asked him quietly to please take me home, that I didn't feel good.

But Ben got on the turnpike and headed north to South Portland. When I realized which direction we were going, I asked him to please take me home so I could go to bed. Ben responded, "What? You don't like my parents? They invited us for dinner."

Ben's parents don't like me. I've never measured up, never been good enough for their precious Benny. I never seem to say or do the right thing. The first time he took me to their house for dinner, I used the wrong fork to eat my salad, and Ben's mother never let me forget it.

"That gets the serving fork, Isa dear," Carol had cooed when I took the platter of sliced roast to the table at one memorable dinner. "Tongs are for cafeterias."

Now I just wanted to go home and go to bed. I was sore, pregnant, and exhausted. Instead, Ben drove to South Portland and dinner with a bunch of people who really couldn't care less if I was there.

Fixing my hair the best I could, I followed Ben into their house. To look like a doting father, I guess, Ben carried a sleepy Luke.

Carol met us at the door and raked me over with her gaze from head to toe. "You look terrible; you should really be more careful." I just nodded. The local anesthesia was wearing off and I was too sore to talk. She didn't want to listen to me anyway.

I wasn't hungry and didn't feel like eating. Ben said I was insulting them by not eating the meal they cooked for us, but I didn't care.

After everyone had finished eating, Ben and his dad had their usual after-dinner drinks. My head was throbbing, but with Ben drinking, that left me to get us home. I couldn't take the pain meds from the ER doctor. I slouched in a wingback chair in a corner to rest my head while Luke played quietly at my feet. I think he was feeling the exhaustion of the day too.

At one point, Carol came over and pushed an old stuffed clown with stains on it into Luke's face. It scared him, and he started shrieking, and then Carol scolded me for leaning my head on the chair because I might get blood on it. "But of course that doesn't matter to you."

Ben lurched over to us and demanded I quiet "the brat" because he had a headache. I wanted to lose it, to cry and scream out all my pain and weariness, but as always, I pushed my feelings aside, picked up and cuddled Luke, and went out to the car. The cool night air helped to dry my threatening tears, and Luke calmed down. He was asleep by the time I had him secured in his car seat.

The only good thing about the night was when Ben fell asleep—or, rather, passed out—on our way home. I didn't need to listen to him complain about me.

We pulled into our driveway, and I was tempted to leave Ben there to wake up on his own, but that would get me into more trouble, so I woke him up to go inside. I was expecting him to say something mean, but he just got up and went inside and to bed. I collected Luke and put him in his toddler bed. I slipped in beside him, contorting myself to fit, so as not to disturb Ben.

Happy birthday to me.

I'M amazed by how many details I can remember. Your husband forgetting your birthday might not be memorable, but your husband almost drowning your child and then deliberately hurting you leaves indelible marks.

As I wrote, the words flowed as much as my tears. Even though the scar on my head is healed and is easily hidden by my hair, writing down what happened ripped open the emotional scar. The words are like salt being rubbed into the wound to make it sting and hurt. It's a good thing my villa is near the ocean. Now that I've remembered, I will never forget this happened.

I stretch and look at the clock. Morning will be here in a few hours, long enough for me to go back to bed. My head is throbbing from remembering how awful Ben is and what I accepted to keep our family together.

Tidying up the kitchenette, I collect the looseleaf sheets of memories and tuck them safely under the fruit bowl in the center of the table. The next time I go into town, I'll get a proper journal. The villa's first aid kit has ibuprofen, so I swallow several pills with a glass of water and return to bed.

This year my birthday will be special. I will have cake, and I will do whatever I want.

FOUR

March 1, early morning

BEEP, *beep, be-ep, be-ep.*

The sound of a horn wakes me, and I kick off the covers. I lie on my back, staring at the palm-leaf–bladed ceiling fan turning lazily in the cool morning air. My room is still somewhat dark, but the sky is beginning to lighten.

I'm feeling lighter too.

Beep, beep, be-ep, be-ep.

I sit up and hurriedly leave the bed, rushing to the window and peeking through the blinds. Expecting to see a motorbike and wondering how I'd fit on it, I'm relieved to see Jack in a Jeep with no top. He starts another chorus of the beeping song before coming to the door and knocking with the same beat.

"I hope you didn't wake the neighbors!" I say after unlocking and opening the front door of the villa. "But come on in; I'm not ready yet."

I race to the bathroom, where I pull my hair into a loose bun and change into my red two-piece and a sundress. The Isa in the mirror grins and gives me two thumbs-up when I give myself a once-over. I guess I do care how I look to some people. I shrug. Today will be fun.

Jack's eyes are bright and cheerful as he greets me when I emerge from the bedroom, my beach bag in hand. "Hi, gorgeous!" My blood rushes to my cheeks.

He hugs me with his strong arms, and we sway back and forth a little. "Hi."

"You ready to go?"

"I'm famished."

"You're in for a treat then," he says, rubbing his stomach. The movement reminds me of the tight abs I touched and kissed last night, and my hunger for food is joined by a new hunger.

As we near the Jeep, I begin to wonder whether the motorbike might've been a better option. Along with being topless, the dull golden-painted vehicle lacks doors. Its windshield is cracked, and the rear bumper is held on with duct tape.

Jack leads me to the passenger side and extends a hand to help me up. "Hop in, we're going to breakfast."

"Are you sure this is safe to drive?" I shout to Jack as he jogs around to the driver's side. He hops in and turns the ignition in one smooth move, the engine springing to a loud and boisterous life. The Jeep doesn't have a muffler either.

I tap Jack on the arm, his firm bicep feeling good underneath my fingers. Once I have his attention, I mime putting on a seat belt. Jack's forehead furrows for a moment, then it relaxes and he leans over me. As Jack fishes between the door frame and the edge of my seat, I breathe deeply, inhaling the chemical coconut smell of freshly applied sunscreen. At least he's being safe with his skin, if not the rest of him.

He pulls back, the belt caught in one hand. He tilts his

head as if to kiss me, and we hold there, our eyes silently conversing, but then the engine hiccups and he retreats and snaps the belt into the buckle. He leans in once again, but this time only near my ear, and points up to the bar running above us. "This is the oh shit handle," he shouts, straining to be heard above the engine. "Grab hold of this if you want."

I want. A frisson of awareness had curled in my belly when Jack leaned over me, and our night together flashed through my mind.. No matter what he ate, Ben's breath always smelled like onions. After last night's cathartic journaling, I'm ready for something fresh and new. Something like Jack and the rum and orange he tasted of the other night.

As we wind along the island roads, I flinch every time a vehicle approaches, certain we're set for a collision because we're on the wrong side of the road. But then they pass without trouble because they're on the right side of the road. The literal right.

Sitting on the left side of the vehicle but not having a steering wheel in front of me has me off-kilter. I'm glad Jack showed me the oh shit handle. I hold on tightly, feeling more secure than if I were just wearing my seat belt. But I don't know whether the belt will do any good if the Jeep falls apart on the road. Jack talks, and all I can do is nod. I can't hear him over the noise. This feels very dangerous.

I gasp for air when we pull up to the traffic circle in front of the Westin. I hadn't realized I'd been holding my breath nearly the entire trip. Luckily, it wasn't a long drive.

"How are you today, Mr. Jack?" the valet shouts over the noise of the idling engine.

I'm a little shocked that a worker from a high-end hotel knows Jack, as he doesn't strike me as someone who could afford a place like this on a regular basis. Maybe Jack is a former staff member and the two men used to work together? But then, why would he use "Mister"?

"I'm doing great, Alfie. How are you and your wife doing?" Jack asks as he jumps out of the death trap and comes over to help me out. I'm grateful for his steadiness as I exit the Jeep on shaking legs.

"They are doing great, thank you." Alfie grins as he climbs in behind the wheel. "Your Jeep is in good hands, Mr. Jack."

"I know it is, Alfie." Jack has his arm around me now, and he leans across me and the seat to hand Alfie some cash. He says something more, but I can't make it out over the noise from the obnoxious engine.

Alfie pulls away and Jack steps back but doesn't let me go. I'm enjoying being tucked into his side. "He's taking his life in his own hands, don't you think?" I ask with a nervous laugh. Even though the Jeep is out of sight, I can still hear it.

"He'll be fine," Jack says as he takes my hand and leads me toward the resort's entrance. "He's a professional, and it's not the first time he's driven Jolene."

"Jolene? You named that sad excuse of a vehicle Jolene?" I bite my lip and shrink inside, ashamed of having blurted out my opinion. But Jack just chuckles and swings our hands between us as we near the door.

"Hey, don't offend my lady. She's seen some hard times, but she's dependable and gets me where I need to go. And as to the name, well, Jolene of the song had auburn hair, and I figure that's a bit like my Jolene's color."

"Maybe if you squinted?" I'm feeling bolder now; maybe Jack isn't upset by negative opinions.

He leads me into the hotel and I cringe, awed and embarrassed by the luxury. "I'm a little underdressed for this place," I point out.

"Nonsense. You look fantastic! And besides, this place has the best waffles on the island."

The few people in the atrium are staring at us, and my skin is as red as my bathing suit. I wish I had worn better clothing for breakfast. I'm sure Jolene's lack of muffler got everyone's attention, and now they see we're dressed in clothes we could have bought at the secondhand store. Our hair is windblown and wild, in sharp contrast to the well-dressed people preparing to start their day. They seem to have spent a lot of money on designer everything, and they aren't afraid to flaunt it, even at breakfast.

Jack guides me through the atrium and over to Snorkels, a little restaurant on the other side of the hotel, that sits close to the water.

"Oh, I get it," I say as my stomach sinks. "When you invited me to go snorkeling, you meant 'go to Snorkels'."

I pluck at my sundress, feeling like the country cousin I am among all the extravagance. It's Carol Cushing all over again. The lightness from my journaling revelations has fled, leaving me hungry, weary, and humiliated.

Jack throws his head back and laughs, and if I wasn't feeling so miserable, I would've enjoyed watching his expression. He stops abruptly and turns serious when he notices I'm not laughing with him.

"Oh, I thought you made a joke," he says. He looks around, then spies a bench in front of an open window and leads me there. Once seated, he pulls me so I'm standing in front of him, his hands clasping mine. "You heard right last night." Jack squeezes my hands. "I invited you to go snorkeling, and after we eat some of the best waffles in the world, we will meet my friends at the dock. It just so happens that the best waffles are prepared by the chefs here at Snorkels." He releases a hand and reaches up to wipe my cheek, and I realize my eyes are full of tears. "Are you OK, Isa Misha?"

I can't help chuckling, if a bit soberly. "Not my middle name." I sniffle, and Jack pats his hip.

"Aw, man. I'm wearing my swim trunks, and they don't have pockets. I don't have any tissues." He shrugs then lifts the hem of his T-shirt. "Here, you can wipe your nose on this."

My knees wobble, and I plop down beside him on the bench. "Give me a minute, and I'll be fine."

My head is awhirl with all kinds of thoughts. Who offers their shirt to a woman they just met for her to wipe her snot on? Jack is either the sweetest man or the most cunning one. Right now, he feels like the biggest, most adorable puppy.

And then my blood runs cold. If Jack doesn't have pockets, where's his wallet? Who's paying for breakfast?

I clear my throat and try to sound my most mature and stern. "Jack, who's paying for breakfast?"

"Why I am, darlin'." He flashes another of his wide grins at me. "Don't you worry about it."

"But you're not carrying a wallet."

"Like I said, you don't need to worry. I have an account here too." He stands up and holds out a hand, eyebrow quirked as if questioning whether I'll trust him. He wiggles his fingers and backs away slowly. "You know you want waffles," he sing-songs. "Waffles with mango and pineapple and chocolate and pecans and fried chicken—whatever you'd like. And all without costing you a penny."

Yes, but will it cost me my heart?

I do what I do best and shove that thought aside and jump up. "Lead the way. Pocketed pastry is calling my name!"

"MR. JACK! Good to see you again," says the woman at the host stand just inside Snorkels.

"Hi, Amelia. How are ya this morning?" Jack grins at Amelia and wraps his arm around my waist. "A table for two, please. This lovely lady is joining me for breakfast."

"Usual table?"

"Absolutely! I need to show off your waffles to my pretty friend." Jack tightens his hold momentarily, as though I need encouragement.

Ben used to hold me like this when we were in public, but he used it as a method of control. He'd pinch the skin at my waist where no one could see. To other people, we looked like a loving couple who was joined at the hip; they didn't know that my hips invariably bore bruises from being shoved into the sharp corners of our kitchen table. Recalling that bone-deep ache, I rub my hip, making a wish that the memories stay away for the day—or at least until I buy a journal.

Fake it 'til you make it, so I arrange my face into a pleasant expression and join Jack in following Amelia to a table on the edge of the deck. It's just a step down to the sand and a few yards to the water. Over Jack's shoulder, I have a view of a beautiful pool with a waterfall and an island with tall palm trees that provide nice shade for swimmers.

Jack waves away the menus as Amelia says, "It's very nice to see you again. How long are you in town for?" He really must be a regular.

"I'm in between gigs right now. Should be here for while." Jack shouldn't be treating me to an expensive meal when he doesn't even have a job.

"That is wonderful. Glad to have you back on the island. Enjoy your breakfast." Amelia leaves us while Jack pulls out a chair for me and then takes his own seat.

"Your mom taught you some manners." Jack's politeness and care is refreshing.

"My dad always said nothing says 'I like you' like good manners." He smiles.

I feel a pang, knowing my boys aren't being taught authentic, caring manners. Ben poured on the charm until he had me hooked, and when it was too late, I saw the real man. Jack seems like the real deal, but I don't trust myself.

"Do you know everyone on this island? They all seem to know you."

He shrugs. "It's a small island. Everyone knows each other. I've lived here off and on for a while, and it's my home, even when I'm back in Tennessee. I love the people here. I love the community."

"I love the island, but I feel out of place here, in the Westin. I'm really not dressed to be here. I'm a mess."

"You are beautiful, and this is a beach. You are not out of place." His bright blue eyes sparkle with warmth as he compliments me. A gentle breeze off the ocean tousles his sun-bleached hair as he reaches for my hand.

His smile and his warm grasp make me feel... special. Like I'm the only person in the restaurant. I don't think I've ever felt this way before, and I like it. A lot.

Jack squeezes my hand gently. "The mango mimosas are to die for. Would ya like one?"

I accede, and Jack holds up two fingers to a man in a Snorkels polo who nods and heads to the bar.

"You didn't tell him your order."

"I'm a man of habit. They have good food, so I come here a lot." I suppose what he saves in car payments he can spend on dining out. "And I always start breakfast with a mango mimosa."

Our conversation lulls as I watch the bathers in the pool.

Then my eye catches on a large iguana, about four or five feet long, crawling under a row of perfectly arranged chaises along the edge of the pool. When it reaches someone's bag, the lizard tips it over and rips everything out. How destructive!

Then from the top of one of the palm trees on the pool's island, another iguana jumps. It lands in the pool with a big splash, right behind a woman who's talking with a friend.

She whirls around as quickly as you can in waist-high water and lets out a bloodcurdling scream. Everyone at the pool or seated on our deck turns to see what's happening. It sounds like someone is being murdered.

Now people are trying to get out of the pool as fast as they can. And there it is. The large iguana that just belly flopped into the pool swims to the edge, pulls itself onto the apron, and leisurely slinks off into the meticulous green landscape.

"Did that just happen?" I ask Jack. I can't believe what I saw.

"Yeah, we have some iguanas here," he says. He seems amused by what just happened in the pool. "They're taking over the island in some aspects. They're opportunists when they're hungry."

"It kind of feels like Jurassic Park." Now I'm a little freaked out. "If I were in that pool and an iguana jumped in, I would've passed out." I don't let myself think of what would happen next.

"Nah, I wouldn't let you drown."

A flash of memory—Ben and Luke disappearing beneath the waves—and I shake my head, refusing to dwell.

"Gee, thanks. I don't like the idea of dinosaurs running around St. John while I'm here."

"You'll get used to them. They're like big bunny rabbits." Jack laughs. "They'll run from you unless they're cornered."

"Cornered? I have no intention of cornering them."

"Well, just check your toilet. If one finds its way in there, it might feel cornered when ya go to use it."

The server sets two tall footed glasses in front of us.

"Thank you, Winston. How are you and your family?"

"We are doing wonderfully, Mr. Jack. Your usual?"

"Yes, sir, and for the lady too."

Winston nods and heads back to the bar, and Jack turns his smile toward me and lifts up his glass.

"To mangos, waffles, and us." I raise my glass and tap Jack's, then take a sip of my mango mimosa. The sweet-tart flavor of the blended fruit and the champagne bubbles dance across my tongue before tickling my nose, causing me to squinch to keep from sneezing. But the slight discomfort is worth it. This drink is delicious. I want to savor it, so I force myself to set my glass down.

As I do, Winston sets a steaming plate in front of each of us. My breakfast is a feast for the eyes as well as my stomach. Two golden-toasted waffles are overlapped in the middle of my plate. An assortment of fresh tropical fruit diced in tiny cubes has been arranged across the pastries, and whipped cream has begun to melt into the crispy crannies.

I fork up a bite of waffle, fruit, and cream, and my eyes close as I savor the contrasts—warm waffle and cool cream, the burst of flavor as firm pineapple and fluffy pastry give way between my teeth. This is the best thing I've eaten in months. Probably years.

When I look up, Jack's focused on me. His eyes are narrowed in an expression I haven't seen in a very long time.

"I take it you like it?" he asks, his voice a low growl.

I squirm as I nod. The rising sun is beginning to warm my shoulders, but it can't compare to the heat of Jack's gaze.

"This is really great," I stammer, then take another bite. If my mouth is full, I can't say anything else.

"See, I told ya. These waffles are amazing, but not as amazing as you."

I lay my fork on the plate and give Jack my full attention. "Please stop with the flattery." I'm not used to people complimenting me; it makes me uncomfortable.

In a blink, Jack turns serious. "You must know you're great stuff, Isa. Don't let anyone tell ya different. Besides, I wouldn't say these things if I didn't mean them." He holds my stare, and I make myself resist the urge to look away. "But you've made a boundary clear, and I always respect boundaries. Now, if you'll excuse me."

Jack pushes himself away from the table and stands up. "I'll be right back. Need to use the restroom." He walks into the hotel, and if his shoulders aren't as straight and square as usual, well, the many diners watching him won't know the difference.

Pleased that Jack's promised to respect my wishes—how rare that is makes me want to sob, but the view is too nice—I enjoy my breakfast. I've just taken another sip of the mimosa when I hear my name.

"Isa?" I turn toward the voice and encounter a face reminiscent of one I haven't seen in ten years. "Isa? That is you!" A perfectly dressed woman with perfect hair and perfect makeup is approaching from a nearby table.

I get a closer look and... "Suzanne? Hi! I haven't seen you since graduation. Of all the places to run into someone! How funny to see you here. How have you been? You haven't changed a bit." I slam my mouth shut to hold back more word vomit and paste on a smile to show that I'm happy to see someone who's a reminder of my awkward past, but I'm sure she sees right through it to my personal failings.

"I just got married!" The statement ends on a tremolo almost like the one given by gray kingbirds plentiful on the island. Suzanne shoves her hand in front of my face so I can see her wedding band and the huge diamond on her engage-ment ring. "My husband and I are on our honeymoon." Wow, that's a rock and yes, this well-to-do woman has reverted to her cheerleading days and is practically jumping up and down.

Suzanne was annoying in high school. She was loud and boisterous, not letting me know a moment's peace to cope with the issues in my life. But I grudgingly found that her perpetual cheerleader mode and unrelenting passion and spirit strangely endearing. Her smile was utterly infectious. She might be dressing much better now, but I can already tell she hasn't changed very much.

"Congratulations," I say, and leave it at that. I don't want to address marriage.

"Are you on vacation? Are you here with your husband?" She cranes her neck around, as if to find him. Seeing none, she turns back to me, and I endure her scrutiny, immediately uncomfortable. She looks so successful and well put together and I'm not, especially after my failed marriage.

"No. Actually..." And just as I was going to make some-thing up because my truth would make her ego even bigger, Jack appears behind me and kisses me on the top of my head before resuming his seat.

"Sorry for taking so long, Isa," Jack says. He reaches across the table and takes my hand and, giving it a little squeeze as though telling me to play along. "I see you met a friend."

I'm stunned, but not as shocked as Suzanne appears to be. Jack extends his other hand to shake hers, but she stares back, wide-eyed and slack-jawed, the stillest I've ever seen her.

Excuse me. My ire rises. Sure, we aren't dressed as fancy as Suzanne is, but she doesn't have to be so surprised a handsome man like Jack has taken me out for breakfast.

"Isa, *this* is your man?" Suzanne hisses the words at me, still goggling at Jack. "Do you know who this is? This is Jack Kendall. You're with Jack. Freaking. Kendall."

What?! It's now my turn to be shocked, and I face Jack full on.

The unassuming beach bum I've been chatting with at the bar couldn't possibly be who Suzanne says he is. But as I study Jack's tanned features more closely, imagining him in a plaid shirt, Western hat, a pair of tight-fighting Wranglers, and a guitar slung over one shoulder, I'm convinced. Jack is Jack Kendall—*the* Jack Kendall—who I hear on the radio and who's sold out shows at the Grand Ole Opry and arenas around the globe.

Jack has dropped his hand back to the table and settled back in his chair. He's wearing an impersonal smile as he looks at Suzanne. "Nice to meet you, uh...?"

"Suzanne," I fill in the blank.

"Nice to meet you, Suzanne," Jack says cordially and looks at me, a real smile on his face this time.

"You two are visiting the island together?"

Jack answers for me. "Yes, we are." He raises my hand to his mouth, and he brushes his lips over my knuckles. I swoon—or I would if I were the swooning type. My heart beats faster, although I'm unsure whether it's because of the intimate contact with a man or that country music star Jack Freaking Kendall has kissed me twice.

"Can I get a picture with you? You know, for my Instagram?" Suzanne begs, pulling her phone out of the pocket of her shorts.

"Sure, that won't be a problem." As Jack stands, he guides me up to stand next to him. Suzanne grimaces a bit, apparently displeased she has to share her picture with me. Jack motions to Winston, who comes over and accepts the phone from Suzanne.

We stand there, our backs to the beach. Jack's in the middle, his arm around my waist, and Suzanne on his other side. She puts her hand on his shoulder, but he angles himself toward me and leans in to kiss my cheek—my third today, not that I'm counting— as we hear the digital shutter click. Winston returns the phone and we look at it: Two shabby yet happy people and a perfectly coiffed and attired sourpuss.

"We look so cute, Isa," Jack says.

"Thank you, Jack." Suzanne's voice is cool. "My husband is back from his call; I'm going to go join him. Nice seeing you again, Isa. Very nice to meet you, Jack."

"Always happy to meet my fans." Jack pulls me close so he can wrap both arms around me. He rests his chin on my head.

"Wow, that was fun," he says with a low voice only I can hear. "Good job."

"Thank you for that." Suzanne has sat down at a table with an older man who looks like he's ready for a round of golf. Hmm. Could it be that we might have something in common? We're both interested in older men.

The thought makes me stiffen, and Jack drops his arms from around my body. We return to our chairs, Jack holding mine for me again. He sits down and reaches for my hand again to keep the charade going.

"I saw her making you squirm, and I didn't like that." He's keeping his expression pleasant, but his voice is stern. I've noticed he drops the smooth Southern drawl when he's serious. "You looked uncomfortable. Figured we could really turn the tables on her."

"Thank you. Suzanne has always been everything I'm not."

"I'd contradict you, but someone told me to stop complimenting her."

I groan. "I said to stop flattering me! Sincere compliments

are different." Hearing myself flirt with Jack Freaking Kendall is surreal. In what world is this happening?

"By the way, you're Jack Kendall?"

"You didn't know that? I thought Sarah would have told you."

"No, I had no idea," I say, my mind buzzing.

A shadow falls over our table and I brace myself for another fan, but it's Winston. "Can I get you anything more?"

"I think we're good. Thank you," Jack says. "Everything was excellent as usual."

Winston smiles, and I snag the last bite of waffle with my fork as he clears our empty plates.

"They clear pretty quickly. They don't want uneaten food left on the table," Jack says.

"Oh yeah? Why's that?"

"Iguanas will finish what's left." Jack looks up into the trees, pretending to be worried. "Drinks too."

"Not what I want to hear." I look up too, but see nothing more than greenery. "Cut it out."

Jack is laughing at me now. "I'm just having some fun."

"As long as you don't actually see more iguanas." I shudder. I like the teasing, but not the iguanas.

"No, seriously, the iguanas will rob the tables. And, if there are flowers on the table, they'll eat those too."

"Wonderful." I can only imagine what else they do. "I'll have nightmares about them tonight."

"If you do, call me." Jack winks. "Ringo and I'll come right over."

I cock my head. "Who's Ringo? Your drummer?"

"He's my pup."

"So if I had a nightmare that I was getting attacked by iguanas, you and Ringo would come over?"

"Absolutely!" Jack nods emphatically.

I smile at him. I think I would like that.

FIVE

March 5

THE CEILING FAN is clicking and the moonlight stripes the wall next to me as I look at the boys' picture on my phone. As much as I don't want to interact with Ben, I hoped I could talk with Cole before the boys' bedtime. My baby turned three today.

Nothing.

When I put down the device, it buzzes several times. I flip it over, and it's Jack blowing up my phone.

Hey girlfriend!

What ya doin?

I'm sitting here, thinking of ya

A series of hearts follows the messages.

I smile to myself. Jack is fun—I'll give him that. I had a great time with him and his friends, first paddling out to the reef, then tethering our kayaks to each other before submerging to see the underwater life. The crystal-clear water was illuminated by the sun, affording me views of bumpy coral, spiky urchins, and smoothly fluttering rays. I could've stayed there for hours.

When he dropped me off at my villa afterward, Jack confessed that when he'd excused himself at breakfast, he'd called some of the greatest troublemakers in their group and told them to be on their best behavior. *No flirting*, he'd said. *Don't scare her off.*

The guys must really like Jack because everyone was respectful and courteous. What was that I learned about green flag behavior in those library books?

That's sweet, I text back.

A knock at the door startles me. I guess Jack couldn't wait for an answer and decided to ask me in person.

I open the door.

"Hi, Isa."

"Suzanne?" I ask, surprised. "How did you find me? Why are you here?"

She steps closer to the porch light, and I think I see tear tracks on her cheeks.

"I'm not stalking you, I promise! I asked at the Westin where Jack Kendall takes his dates—other than Snorkels—and they suggested We Be Jammin'. I told the bartender we were supposed to meet up but I'd lost your address. She didn't know where you were staying, just that you were in a villa. I've been knocking on doors, and you're my fourth. Please don't be mad."

"So that's how you found me, but not why you're here. Still, I suppose you should come in."

I stand aside and she steps past me, expensive perfume wafting in with her. I turn on the lights and can confirm she's been crying. "Sit down." I guide her to the small table near the kitchenette. "Can I get you some water, juice, maybe a soda? Sorry I don't have more to offer you."

"I'll take some water, thank you." Suzanne is quiet as I fill a glass of water from a bottle in the fridge.

"I don't have anyone to talk to," she blurts. I set the glass in front of her and sink into a chair across from her. "Henry has no time for me. We've only been married for two weeks. We're still on our honeymoon, for fuck's sake. All he does is talk on the phone. He talks to everyone but me. He's interested in everybody except me."

"How long are you supposed to be on your honeymoon?"

"A month." Suzanne sobs into her glass of water. "But we're supposed to be spending it together. We're supposed to be in love. We're supposed to be"—she hiccups—"happy."

A *month*? I can't imagine a weeklong honeymoon, much less one that lasts a month. The economic difference between Suzanne and me is enormous. But, I can relate with the honeymoon that doesn't meet expectations and the neglectful spouse.

"It's all work stuff, I guess. But I really don't know?" The question ends on a wail, and Suzanne turns tear-filled eyes to me.

I rise and look around the villa for tissues, finally resorting to snagging a roll of toilet paper from the bathroom. Back in the kitchenette, I hand the roll to Suzanne, who winds off a wad to blow her nose and wipe her eyes.

"I wish I knew what to tell you. You're so lucky he's able to travel and take that time off for so long for your honeymoon. But, maybe, there's some sort of emergency at work?" Her sobs are slowing as I offer another perspective.

"You think so?" She looks relieved.

"Perhaps he's under a lot of pressure trying to balance you and his company? Has he spent *any* time with you?" My late-night visitor visibly relaxes.

"We've had some good times together. He took me to this incredible restaurant on the other side of the island when we first got here, but then he disappeared into the kitchen for a while." She laughs nervously. "Talk about awkward."

I know awkward.

"Anyway, thanks for listening," Suzanne says. "Wow, what are you, like a marriage counselor or something?" She wipes her nose and smiles.

"No." I laugh to myself. I'm in no position to counsel anyone on how to be married.

"Where's your hottie? I can't believe you, Isa Cushing, hooked up with Jack Kendall."

"We're not hooking up." I'm not sure I want to have this conversation with Suzanne. "We met a week ago; we're just friends."

"I just saw him over at the bar turning away women. Telling them he has a girlfriend?"

"That's probably what he says all the time to women who throw themselves at him."

"He has a reputation, you know. Don't you read *People*?"

"No, Suzanne, I don't read *People* magazine." I suppose I could've while the boys and I visited the Kennebunk Library, but I stayed too busy keeping after them and researching solutions for gardening problems like tomato blight. "I didn't even know what Jack Kendall really looked like." I lean in as if to tell my guest a secret. "When I met him, I thought he was some beach bum living on the island trying to avoid real life."

"You didn't!"

"Yep. Not kidding."

"To be fair, the pictures they ran with the article were from his concerts, so maybe you wouldn't have recognized him anyway. But Isa!" Now it's Suzanne's turn to lean in. "In the article, he said he's thinking about quitting the music scene since he's nearly fifty. That he's done with his hectic schedules and just wants to be left alone. Besides, he hasn't come out with a big hit song in a long time."

"Oh, I didn't realize he was that much older than me. That must explain why he's been such a gentleman."

"Well, you and I are what, nearly thirty? Henry's quite a bit older than I am too. Get it, girl!" She reaches across the table for a high five, which I reluctantly give her. "But back to Jack. He's never been married but always has a woman on his arm." Suzanne sits up straight and looks proud of the research she's done. "*People* magazine says—"

"I'm not sleeping with him"—it was only one time—"and I'm not his latest flavor of the week. He's just been kind, showing me around."

Suzanne opens her mouth as if to speak but must change her mind because she takes a drink instead. She sets the glass on the table and squares her shoulders, her gaze wary.

"We're supposed to be here for another week or two. If Henry keeps having these work emergencies, I'll have lots of free time. You and I could hang out and reconnect. We could become great friends!"

She wants to be friends with me? Is she really that lonely? But I've been where she is. I could've used a friend the past few years. "Sure. That sounds nice."

"How long are you here?"

"To be honest, I have no idea. I have no real plans to head back to Maine."

"Do you have anything else to drink?"

"Just the complementary juice and soda."

"Want to head next door? Henry won't miss me."

"Sure, let me change."

I pull on cutoffs and a clean tank, and brush my hair. "Let's go."

"You aren't going to put any makeup on?"

"Uh, no?" I don't have any, but she doesn't need to know that.

Suzanne shrugs. "Well, can I use your bathroom to fix mine?"

I gesture the way. "Be my guest."

I slip my flip-flops on and step outside onto the porch to wait for Suzanne. When she comes out, she's washed her face, and except for the redness in her eyes, she doesn't show any signs of crying. I lock the door, and we head down the sandy, moonlit path to Jammin'. The breeze is warm and heavy, and the salt smell from the waves breaking on the beach is intoxicating.

A modernized version of Hank Williams's "Honky Tonkin'" greets us as we near the bar. Suzanne eyes me expectantly, her eyebrows raised. "Oh, pshaw. It could be anyone playing," I say.

"Or it could be your hot country star."

"For goodness' sake, Suzanne. He's not 'my' country star."

"So you're not denying he's hot."

I throw my hands into the air and enter Jammin', wiping my feet of sand as I do so. When I look up, I lock eyes with Jack, who's finishing up honky tonkin' around town. When the final chords die, he removes his guitar and sets it on a stand, then leans into the microphone and announces a short break. Canned music plays through the speakers overhead as he jumps from the stage and makes his way to us. All eyes in the bar that were once on Jack alone are now on Jack and me.

"I didn't think you were coming out tonight. Did you get my texts?"

"Ah, yes. I saw you texted." Honestly, I had forgotten about his messages what with Suzanne and all her drama. "I'm sorry I didn't respond. Suzanne stopped by and needed to talk, then we decided to come out for a drink. I didn't know you were playing tonight."

Jack wraps an arm around me and kisses my cheek. "I was hoping I'd get to see ya tonight," he whispers in my ear, his breath stirring my hair and making shivers run down my spine.

My belly heats with warmth. I don't want a repeat of my experience with Ben, but I can't stop my reaction to the attention of this man.

"Well, now, let's hear some music," I say as I pull away.

"Hiya," Jack acknowledges Suzanne, then returns to the stage and climbs onto his stool, where he starts singing about falling in love with a stranger on a Mexican beach.

We find a couple of seats at the bar. The first thing out of Sarah's mouth is, "He's been waiting for you to show up all night. I've never seen him like this. He's never this intent on waiting for anyone. He picks up a lot of women, but he seems pretty smitten with you."

Huh. I swing around and look at Jack, who winks when he notices me looking at him. My body heats and I turn back to Sarah. A painkiller is just what I need tonight.

As Sarah blends Pusser's dark rum, pineapple and orange juices, and cream of coconut, she nods at me. "Looks like you found her," she says to Suzanne. "Everything OK now?"

Suzanne straightens up. "It is, thanks again."

"Suzanne and I went to the same high school a long, long time ago," I say. "We ran into each other when Jack and I were at breakfast the other morning. She and her new husband are staying on the island for a bit."

"Where's your husband tonight?" Sarah asks as she grates fresh nutmeg onto my drink.

"He has to work, but I texted him to join us later."

Sarah slides the glass to me and moves away to wait on another couple across the U-shaped bar.

Up on the small wooden stage, Jack is talking into his microphone. "I only have time to play one more song. I just wrote it, and I've been waiting for her to be here to sing it. So here it goes. Let me know what you think."

Jack picks a slow but catchy tune on his worn guitar. "This is called 'Old Beaches,'" he says and starts to sing, his gaze never leaving mine:

SHE HIDES THE BRUISES BENEATH HER SLEEVES

A BROKEN HEART

HER SPIRIT SHATTERED,

HER DREAMS DESTROYED

OLD BEACHES OF THE NORTH

SHE ALMOST LOST IT ALL

BATTERED AND BROKEN BY THE WAVES

SHE HAS BETTER SANDS TO RUN ON

SHE'S STRONGER THAN SHE KNOWS

SHE WAS TRAPPED

THOUGHT SHE COULDN'T SAIL

TO GET OFF THE OLD BEACH

AND WHEN SHE FOUND HERSELF

AND RAN ON GLIMMERING SANDS

SHE'S ON THAT BETTER BEACH NOW

BATTERED AND BROKEN BY THE WAVES

SHE HAS BETTER SANDS TO RUN ON

AND SHE'S STRONGER THAN SHE KNOWS

SHE'S ON A BETTER BEACH NOW, FREE TO GROW

SHE COULD DO IT ALONE

THERE'S A WORLD OF LOVE

SHE'S NEVER EVEN KNEW

THE SHORE IS LONG

AND SHE'S NO LONGER RUNNING ALONE

SHE'S ON A BETTER BEACH

THE BAR IS quiet when Jack finishes, then bursts into applause.

"What do y'all think? Is it something I should record?" Jack asks.

"Sounds like your next hit, Jack!" someone at a table screams.

Jack removes his guitar and sets it in the stand again before heading my way. Mortification clings to me like a shroud. I haven't shared my inner thoughts with anyone, at least not in that detail, and Jack not only knows, he wrote a song about them.

"How much did you read?" I stare at Jack.

"Your story was heartbreaking," Jack says. "I wanted to give you something positive after all that."

"You read my notes?"

"I was fidgeting with the fruit bowl while ya showered, and then the notes started to scatter, so I collected them, and one thing led to another." He takes my hand; I'm so numb I don't resist. "What you described—your emotion, your pain—I'm so sorry that happened to you. You're so strong. And amazing."

"Jack, that writing was personal." Calmly, very calmly, I stand up and look at him. I'm hurt that he read something I wasn't ready to share. I'm not ready to share it with anyone.

"Isa. Please," Jack pleads. "I didn't mean to hurt you. I didn't know what it was."

"Then why didn't you stop reading once you realized it was personal?"

"I wanted to get to know you better."

Angry, upset words fill my mouth, but I hold them in. Getting angry with Ben always backfired on me. Ben screams a lot louder than I ever could. Finally, I find something safe to say.

"Did you ever think about just asking me?"

Jack seems to wilt, his muscular swimmer's body now crumpled at the edges. "I really am sorry you're upset, Isa. I thought you'd like the song."

"Even if I liked it, now everyone knows something's wrong with me, that I'm damaged." I move past Jack, my destination the solitude of the beach, but he reaches out, grasping my wrist. I brace myself, ready to be shaken in punishment, but Jack just holds on. I dredge up courage from my weary soul and pull away—"Please leave me alone"—finally making my escape from the bar and my humiliation.

I walk back to my villa alone. No one chases after me. No one tries to stop me. No one tries to apologize to me. Jack knows I'm mad and I'm hurt. I hope he doesn't share where he got the inspiration for his song with anyone. I don't want my new friends to know that Isa. How could women like Sarah and Suzanne spend time with a disaster like me?

What started out being a nice evening has ended being a crappy one.

I pull on my oversized T-shirt and climb into bed.

My phone buzzes with a text message from Jack.

I'm sorry

Please forgive me

I feel bad now. Did I overreact? I did leave my notes out in the open where visitors could read them, but still he should have asked me, not written a song.

Am I being overly sensitive? This is all new to me. A disagreement without yelling. I don't think Jack realized he violated my privacy. Ben wouldn't have cared. Now that I have some physical distance between us, I realize Ben never cared. At least, he never apologized. Jack said he's sorry. If I were in his shoes, I'd feel terrible. But this is *my* past, and it's my decision when to deal with it. Now is not that time.

I stuff the shame and the fear and the guilt down and fall asleep, the clicking of the ceiling fan and the tune of Jack's new song playing over and over in my head like a broken record.

SIX

March 9

HER INATTENTIVE HUSBAND ASIDE, I envy Suzanne. Staying in St. John indefinitely would be the fulfillment of a dream I didn't know I had but for two things. Well, three. First, I'd lose any chances to run into the boys in town or even to get them back. Two, I'd have to find a job. Island life isn't cheap. And third? I shrink against the rock wall adjacent to the road as another vehicle roars past. Driving on the wrong side of the road.

Habit has me walking on the left side of the road, and back in Kennebunk, I'd be facing oncoming traffic. Here, though, I'm always surprised by a vehicle approaching from behind. Once they're safely past me, I scurry across to the other side so I'm traveling against traffic. I'm in constant fear of being hit by a Jeep while I walk, yet I can't seem to break my habit.

St. John has been occupied for centuries, and the roads expanded for motor vehicles have eaten up sidewalks and shoulders. When I walk into town, I press against thick brush or stone walls to make myself as small as possible. There is no room for error. Nowhere for me to go if I realize at the last minute that I'm in the wrong and need to get out of the way.

This morning, a rumbling stomach woke me up, interrupting a wonderful dream of eating waffles. I stumbled over to the fridge to see if there might be anything to eat. But when I opened the door, it contained the same juice and soda it had yesterday. I grabbed a bottle of a juice blend, hoping the sugar and light pulp would quiet my stomach temporarily.

I changed into a T-shirt and cutoffs and slid into my flip-flops and headed out to a little café just a short walk away.

I'm nearing the café when I hear a horn blast.

Beep, beep, be-ep, be-ep.

I flatten myself against the wall so I won't get hit by a driver traveling the narrow road. As the vehicle nears, I recognize the deafening sound of a missing exhaust. When it stops next to me, I'm relieved to see Jack behind the wheel, his body vibrating with the rough engine. He waves a hand and smiles, but it's not the sun-rivaling brilliance I've seen from him before. Jack checks that no one is behind him or ahead, then turns off the engine.

"These roads aren't safe for you, Isa," he calls. "Jump in! I'll take ya where you need to go." He swallows. Looks down, then back up at me. "That is, if you forgive me."

I made up my mind that I wouldn't spend more time with Jack, but he seems contrite, and until he sang that song, I'd felt more like myself than I had in years. So maybe the safest decision is to accept the offer of a ride. I survived our previous trips together, though his Jeep looks like it's falling apart.

Peeling myself off the stone, I brush myself off and carefully cross the road and round the front of the Jeep. I climb inside, then snap on my seat belt before I do anything else.

"I'm so glad to see you! These roads scare me."

"I wasn't expecting you would ever talk to me again," he says.

"I forgive you," I blurt out. Jack's face brightens. "Thank you for leaving me alone last night."

His eyebrows knit in confusion.

"You didn't blow up my phone begging for forgiveness," I say. "Well, *after* you blew up my phone earlier in the evening, I mean."

"I'm so sorry."

"I know you are. Your song was really nice. It was just awful of you to read my private thoughts."

"I apologize, and I won't sing it again until you say it's okay for me to sing."

My heart swells. This is how it's supposed to be. Jack is remorseful. Ben never showed remorse.

Jack's eyes crease in the corners as he squints against the morning sun. "Where are we going?"

"Well, I had a dream about waffles. I'm so hungry." I sit back in my seat and grab the oh shit handle as Jack puts his hand on the key. I don't want to think I'm going to die every time a vehicle passes us, but I know it's a high likelihood I will. "I was headed somewhere to get breakfast."

"Just waffles?"

"Yep, but I don't have the budget for Snorkels, so I was hoping the café up the road would have some more in my price range."

"I know just the place."

Jack turns the key and puts the Jeep in gear. As we drive, I can't hear anything else he says. I just smile and nod and hold on for the ride. When an oncoming Jeep passes us, Jack beeps and waves, returning the beep and wave from the other driver.

Minutes later, we pull into the parking lot of a cute little shack-type eatery that overlooks Galge Cove. Jack turns off the ignition and takes my hand. His hand is warm and strong, and the calluses on his fingers, which I now know are from playing guitar, are rough against my skin. Butterflies spring to life in my stomach, and I realize I'm nervous, but also incredibly excited. We made it through our first disagreement. *See Suzanne,* I imagine saying to her. *He's just a respectful, helpful gentleman. Nothing else to see here.*

"I'm so glad I ran into you this morning," he says with a squeeze of my hand.

"I'm glad you didn't run into me." I pull my hand from his. "But I'm happy to see you. I'm starving!"

"Let's get ya fed." He leads me around to the back of the building. Its large, covered deck high up on the hill has a beautiful view of the bay.

"Are there any restaurants here that don't have a perfect view of the water?" I don't think I could ever get used to how beautiful this island is.

"Would you like to sit over here?" Jack guides me to the high top at the far edge of the deck, away from the few diners who are enjoying a late breakfast of their own. "Is this OK?" I nod, and he pulls my chair out for me.

"Thank you." He helps me climb up on the tall chair, then sits down across from me.

A server approaches immediately. "Hello, Mr. Kendall." This man knows Jack too? He turns to me. "May I bring you some coffee?"

"Yes, that sounds perfect. Thank you."

"Make that two," Jack adds. The waiter sets menus on the table and hurries away.

"Is there anywhere on the island that people don't know you?" I look at him with curiosity and a little bit of amazement. This is Jack Kendall, performer of some of my favorite songs, but I had no idea who he was. And for some reason, he likes spending time with me.

"It's a small island, like I told ya, so everyone who lives here knows everyone else."

"I know. But like when we were driving and the guy beeped, and you beeped back."

"That's what everyone does here regardless of whether you know the person or not. Besides, it's not just an island thing. It's a Jeep thing."

"Well, you should stop it."

Jack chuckles as the server sets down coffees, an assortment of sweeteners, and an insulated pitcher of cream. "Why?" I indicate the pitcher, and Jack proceeds to add cream to my coffee before handing it to me.

"Well, it's dangerous. Beeping your horn all the time could set your airbag off." At least, that's what I've been told. All I can think of is him beeping the horn for some frivolous reason and the steering wheel exploding in his face, breaking his beautiful nose and front teeth.

Jack is outright laughing at me. "That's not how airbags work, but even if they did, ya don't have to worry. My Jeep doesn't have airbags."

"What? It doesn't have any airbags?" My brow lowers and my voice flattens. "It's more dangerous than I thought."

"Don't worry. I'm a good driver. I won't let anything happen to you."

"It's not your driving that worries me, it's your vehicle."

I can't believe I'm arguing with a country music star about his car, or that he's being so nice about it. Ben would have never allowed it.

For something to do, I look through the menu, and I'm glad I did. This kitchen offers waffles with mango syrup and mango-glazed bacon. I've learned on my trip that I like mango, so I'm all in on those two items. Our server comes back to take our order, and I sip my coffee while Jack orders for us. My stomach grumbles with the words "waffles" and "bacon."

"May I bring you anything else? Perhaps one of our morning cocktails?" The server is almost too polite and professional for this casual restaurant.

Jack and I look at each other. "Isa, would you like anything? You *are* on vacation."

"I will if you will." I shrug and set my coffee down. It appears I set a precedent at Snorkels.

"Let's make it a trifecta for my guest. Two mimosas, mango if you have it. Thank you." The server confirms mango mimosas are indeed available, then walks off, leaving us to stare at each other.

This is now the fifth time I've seen Jack, and every time, I've noticed something new about him. Today, his hair has caught my attention. It's a silly thing to focus on, but he really does have nice hair. I'm glad he doesn't wear a hat like some men do.

"So." Jack reaches both hands across the table, palms up. I've also noticed he likes to touch. I think of what Suzanne said about Jack always having a different woman on his arm. He's spent time with me—even wrote me a song, misguided as he was—and treated me to breakfast twice now. I'm sure my time with him is up soon, so I'll enjoy the royal treatment while I can. I slip my hands into his and grin. "What's your plan for the rest of the day?"

"I was just gonna get something to eat and then go back to the beach." My thumbs stroke his knuckles. "I picked up a notebook, an actual journal, at the stationery store near the library. Also bought a glue stick and pasted those sheets in it so I don't lose them. I'm going to do some more journaling this afternoon when the sun gets too hot."

"Why don't ya hang out with me today?" Jack smiles warmly at me. "I want to show ya the island."

"You don't have anything better to do than show some tourist around?" I laugh at the word "tourist" because I'm enjoying my new identity.

"I would like nothing else. I can't think of a more perfect way to spend my day."

The server returns with our mimosas. "Your meals should not be long."

"Thank you," I say, realizing how hungry I am as he leaves.

"Sounds like fun. I'd love to go," I say to Jack. "But what about your dog. Bingo, was it?"

He smiles, and my heart skips a beat. His smiles make me feel special. They're real smiles, not the practiced, professional one he used with Suzanne.

"Thank ya kindly for asking after my pup. His name's Ringo, and he's well cared for."

Our meals arrive and I dig in, drowning my waffles in mango syrup and spreading around the real whipped cream before I take a massive bite.

"Mmph-mm," I say, my mouth too full to speak.

Jack laughs. "I take it you like them?"

I nod emphatically, and swallow. "Oh my gosh, they're so goooood! Crispy and fluffy and the sweet-tart sauce?" I groan. "I could eat these every day."

"I like a woman who likes to eat. I'm enjoying watching you enjoy yourself." His words finish on a growl and heat flares low in my belly. My heart thumps. "I like a woman who appreciates good... food."

My mimosa is in my hand and I've swallowed a huge gulp before I know it. Did I say I was feeling heat? I didn't know I could incinerate this quickly. Maybe Suzanne was right about Jack. "Oh, well, you don't have to worry about that with me."

My voice is light and floaty, almost as if it's coming from outside my body.

Jack shifts in his chair, stretching out his legs, then asks, "How's your bacon?"

I snap a piece of the caramelized meat between my teeth and savor its layers of flavors. "So good."

Our meal finished, we head out to the Jeep. "Please, don't beep the horn," I beg before Jack turns the key and won't be able to hear me.

"If it makes ya feel safer, I won't."

I'm reaching for my seat belt when, "Isa Lane," Jack says solemnly. A peal of laughter erupts from me, and I turn toward Jack.

"Silly goo—" His expression is more serious than I've ever seen it. "What? What's the matter?" Now I'm worried. Is he upset about my fear of an overused car horn? I know now it's irrational—I don't think Jack would've lied to me about how an airbag, of all things, works—but I can't help my fear.

But no, he gently lays a hand on my knee and cradles my face with the other. I can't move. Is this really happening? Is Jack Kendall about to kiss me?

"Is this OK?"

I nod, knowing what's coming but not able to stop it. I don't want to stop it. Oh God, I've been divorced just a month and now—

His lips cover mine. Softly. Tenderly. I allow my eyes to close as I savor this kind connection. It's warm. And safe. That thought thrills me even more than the arousal that floods my body. My heart races, and I reach for his neck to hold him close. I've just begun to open my mouth to deepen the kiss when a Jeep pulls into the spot next to us, destroying our moment.

"You're so sweet," Jack murmurs in a low voice as he backs off.

"That's the mango syrup," I reply, breathless.

We settle into our respective seats and Jack turns the ignition, the biggest grin on his face. The cacophony of a mufflerless combustion engine starts right up. "Buckle up!" I shout, and we pull onto the narrow road where he found me earlier this morning.

Jack drives us along the scenic island loop that follows the perimeter of St. John. Every time we arrive at a beautiful beach or an overlook with a breathtaking view, Jack stops the Jeep and we get out to gaze at the view or explore. Signs posted around the island remind us not to leave trash or take shells or coral as souvenirs. I focus on collecting memories instead.

Jack tells me facts he's collected over the years he's stayed on St. John, punctuating the trivia with kisses on my cheeks, my forehead, and once even my nose. I wonder what he's thinking, why he won't kiss me for real like he did back at the breakfast shack. Is he finally realizing I'm too young and naive?

Jack pulls over near a group of imposing buildings and athletic fields and turns off the noise. "What's this place?" I ask.

"It's the Gifft Hill School." Jack puts on his tour guide voice. "It's a private school. Preschool to twelfth grade. If I had kids and lived here full time, they would attend here."

That last bit sounded wistful. The jovial Jack that was here a minute ago is gone.

"Do you want kids?"

"I don't have any that I'm aware of anyway. Besides, it wouldn't have been fair with my lifestyle and all. I do have regrets."

"There's still time. You can still have a family."

"Oh, I wish I could." He looks at me. "I have a confession, but I don't want ya to run."

Sound ominous. "What?"

"You're young. A lot younger than me." I nod. "And you

must know I'm enjoying our time together. What I'm going to say might make ya think bad of me." He pounds his fists on his muscular thighs as he heaves a breath. "I had a vasectomy early on in my career. I didn't want to risk fathering a child with someone who..."

"I can fill in the blanks." I'm torn between excitement that Jack enjoys my company and sympathy for him.

"I led a fast life, never settled down."

"And now?"

"And now, I'm tired. I missed out on a lot. Don't get me wrong—I've had a great life. I love singing, but I've missed out on having a family. So, I had a revision."

"A revision? They can do that?"

"The doctors reversed the vasectomy. Well, they tried, at least. They don't think they were successful. There was a lot of scar tissue." Jack's blue eyes dull as he stares down at his empty hands. "I was hoping to meet someone and..."

How does he know that the revision didn't work? Is there some sort of test? Or did he try to start a family with someone and it didn't work out? I have so many questions, but it's not the right time to ask.

"Why can't you still have both?" I meet his eyes. From what I've seen, he could be a wonderful husband. He'd treat his wife miles better than Ben treated me on his best day.

"It wouldn't be fair." Jack shrugs and looks out at the school. "A wife and babies now? Men my age are becoming grandparents, not first-time dads." Jack sighs. "I don't want to be selfish."

"Then don't be." For a man with the resources I assume he has, parenting would be a breeze. "Jack, there are plenty of things you can do."

Funny that I'm the one giving advice. But what I've gone through has made me stronger,

"What do you mean?" he asks, his voice small.

"Do you want kids? I'm sure you could get a second opinion. Or adopt. Marry someone who already has kids." I deliberately don't think about how I resemble that last option. "You could retire, write songs, write a book, open restaurants." I make my voice light and teasing when I add, "You should be writing my ideas down."

"I should be; you're right." Jack laughs. "It's getting late, and we missed lunch. Wanna hit up our place for an early dinner on the beach?"

"Sounds delightful."

As we busy ourselves with refastening our seat belts, I say, "You're right, by the way. This is a nice school. If the teachers are as nice as the outside, I'd love to send my boys here. It's so pretty and peaceful." Although, with a tropical beach so close, how can the students get any studying done?

Jack grins at me before he starts up the Jeep and we head back to what I'm beginning to think of as home.

SARAH WAVES when we walk in. "Hi, guys!" We sit down in my usual spot, and she comes around from behind the bar to give me a hug. What a sweet person. Friend hugs feel good. "You got some sun on your cheeks."

I check, and she's right—the skin on my face is feeling toasty. I've been good about avoiding sunburn so far, but my luck might have just run out. "Jack took me on an impromptu tour of the coast road. I didn't expect to be out so long, so I didn't apply sunscreen. It's worth it, though. The shoreline is so pretty." I lean over and bump Jack's shoulder with mine. "And this guy could have a second career as a tour guy."

"Usual?" Sarah asks Jack, but it's not really a question.

"Please." There's a stillness to him that worries me. What he told me must still be weighing on him. But as if he's reading my mind, he sits back and says, "Enough about me. I'm depressing. Let's talk about you."

"You aren't nearly as depressing as me," I say. "I'm on vacation, so I hide it better."

"Indefinite vacation?"

"I like to think of it as an 'open-ended' vacation."

"Like an open-ended airline ticket?"

"Exactly." I take a big sip of my drink and enjoy the warmth of the rum. "When I'm close to running out of money and if I still don't have a plan, then it's time to go back to Maine. But I don't want to go back, so that should help me make a decision before then."

"So we need to work on you too." We smile like fools at each other, and as if by mutual agreement, set aside talk of serious things and just enjoy each other's company. "Thanks for today."

"What do you mean? You're the one who drove me around. Thank *you*!" I reach over and give his hand a little squeeze.

We order spicy peel-and-eat shrimp for dinner. Eventually, the day catches up to me, and I'm ready for a nap.

"Walk me back to my villa?" I ask after returning from washing my hands.

"Sure. Let me make sure Sarah puts both our meals on my tab."

My instinct is to protest—I don't want Jack to think I'm spending time with him because he's wealthy—but prudence wins out. Allowing Jack to pay allows me to conserve my cash, which means I can stay longer on the island.

"Thanks, Jack. See you tomorrow, Sarah?"

"I'll be here." Giving her a wave, we step out from under the thatch of the bar's tiki-style roof and onto the beach.

Jack wraps his arm around me, and although the late afternoon sun is bright, I snuggle in. It's been an emotional day. At my door, Jack turns toward me and looks deep into my eyes. This close, I can see dark flecks in his clear blue irises. There's a bump on his nose; I wonder whether he broke it as a child.

"Thanks again, Isa." I nod as he adds, "You don't know how nice it is to have someone I can talk to, but vulnerable with. Your treatment of me hasn't changed now that ya know who I am. You push back." He grins, and the skin beside his eyes crinkles inro rays of happiness. "Give me hell about vehicle safety." Then he sobers. "You're someone who doesn't have something to gain from me. You're not angling for me to get your demo to my label, wear your latest Western fashion on tour, or have me sign fifteen T-shirts. Heck, I don't even know whether ya *like* country music."

"It's OK." I shrug, then laugh at his glum face. "Yes, silly, I like country music. I like *your* music. And I like spending time with you too."

Then I prepare to do something I haven't done in at least seven years. "Stay."

"You want me to?" Jack asks, surprised.

"Yes, take a nap with me."

I lead him into the villa, where I busy myself getting each of us a bottle of water. Jack undresses down to his boxers, and I shimmy out of my shorts and unhook my bra, letting it fall from under my T-shirt. We climb into my bed and lie facing each other.

"Hi." I giggle.

"Hi," he says and runs a finger over my eyebrow. "I like the way your pillows smell. Like you."

"Is this pillow talk? I haven't slept with anyone other than my ex."

"Ever?"

I nod, shy, my senses on high alert. He likes my smell? Right back atcha. His scent is all that fills my nostrils.

Jack encourages me to roll over, then pulls me to himself, his arm solid and secure. "I'm just gonna hold ya."

Our bodies fit perfectly together. His body aligns with my curves, leaving no space between us. Some people might find this claustrophobic, but not me, not today. I need to be touched, and I think Jack does too.

"You're wrong," I say with my eyes closed, half asleep.

"I am?"

Yawning, I mumble, "I do want something from you."

"What's that?"

"I want you make the Jeep a little safer, maybe put a door or two on."

Jack chuckles. "I'll see what I can do." He squeezes me gently, and I can feel his breath on my shoulder as he speaks. "Now sleep, Isa Diane Cushing."

"Nope, still not it." And I drift to sleep.

"YOU'RE PERFECT," Jack whispers in my ear.

"Hmm?" I stretch, and he leans in to kiss my shoulder.

"Are you awake?"

"No." I clench my eyes tight. "Go back to sleep."

He props himself up on his elbow to lean over me. "Well, I'm wide awake."

"What time is it?"

"Six-fifteen." He runs his fingers down the length of my exposed arm to the tip of my index finger, my skin pebbling in his wake.

"That was the best nap I've ever had. I refuse to let it end," I protest.

Jack snorts softly as he laces his fingers with mine. While we slept, my T-shirt scrunched up, exposing my back to Jack's hard, naked chest. His body blazes with heat, and his heart beats steadily against my back.

"Sorry, but I need to go. A conference call with my producer." He grimaces.

I roll to face him instead of continuing to strain to see him. "Have you told them you're thinking of retiring?"

"Not yet. I'm still thinking about it." He tugs on a lock of my hair. "But I'm thinking about something else now."

"Oh, yeah?"

His fingers wake my nerves, sending pulses of electricity through my body as they travel down my side, tracing a path to my hip. He pauses when he comes to my white cotton panties. They're more gray than white, having aged along with me. I'd splurged on sexy lingerie when Ben and I were dating, but after we married, there wasn't any room in the budget to replace pieces as they wore out.

When I don't resist Jack's touch, he plays with the waistband. Running his teasing finger along the inside, sparks trailing his fingertips. My head might not be fully awake, but my nerve endings are making up for it.

Finally, his fingers move away from my waist, and I think I'll finally get some relief from the electricity of his touch, but the ache that's building low in my belly grows as he drapes his arm over me again and drags his hand up my back. The calluses from years of playing the guitar catch on each bump and hollow of my spine. He combs through my hair, stroking it before he brushes it away, exposing the side of my neck.

Jack leans down and kisses my sensitive skin, and my gasps push my breasts against his firm chest. The temperature in the room is warm, but I have chills. No chance of falling back to sleep now.

Jack's arm muscles flex as hugs me, and I can feel that he's hard, pressing against my thigh.

"I wasn't expecting this," I say softly, not wanting to spoil the mood. "I wasn't expecting you."

"I've wanted you since I bumped into you that day in the water."

"Really?" I'm sure I looked a mess next to his spectacular good looks.

"When I saw you later, I knew I had to get to know you better." He kisses behind my ear, his breath stirring my hair. More chills. "When I saw you, my heart raced. I didn't know what to say. I felt like an awkward school boy."

I giggle and relax into his hold. "I thought you were an Olympic swimmer." Feeling brave, I place my hand on his side, and the soft skin twitches under my palm. "A *hot* Olympic swimmer."

Jack moves his hand to my belly just above my panties. I release his body—his hard, muscular body—and guide his hand beneath the cotton, letting him feel how wet he's made me.

"I guess you like *hot* Olympic swimmers."

SEVEN

March 13

SUZANNE and I are lying on the teak deck of the boat Henry chartered, staying out of the way of the two men who are working on the engine. Our bodies contour to the sides of the boat, and our heads meet at the bow, creating a V. I'm port; Suzanne is starboard. I'm learning boat lingo fast.

Ringo keeps coming over and licking my face to let me know he has an eye on me. He's been hanging out with me for the past three days. Jack's conference call led to him leaving the island. He offered me the company of his dog, and I've been glad to have it. If Ringo ever gets to be too much or something happens, Jack gave me a number to call for one of his staff members to take over. If that doesn't make me feel like I'm in a dream—Jack has *staff*.

Suzanne lifts her head and squints at Ringo. "He doesn't let you out of his sight."

"It's nice to have a protector." I open my eyes and see

Ringo, in his shark fin life jacket, lying in the shade by the cabin.

"I really think he likes you."

"He's a very sweet dog. Jack rescued him from the side of the road two years ago. They've been best friends ever since. It's helpful Ringo likes me too. I was beginning to miss having someone or something to care for."

"No, I think *Jack* really likes you." Suzanne rolls onto her side so we are face to face. "I can tell he's in love with you."

"I really doubt that. We're just friends." Friends who take naps together and spend nearly every day with each other. "There's too much uncertainty in Jack's life. I don't think either of us is looking for a relationship. I definitely don't think I'm ready."

"I'm telling you, Jack doesn't take his eyes off you when you're together. And look. He *is* entrusting you with his best friend." She giggles. "You said he takes Ringo with him when he travels, and now he's left him with you?"

"That's ridiculous." I laugh too, but Suzanne is right. I have noticed Jack staring at me, and Jack sharing Ringo with me? With someone he met less than two weeks ago? I've found myself counting the hours until I next see Jack. I do like him looking at me. The thought of there being a deeper meaning behind his attention bothers me, so I shove it aside. "I'm getting hot. Let's go for a swim."

I stand up and dive into the crystal-clear water. Once I surface, I yell to Suzanne, "Jump in! It's so nice!" Ringo takes that as his cue and, barking, jumps off the boat to join me.

Just as Suzanne hits the water, her bikini top falls off. I swim over to shield her from the workers on the boat while she recovers herself. Suzanne seems annoyed by my efforts to help.

"Don't want to give any free shows!" I say to break the tension. I'd be mortified if it happened to me.

"Anyone who wears a bikini top knows there's a high chance of it falling off when they jump into the water," she says. "Besides, I have great breasts. If we could take the boat out to sea, I could sunbathe nude. Henry thinks it sexy that I don't have any tan lines."

So Henry has been paying attention to Suzanne. I'm glad to hear it. But why spend all day on the water when you could be in it instead? I envy Ringo, paddling circles around us, having fun in his shark fin.

We swim over to a sandbar where it's shallow enough to stand. Ringo keeps up with us, splashing. "So, Isa. You've heard all about my troubles. Tell me about you. What've you been doing since we graduated?" She doesn't know about Ben and the divorce. She doesn't know about Luke and Cole.

"Well"—I hesitate, not wanting to feel the pain of remembering—"I got married, and it didn't work out the way I hoped."

Suzanne's eyes widen. "Really? You were married? To who? Anyone I know?"

"I doubt you'll know him. He's from South Portland." I really don't like talking about Ben. I hope Suzanne will lose interest in this topic.

"Oh? I've been to parties in South Portland."

Maine seems so far away. I'm standing on a sandbar seventeen-hundred miles from the chaos I was in a few weeks ago. Then, I was living a completely different life. Until a few months ago, I was a full-time mother to two beautiful boys.

"Ben Cushing," I say, acid filling my throat at the thought of all the years I wasted on him.

"Oh! I know who he is. But I didn't think he was married. I must have met him after you guys got divorced."

"No, I highly doubt it. Why?"

"Well, last summer, I was out with some friends in Kennebunkport and ran into him at a bar," Suzanne says, excitement warming her tone, but then she sobers. "He was really drunk, and I think he was hitting on me." She's quiet for a moment, then she smiles. "Nope, he was definitely hitting on me. And when I turned him down, he just moved on to the next girl."

"Next girl?" I'm not actually surprised.

"He basically hit on every girl at the bar until he got takers. And he definitely got takers."

"Takers? More than one?"

"Oh yes. He left there with a couple girls. I think they were friends, but whatever. I didn't want anything to do with him."

"We were still married," I say flatly. I remember last summer when Ben had to work late and ended up sleeping in the back room of the restaurant. Or so he said.

My arms are suddenly full of wet dog as an exhausted Ringo tries to climb up on me. I step back to regain my balance, and sharp pain shoots through my left foot.

I hop back to get away from the pain, but that only makes it worse.

"Ouch! What the hell did I step on?"

I lift my foot to look at it. Two black spines are sticking through the top, and a spiny sea urchin is hanging from the bottom. My foot feels like it's on fire.

Suzanne is quickly by my side to keep me upright and balanced on my right foot. "Hey, guys!" She waves her arm to get the mechanics' attention. "We need help over here!"

Ringo barks as if to add his voice to the call.

The chaos around me blurs as the pain commands my focus. Shaking my foot does nothing to dislodge the urchin. Don't overreact, I remind myself. Try to stay calm.

The salty air gives way to the pungent smell of gasoline, and I look up. The two mechanics have powered their skiff over to us. Leaving the outboard idling, the man with the blue shirt jumps into the water and helps me climb into the skiff.

Once I'm in, the other man pulls the urchin off my foot and tosses it back into the water. Unfortunately, a lot of dark spines are still stuck in my instep. The man still in the water helps Suzanne and Ringo into the boat and then pulls himself aboard.

"Thanks, Bluey," I breathe out through the pain. His shirt makes my delirious brain think of the show my boys like to watch.

Bluey laughs. "Cute nickname. I'm Reed. And those urchins are nasty, nasty creatures. They cause a lot of problems to a lot of feet. Let's get you to the clinic."

"I hope you don't have to pee on my foot." That would be absolutely gross.

Bluey—no, Reed—laughs again. "No, that would be for jellyfish stings. Completely different animal."

I would feel ashamed of my ignorance, but I hurt too much. I grit my teeth and keep silent. Suzanne is sobbing enough for both of us. A cold nose pokes my arm, and I look down. Ringo, with his shark fin, looks so sad, and soon I have a lapful of wet dog licking away my quiet tears.

Reed's co-worker, whose sunglasses reflect the ocean, has opened up the skiff's motor, and we're at the dock in no time.

"Thanks, Sunny, for getting us to shore." I'm grateful they were there to help.

Sunny, who tells us his name is Freddy, jumps onto the dock and ties the skiff off while Reed picks me up and carries me to their truck with little effort. He straightens my leg out so my heel is resting on the dash and the bottom of my foot doesn't touch anything.

"Keep it elevated. I'll be right back," Freddy instructs as Reed gets behind the wheel and starts the engine. He runs over to a couple of nearby trees just a bit taller than him. Grabbing a knife from his belt, he cuts off a few of the oblong fruit and runs back to us. "Hold on, I got these for you," he says as he drops the fruit into my lap.

"Thanks, but no thanks. I'm not very hungry right now." I just want to get this ticking time bomb out of my foot before it explodes.

"They aren't to eat. I'm going to squeeze the juice onto your foot. It will help with getting rid of the spines."

"You really think mango will help?" I'm skeptical about squeezing tropical fruit into my open wounds.

"It's not mango; it's papaya. It helps, trust me."

"Okay, you can squeeze it on, but I'd still like to go to the clinic afterward."

Freddy uses his pocket knife to cut a slice of papaya and squeezes the fruit over the spines stuck throughout my foot. At least the juice doesn't make my injury hurt worse. He proceeds to squeeze the juice of both papayas onto my foot before climbing into the back seat.

"How far is the clinic?" I ask Reed as Suzanne slides into the back seat on the other side.

"The clinic is less than a mile away. There are some dry towels back there." Freddy hands one to Suzanne and opens another for me.

My foot is throbbing, and I start breathing like they taught us in birthing classes. *Hee hee, hoo.* It doesn't relieve the pain, but it gives me something to focus on as we drive over bumpy roads to the clinic.

At the front entrance, Reed parks and carries me into the lobby. Suzanne follows us with Ringo. My tears have stopped, but the throbbing has turned into a pounding.

A staff member directs Reed to take me into the examining room behind the front desk, and our ragtag group traipses into the room. He helps me onto the exam table and then leaves with our profuse gratitude. Suzanne takes Ringo's shark fin off and hands him to me for comfort.

"Looks like you met one of our sea urchins." Dr. Easton looks over his black-rimmed glasses at me, then down at my foot, focusing through his lenses on the spines.

I cringe as he examines my foot. "Yeah, a mean one." Not that urchins are mean, but they do cause a mean injury. "Those guys put some papaya juice on it; they said it will help."

"It can help a little with shallow spines. The ones in your foot are very deep." Dr. Easton gives Ringo a little scratch on his head and goes over to wash up. I guess comfort dogs are welcome here.

"Jack told me to make sure nothing happens to you, and now look." Suzanne sniffles.

"I need to remove the spines and clean the wound to prevent infection and cellulitis," the doctor says, and then I'm overcome with pain as he uses pliers to pull out the spines one by one. Suzanne squeezes my hand as her tears start to fall again.

"Looks like about fifteen or sixteen spines, maybe more. I want to take X-rays to locate any spines that may have broken off in your foot. Any chance you could be pregnant?"

"What? No, I don't think so."

"Do you mind if I run a quick test?"

"Do what you need to do. It hurts so much; I just want it to stop." My left foot is swollen to twice its size.

Dr. Easton nods. "I'll get the nurse."

A nurse with a nametag that says Pieter walks in through the open door and pulls a privacy curtain around Ringo, Suzanne, and me. "Are you able to get up to use the restroom?" I nod, and he helps me up. With Suzanne on one side and Pieter on the other, I make it into the bathroom attached to the examining room and sit down on the toilet. I keep my leg straight and resting on the heel.

Pieter opens a cabinet and hands me a plastic jar with a lid. "Here you go; leave it on the counter when you're done and give me a shout so I can help you back into the bed."

Once he leaves, Suzanne asks, "Do you need help?"

"No, thanks. I'm good." Suzanne looks the other way so I can be done with this. I pull the gusset of my bathing suit to the side and fill the cup halfway before snapping my suit into place.

She calls for Pieter, who helps me back to the exam table, then collects my sample from the bathroom. "This shouldn't take too long."

Several minutes later, Dr. Easton returns. "Looks like we're going to have to do this the hard way."

"What do you mean?"

"Looks like you're pregnant. No X-rays. No good painkillers. Just Tylenol," Dr. Easton says, looking down at his clipboard, which must contain my results. "We can do a little lidocaine to numb the area, though."

"I'm what?" I blurt as Suzanne asks, "She's what?"

"Oh, yes. We can discuss that later. Let's take care of your foot first."

All I can think of is Ben the night before our court date. Oh my God, I can't be pregnant. The pain in my foot fades as dread curdles in my stomach.

Suzanne grabs hold of my arm when she sees how scared I am.

"I can't be pregnant. This can't be happening. I reach for Ringo and run my fingers anxiously through his short, damp fur. "Please don't say anything. Don't tell anybody."

"I won't say a word," Suzanne assures me and wipes away a tear running down my face.

Dr. Easton digs through my foot, removing all the spines he can. "I hope I got them all. Pieter will come in and bandage you up and give you a tetanus shot. Tomorrow, I want you to soak your foot in warm water with a little bit of vinegar. It will help to neutralize the venom and break down any pieces I may have missed. Take Tylenol for the pain and elevate your foot to keep swelling down." Dr. Easton pats my ankle. "And stay off it for a week or so. I'll lend you some crutches. Are you a tourist?"

"She's visiting," Suzanne answers for me. "She's Jack Kendall's girlfriend."

Dr. Easton smiles. "Oh? How's Jack doing?"

"He's doing great. Can I go home now?"

"You're good to go. Please keep an eye on it to make sure it doesn't become infected. And it would be good for you to see an OB to make sure everybody is okay."

I nod. What else can I do? Pieter comes in with crutches and shows me how to use them.

"Thank you for everything," I say, although my foot is throbbing and I'm nauseated—not because of the spiny urchin venom or pregnancy symptoms, but the fact that I'm pregnant. I can't even think about the conversation I'll have to have with Ben.

When we go out the front door, Sarah is waiting for us. "A half mile is a little too long for someone just starting out on crutches," she says. Suzanne has stopped crying now that the drama is over.

"Aren't you supposed to be behind the bar right now?"

"I called in an employee when Suzanne texted me. Let's get you to your villa."

We pile into Sarah's car, and she drives me home with care. I hobble inside with a woman on either side of me, gratefully sinking into the sofa near the door.

Suzanne goes into the bedroom to get me something to

wear. "Where are all your clothes?" she asks as she comes back, her face disapproving. "We seriously need to go shopping." She tosses a T-shirt that's wearing thin in spots to me, then holds up a pair of my Walmart special panties and laughs. "If you're gonna date Jack Kendall, you'll need sexy underwear."

I burst into tears. Sarah looks at Suzanne as if to ask what's wrong.

"I just found out I'm pregnant," I explain between sobs. Suzanne ducks into the bathroom and brings out a roll of toilet paper. Guess we've created a routine.

Sarah sits down next to me and takes my hand. "When does Jack get back?" I wipe my eyes, and when I'm done blowing my nose, she continues, "Is this his baby? Are you going to tell him?"

I look at Ringo, who's staying right by my side. "I have no idea. I have absolutely no idea."

BZZ-BZZ-BZZ

Between the throbbing of my foot and being a side sleeper forced to sleep on her back, I've only just fallen asleep. And now my phone is going off.

Bzz-bzz-bzz

The sky outside my bedroom is lighter, but the sun isn't up yet. Who could be texting me this early? Did something happen to my boys?

Eyes glued closed, I feel around the bedside table until I find my phone. My eyes unstick enough to be blinded by the brightness of the screen, and I immediately turn it down. I can see there are eight texts from Jack. That, and it's six a.m.

11:04 p.m.

Isa Jane Cushing are ya OK? How's your foot?

2:43 a.m.

Isa Willa Cushing? You are worrying me! Are ya OK???

2:45 a.m.

Isa Mia Cushing I am so worried! I'm flying home now to see ya

3:15 a.m.

I just took off. I'll be there soon.

3:16 a.m.

Pilot says we should land at STT around 5:30

4:30 a.m.

Isa Ivy Cushing, I can't wait to see you!

5:25 a.m.

Landed! Headed your way!

5:55 a.m.

On the island

The knock at the door seems a little too soon. He must've timed his arrival and the ferry departure perfectly. My foot is sore and throbbing when I try to sit up. "Shit!"

"Isa!" Jack calls from the porch.

"The key is out there somewhere," I yell to him. After putting me in bed last night, Sarah and Suzanne locked the front door, then hid the key. I hear Jack rummaging through the items on the porch, and then it's quiet except for the skittering of Ringo's nails on the tile floor as the door is unlocked and pushed open.

Jack, backlit by the rising sun, rushes across the threshold to my bedside.

"Oh my God, Isa, are you okay?" He bends over and hugs me and doesn't let go. Ringo's wagging his tail and looking up at me as if to say everything will be just fine now that his owner's back.

"I'm not dying, Jack, but I do have to go pee."

"Let me help you up." Jack is careful with my wrapped foot and hands me the crutches on loan from the clinic.

"Give me a few minutes to freshen up." I hop over to the bathroom and close the door.

Telling Jack I'm headed back to Maine will be one of the hardest things I've done. But I can't stay here, not in this condition. Not while I'm pregnant with someone else's baby. I came here to figure out what to do, but now my future has been figured out for me.

I open the door and crutch my way over to the couch, where I prop up my injured foot. It looks like a loaf of bread. The swelling hasn't gone down much, so I ask Jack to give me a few Tylenol from the packets Dr. Easton sent home with me and get me a bottle of water from the fridge to wash them down. He's happy to help.

"I rushed home as fast as I could; I've been so worried about ya. When you didn't respond to my texts, I called Sarah to see if everything was OK. I just had a bad feeling." He drags a chair over so he can sit in front of me. "I don't want to be away from you."

"You didn't have to do that." I know I can't continue whatever this may turn into with him.

"The thing is, I wanted to. I've never wanted to put my career aside before for anything or anybody, especially a woman. But you"—Jack brushes my slept-in hair off my face and tucks it behind my ear.—"you have swept me off my feet. You've come into my life at the exact time when I was at a crossroad that I didn't even know I was at."

"What? What crossroad? Don't you have Google Maps?"

"Isa, I'm serious. A crossroad in my life. I didn't realize it until I left the island. Until I left you here. I want to quit my business, or at least slow it down. I want to focus on me and you. I want to live the things I sing about, not just sing about them."

"Jack, I'm pregnant." I just say it, monotone. No enthusiasm. No excitement. "I'm going to be leaving soon."

I brace myself for Jack's wrath, to be yelled at or called some kind of name. I'm sure whatever island fairy tale he conjured up of us living happily ever after has disintegrated in front of him.

I look down to hide the fact that I have lived this before. I've been in this position where all I want to do is leave. I know I can't fix a shattered dream, especially someone else's shattered dream. "I'm sorry," I whisper. "I'm so sorry."

"Oh, Isa!" Bending forward, Jack hugs me. His fingers gently pinch my chin and move my face so we are eye to eye. "I want to help." Jack's voice has taken on a serious tone. "Please let me help you. I don't want to lose you."

"Jack, I don't know what to say. That's so unexpected." I break my promise to stay strong and stop crying as I allow myself to be wrapped in his arms. To be kept from falling apart. "I don't know what I'm going to do."

"It will be OK. Let me make it OK." He pulls back to brush my hair away and wipe the tears from my cheeks. "Give me a chance; I won't disappoint you. I don't want you to have to worry about anything except getting better and making sure your baby is healthy." Jack flashes his bright smile, and I bask in its light. He feels good, and maybe this is right.

"I don't know," he continues. "I feel like I spent all my life putting everything I have into my music and touring. I never had any desire to settle down with anybody, let alone start a family. I could never see myself with one person." I pull away so I can watch his eyes while I listen.

"It's not that I'm selfish or anything, or I don't think I am. I just think I'm honest. I wouldn't expect anyone to put up with a schedule like what I keep when they want me to be a full-time husband or father. I couldn't do it. It wouldn't be fair to anyone." As Jack speaks, he loses the sparkle in his eyes. "And now, I'm forty-eight. I've led an amazing life, and now I would like to sit back and enjoy my accomplishments. Slow down. Just relax and enjoy what I sing about. Now I'll have time to be a boyfriend and maybe a husband or even a father."

Sometimes pieces to a puzzle fit the first time you try them. It doesn't happen often, especially if you're not very good at puzzles and you're constantly trying all the wrong pieces. My whole life, I've been trying the wrong pieces and they never fit. So far, Jack and I fit in every way. He's kind and gracious, and he makes sure I know he's thinking about me, in a good way. I love his voice and what he says. And to top it off, physically, we fit together perfectly.

I am at the point where I need to make a decision. I need to put the puzzle piece into the puzzle.

Jack traces my lips with his tear-dampened finger, preparing them for his soft kiss. My eyes fly open; I'm shocked that his gentle kiss feels so intense. As if every cell in my body is about to explode. I'm ready to let myself fly, but Ringo barks once and runs to the door to tell us he needs to go out.

"Hi, buddy." Jack jumps up, out of breath, and opens the door for Ringo. Then he turns to me. "You look famished. Would you like to come up to my house for some breakfast? We can talk some more there."

"Yes," I whisper. "Let's talk at your house."

"I'll grab some of your things and help you get some shorts on, although I don't mind you going shorts-less." Jack pulls clothes from the dresser and throws them into the bag I've been using for the beach before going into the bathroom to grab my toiletries.

"Are you expecting me to spend the night?" I ask with a

girlish grin. It feels good to have Jack packing an overnight bag for me.

"I thought you might want to get a shower when you get to my house. That's it. No pressure." The sparkle is back in Jack's eyes as he slings my bag over his shoulder, then helps me stand and step into some shorts.

I brace myself for a loud, rattly ride in Jolene, but to my surprise, when he opens the front door, a brand-new black Ford Expedition, with doors and everything, is parked outside. "Whose is this?"

Jack shrugs, somewhat bashful. "They left it for me at the airport so I could get home in the middle of the night."

"They?"

"My security. You'll be comfortable and safe." Jack helps me hop to the passenger side and slide onto the oversized black leather seat.

As Jack races around to the driver's side, I fasten my seat belt. The engine purrs like a house cat when Jack starts it up.

"It's so quiet compared to what you normally drive," I say. "We don't have to scream. And I don't feel like I'm going to get thrown out of the vehicle at any given moment."

Putting the Expedition in gear, he says, "You'll be much more comfortable in this." The air-conditioning blows cool air, and country music starts playing mid-song from high-quality speakers, whose sound is complimented by the luxe sound-proofing of the interior.

We glide out onto the road, whereas we bounced on every bump when we were in the Jeep. We drive for a while until we come to a small driveway that winds up a hill. Halfway up, a gate of silver bars adorned with starfish blocks our way.

"Oh, how pretty! Starfish are my favorite animal," I exclaim.

Jack grins at me, then turns away, lowering his window so

he can reach out to enter a code on the keypad at the side of the gate. A pole-mounted security camera next to the keypad observes the transaction, and the gate swings open to allow us to drive through.

The palm tree-lined driveway leads us to the front of an enormous traditional island home. I'm in awe. I knew he had some money, but not like this. Not as jaw-droppingly extravagant as this.

"You live here?"

EIGHT

March 14

"WHY DIDN'T YOU SAY SOMETHING?"

"I don't know." Jack and Ringo jump out and he shuts the door with a soft *thunk*, reminding me I'm in luxury. In no time, Jack's helping me out and up the stairs to his grand covered porch that appears to wrap around his entire house. The ceiling's light blue color complements the island vibe.

"Jack... This is stunning."

"Thanks. It's home," he says as he pulls the screen door open. "I can hide away here. Write some songs."

"I love this color."

Jack follows my eyes upward. "That's haint-blue; it's meant to ward off the evil spirits that might want to harm the people who live inside." Jack laughs. "It's also supposed to help ward off bugs. But hey, let's get ya inside."

He opens the heavy wooden doors into a huge, open room with matching dark wood floors. Walls of windows reveal an expansive view of the Caribbean Sea. Jack helps me over to a slipcovered white sectional, his muscular arm keeping me from losing my balance.

"Sit down, sweetheart," he says, guiding me into a corner of the U-shaped sofa. Jack helps me turn so I'm resting against the back and my leg is stretched out on the cushions, pillows elevating my foot. "How ya feeling?" He softly kisses my forehead, and I fist a hand in his T-shirt, the fabric thin and torn from years in the sun and salt.

"I feel better when you do that." I smooth the crumpled fabric as I let go, Jack's tanned chest warming my palm from beneath.

"You do?" I get another kiss with that answer.

"I'm actually feeling a lot better. I'm pretty certain the doctor got out all the spines. It's painful, but it doesn't feel infected. I should be good to go soon."

"You'll feel even better once I open the doors." Jack unlocks the latch on the sliders and pushes a button on the wall. One by one, the panels collapse upon themselves like an accordion until they vanish into a pocket into the wall. It looks like there were never any doors there to begin with.

With the doors hidden away, the breeze brings in the fresh air, heavy with the scent of salt and flowers and nutmeg. The aromatic mixture should be bottled and sold to tourists as a souvenir of their trip to St. John.

"How's that?" Jack asks as the spicy sea breeze blows through our hair. He sits on the sofa with me. "Is it too much?"

"Oh no," I say, brushing my breeze-blown hair out of my eyes. "This is perfect."

"Are ya hungry?" Jack leans in close and kisses me gently. "Do ya want some eggs?" he asks softly.

"Sure." I've never been kissed this sweetly.

"How do ya like them?" he asks, staying close and soft.

"However you like to make them," I whisper, and I linger on his lips a little longer, delaying breakfast.

"Do you like jalapenos?"

"I don't hate them."

"Scrambled with jalapenos and a little cheese. It's a great way to start the day. Coffee too?"

"Sure. I don't think anyone has ever waited on me, except once when I was little and home from school sick. My mom took care of me."

"Well, give me the opportunity. I'd love to take care of you." Jack moves over to the kitchen island behind the sofa where he begins assembling our breakfast.

He opens and closes his six-foot-wide stainless refrigerator/freezer numerous times. "I really like cooking, and I don't get to do it often," he calls out to me.

Jack is busy at the stove, but he's able to run a cup of freshly brewed coffee over to me to sip on while he finishes making breakfast. He remembered how I like it, with a little cream. Jack has a good memory, and the coffee tastes delicious.

Ringo must have slipped in through a dog door because he appears out of nowhere and joins me on the couch for his early morning nap. I stroke his fur distractedly as I think about my current circumstances. I could get used to this. Being in a relationship with someone who wants balance, who doesn't demand I cook hot meals for him three times a day? I could definitely get used to this.

"Breakfast is served." Jack walks over, carrying a full tray. I rouse Ringo and encourage him to the floor, then Jack sets the tray on my lap.

"Oh, yum. This looks amazing." Intensely yellow eggs, scrambled with bright green jalapeno slices and cheese, have been plated attractively with a small bowl of tropical fruit cut up for easy eating. "You really outdid yourself. Thank you!"

"I always have jalapenos for breakfast. I feel they rev up my metabolism for my workouts. You should eat them too; they're high in folate, and ya need that now more than ever."

"Oh yeah?" If this is a dream, please don't wake me up. I take a bite of the eggs. They are so good, I eat the whole plate and start in on the fruit.

"I meant it when I said ya could stay here. I live here by myself. Well, I have staff—Ramone and Gabreille. But other than them, it's just me."

"I'm just so unsure about everything. Last night, I was ready to book my flight back to Maine, but where do I go from there?" I sigh and put down the fork that's loaded with a piece of pineapple. "I really have no place to go. And I don't want to impose on you. I don't want to impose on anyone." I look down, trying to stay calm and not let him see how overwhelmed I am.

"What?" He lifts my chin up so I have no choice but to meet his eyes. It's then I realize they are haint-blue, the color of protection.

Jack is a protector.

My protector.

"I would miss you," I whisper loud enough for him to hear.

"Ooh, I like hearing ya say that." He grins, and I roll my eyes. "I would miss ya so much if you left." He moves closer, careful not to disturb my elevated foot. "Please don't go anywhere. Stay and figure things out."

"Is this how you make breakfast all the time?" I pop the fork into my mouth and smile with a mouth full of sweetness.

"Is that a yes?" Jack moves in and wraps his arms around me.

"Trial basis?"

"Absolutely! Whatever ya need." He bends down and kisses me. "I'll take good care of ya."

Ringo must have had enough of us because he scampers

from the room, his nails clicking on the hardwood floor as he trots out of sight.

I run my hand through Jack's hair. Feeling brave, I add my other hand, burying my fingers in his unruly golden locks. Jack leans into my palms, and I pull him up to me. I look into his dancing haint-blue eyes and feel relief that I am in a good place to heal my body. And just maybe, my soul.

He kisses me, heating my lips with jalapeno, and scratches my face with his unshaven cheeks. Warmth floods me, rekindling the flame he first stirred to life a week ago.

And there it is, the attraction I've been trying to deny. Something that has been growing between us the whole time I've been on the island and I missed when he was gone.

Jack's right. We could be perfect together, and if I give this a chance—no, if *we* give this a chance—we could be great together. I lose myself in his kisses and shiver with his touches.

My breathing changes; my exhales are short. Keeping air in my lungs is difficult. His muscular arms wrap around me, creating a framework of support and care I never want to leave.

The strength of his muscles contrasts with the gentleness of his soft kisses. I really love both of them.

Jack rises and stands above me, blocking the sun from my eyes. He stretches out his hand for me to take.

"Come with me. I want to show ya our room." I reach up and take his hand. His grip pulls me from the couch and into his arms. "Lean on me; I don't want ya to put any weight on your foot."

I nod breathlessly and lean on Jack, holding onto him. I'm dizzy with arousal. "I might fall over."

"I won't let that happen." Jack's voice is low and his eyebrows flattened. The haint-blue has deepened.

"Are we alone?" I pant, weaving my fingers into his sun-bleached hair. Feeling his body against mine is setting off ripples deep in my abdomen.

"Everyone is in town." I love the baby kisses he's sprinkling all over my face. "They won't be back for a while." Jack finds my mouth with his, and his arms hold me tighter as I start to fall.

"I'll show ya the bedroom later." He picks me up, an arm under my knees and the other behind my back, and effortlessly carries me back to the couch. "Scoot over. I'm gonna join ya."

I slide over so my back is against the sofa, and Jack lies down facing me.

"Comfy?" His muscular arms are around me, pulling me close to him. I love his hard body against my soft one.

"Very," I say, snuggling against his chest. I trace his nipple around and around with my index finger, smiling when the nub becomes erect.

"Where were we?" Jack kisses my forehead, lowering his lips to my nose and then my lips, playing first with my upper lip, then the lower.

"You're one of the strongest people I have ever met," Jack says in between kisses.

"Why do you say that?"

"Well, also the smartest and one of the most loyal people I know."

I kiss him back, deeply. "What would you say that for?"

Jack pulls himself off my lips and his haint blues look at me. "I apologized for reading your diary notes, but they gave me extra insight into who ya are, what ya value. You love your kids, more than anything. You gave up everything to stay with them. And ya stood by your ex-husband, even though he was a fucking ass to ya. All ya wanted was your family to stay togeth-er." Jack brushes my hair off my forehead to make way for more kisses. "You survived by being smart and keeping your head down.

"Now ya don't need anyone to make you happy. You can make yourself happy. You don't need anyone to make plans for ya; you just need to make them and follow through."

"Why are you bringing this up now?"

"Because I think you should know." Jack's lips caress mine. "I'm sure Bob never complimented you about anything."

"Ben."

"Huh?"

"Ben. My ex-husband's name is Ben."

"Alright, I'm sure *Ben*"—Jack distorts Ben's name to make him sound like a villain—"never complimented ya for anything."

"No." I pause for what seems like a long, awkward moment. "I can't remember a time he has."

"But you're still open to new experiences and new relationships." Jack smiles and rubs my side. "You aren't broken, ya still like people, and ya still have a sense of humor."

"Because I haven't given up yet."

"And ya had no idea who I was, like that I sang and stuff."

"No, I still think you're an island bum."

"Oh, that's what I want to be, believe me." Jack laughs. "But ya took a chance on me without knowing everything about me, and I really, really love that."

"I almost ran back into the villa and locked the door when I saw the Jeep."

"But ya didn't."

"What was that? Like a test or something?"

"No! I just really love driving Jolene." Jack looks serious again. "But you wanted to stay with me for me."

"You're funny and I like being around you." Jack really likes my response, because he squeezes his arms tight, almost breaking me in two. When he lets up on his grip enough for me to speak again, I squeak out, "And I think you're really hot."

"Yup, I knew ya thought I was sexy." I slap at him and he shields himself several times before grabbing my wrists as we laugh at our mutual attraction for each other. And then we're kissing heavily again.

Jack's hands lift my shirt, exposing my breasts. "I love these." He cups them in his hands, teasing my nipples with his thumbs while keeping my lips engaged with his. I feel his arousal grow hard against my thigh, and I can't help but notice how wet I have become and how much I want to have him inside me. I guess that's where the term "wet and willing" comes from because I am certainly both.

I bend my upper knee and slide my leg over his hip. His hand migrates down to my thigh and holds it tight so it can't move as he feels his way around with his clothed erection.

Jack pulls away from our kiss to breathe. "Oh, Isa. I want you so badly," putting words to his actions. But it makes me want him more.

The front door opens, and a man and a woman walk in, talking as they come right toward us.

Jack grabs the bottom of my shirt and quickly pulls it down to my waist where it belongs before he sits up. I never did put a bra on this morning.

"What are you two doing back so early?" Jack asks the intruders.

"Hello, Mr. Jack. We are dropping off the groceries so they don't spoil," the woman says. "We are going to go back to town after lunch and finish our errands."

"Oh, thank ya for that." Jack takes a deep breath. "I want ya to meet someone." Jack smiles and looks down at me and helps me sit up. "This is Isa Cushing. She's living here for the time being."

"Oooh, hello!" The woman smiles and comes over. She looks at my wrapped foot. "Uh-oh! What happened? Did Jack step on you?" She gives me a big hug. "My name is Gabrielle. If you need anything, you let me know."

"And this is Ramone, Gabrielle's husband." Jack says as Ramone sets a bag of groceries on the kitchen island, waves to me, and heads back outside, I assume to get more.

"I will make some lunch for everyone shortly," Gabrielle says. I'm pretty sure she has no idea what she and Ramone interrupted. "So tell me, Miss Isa. What happened to your foot?" she demands as she opens a cabinet to put away the food.

"I stepped on a sea urchin." I look down at my wrapped foot. *I wonder if Jack is disappointed that we were interrupted?*

"Oh no!" Gabrielle says. Her cheerfulness is gone and concern has taken over. "We will get you better."

"Thank you, Gabrielle." She's a very sweet woman; Jack is lucky to have her on his staff. "Dr. Easton said it should heal up good as new."

"Dr. Easton is a good doctor." Gabrielle turns to face me. "It is so nice to have a woman living here, finally."

"Thank you."

"Alright. That's enough," Jack says. I'm guessing he doesn't want his staff and his girlfriend ganging up on him. He bends down and whispers in my ear, "Pick up where we left off after lunch?"

I don't say anything, just take his hand and grin.

NINE

March 19

"BUT GUYS"—SUZANNE'S tears are dripping into her mai tai—"I'm not ready to leave yet." Sarah looks at me from behind the bar; our little tribe is disbanding just when I've formed special friendships.

I know I'm being selfish, but I don't want Suzanne to go. I need her quirkiness in my life. Plus, she's headed back to a place that's miserable for me.

"We can live anywhere, so why can't we live here?" She sets down her drink, then wraps her arms around me. Her tears dampen my neck. "I don't want to fly out tomorrow."

After being here only a month, I completely understand why she doesn't want to go back to *Maine*: snow, snow, and snow. Oh, and my ex-husband. But why would she want to stay with us instead of going back and being with Henry? Her new husband? Her husband who she's supposed to be on her honeymoon with right now?

I've been so caught up in my own drama, I haven't paid much attention to Suzanne's situation, mostly because she never mentions Henry and I've never met the guy. I honestly forgot she was married.

"Don't you miss him?"

"I guess so." She pulls herself off me and sits up. "I wish he planned to stay home after we get back, but no, he'll just leave me there, then go to his next business meeting someplace far away like Copenhagen."

"I'm sorry, Suzanne. You'll be able to come back down any time, though, right?"

"And you can come up and visit! Stay with me, the both of you." She clasps her hands and looks pleadingly at me and Sarah.

"Of course," Sarah says, discreetly showing me her crossed middle and fore fingers. Sarah, it turns out, owns We Be Jammin'. The only way she's going to leave the island is if a category five hurricane heads directly toward it and a mandatory evacuation order is in place.

"I think we need to have a little going-away party tonight." I'm trying to sound upbeat and lighten the mood. I've been the one who has been moping around, and Suzanne has been the pick-me-up. Now it's my turn to reciprocate. "Too bad Henry returned your charter. Let me text Jack; maybe we can hang out up at his house?"

"You mean your house too?" Sarah reminds me as she rejoins us.

"I guess you're right." I'm not used to the idea of me and Jack, let alone me and Jack living in the same house. I pull out my phone and start texting to planning our farewell party:

Hey, whacha doin?

Jack texts an immediate response:

Thinking about you

I send a few emoji hearts and get a few in return. It's easy to let my guard down around Jack, with everything being hearts and kisses. I'm pretty sure he's trustworthy—wouldn't the paparazzi have dug up all his dirt for Suzanne to read about in her magazines?

Suzanne is flying home tomorrow
would it be ok to have a small get together
tonight at the house so we can say good bye
Promptly, Jack responds
I'll have someone run into town to
pick up food and restock the liquor cabinet
What else can I do to help?

WE FIGURE OUT THE DETAILS, and I work out a time with the girls.

———

"YOU'RE MOVING BETTER," someone says behind me. "Looks like we got them all."

"Hi! Yes, thank you!" I'm a little caught off guard, but in a good way. "Dr. Easton, I didn't know you were coming."

"Simon, Please. Jack and I are friends; we like to go deep-sea fishing when he's on the island." He bends forward and whispers, "But I think he really wanted me to check in on you."

"I'm doing well. My foot is healing up a lot faster than I thought."

"That's what I like to hear! Do you mind if I have a look?"

"No, not at all. It would save me a trip back to the clinic." Simon puts one hand on the small of my back and holds his other arm across his body so I have something to grip. With his support, I walk over to a sofa by the pool, where I plop down and swing my leg up. Simon pulls off my flip-flop and unwraps the bandages that Jack helped me put on this morning.

"Nice. You're a fast healer." Lifting my foot, he brings his face inches from it. Examining it very closely, he says, "How long have you been able to put weight on it?"

"A few days." I watch him closely in case he changes his expression and my foot isn't as healed as he first thought.

"There's no sign of infection at all; the wounds are healing nicely." Simon's face is full of satisfaction. "But I think you should let Jack pamper you a bit longer. How are you feeling with your other situation?"

"The pregnancy? Oh, I'm doing OK." It doesn't seem real to me. Plus, with everything going on, staying on the island, and moving in with Jack, I haven't had time to process it. "Is there a possibility it could've been a false positive or something? I don't feel like I did with my other two pregnancies. I don't feel any different at all."

"There's always that possibility. We can retest. Would you be able to come in tomorrow morning?" He sets my foot back down on the sofa. "Where does Jack keep the bandages? I'll wrap you back up."

"I put them in the cabinet next to the sink where all the cases of Sharpies are." I point through the open wall that allows the outside to be inside and vice versa.

"Sharpies?" Simon asks. "But you don't have a cast to sign."

"No, they're Jack's." I chuckle; obviously I don't have a cast and I wouldn't have cases of permanent markers to sign one. "They're for signing autographs for his fans."

"Ahh, I see. Sometimes I forget what he does for work." Simon rises from the sofa and disappears into the house. When he returns, he has an armful of supplies to rewrap my foot.

Jack joins us as Simon finishes. "How's the patient?"

Simon stands and pats Jack on the back. "Doing great.

Healing up nicely." Then he directs his next comment to me. "No marathons in the next week or so."

I giggle. As if a marathon was ever on my agenda. "Nah, I much prefer to read. I'm looking forward to getting back to the library."

"Oh? You like our little library, do you?" I nod, and Simon continues, "I run the literacy program. We work with kids and adults, teaching them how to read and write."

At this point, Jack pulls a chair over and waves Simon into it. "Looks like ya two have a lot to talk about. Take a load off, Simon, and twist my girl's arm just like ya twisted mine." He slaps Simon on the shoulder and wanders off to help Ramone move patio furniture, and I turn my attention back to Simon with the raise of an eyebrow.

He acknowledges my curiosity and says, "My goal is to make sure that on our small island, everyone has the opportunity to learn how to read and write." His foot is tapping. "Would you like to volunteer with our program once you can get around again?"

Easiest. Decision. Ever. "You can count on me. I would love to help. I used to volunteer in our library back home."

"That's great!" Simon's smile stretches from ear to ear. "We had a couple, husband and wife, volunteers. They just moved back to the States, and we have no one to replace them. Give me your contact info, and I'll be in touch about scheduling your orientation and getting you on the schedule."

A thrill of excitement runs through me as I share my little-used email address and phone number. Simon's joins the five in my contact list: Jack, Suzanne, Sarah at We Be Jammin', Ben, and his parents, the Cushings. My heart aches at the thought of my boys. If I called Ben right now, would he be at home or at work? Who's watching the boys? Who tucks them in at night and tells them they're loved when their father works late? I rub my chest to ease the hurt, and Simon's gaze sharpens.

"Are you OK? It's a little early in your pregnancy to be feeling heartburn, but it does happen."

"No," I wave off his concern and push thoughts of the boys out of my head, "it's nothing. Just getting thirsty."

"Then let's get you something to drink." He swivels as if to check whether beverages have been set out, but Jack's coming our way, full glasses in hand. "Looks like our host has everything under control," he says. "I'm going to duck out."

"Thanks again, Simon. I appreciate your care and your offer."

Simon rubs my leg before standing up and walking over to a table where Ramone has set out some hors d'oeuvres for Gabrielle, who's busy in the kitchen.

"Scoot up a little; I'll sit with ya." I bend forward while Jack slides in behind me, then lean back and rest against him. He hands me a glass of yellow liquid, and I sip slowly from it. Pineapple with some sort of fizzy drink. Soda, maybe. The slightly acidic sweetness hits the spot, and I sigh, cuddling into Jack's firm body.

Ramone and Gabrielle have been busy hanging lights, cooking, setting up the bar, and arranging the patio for Jack's local band buddies. It's a lot of commotion for a little going-away party. "How many people are coming?" I ask when I see all the food that's been prepared.

"Only about twenty-five or thirty."

"I thought that it was just going to be me, you, Sarah, and Suzanne?"

"Oh no, a party is a party." I spin my head around and look at Jack, who is grinning from ear to ear. "I love spending time with friends, and besides, now I get to show you off."

I take hold of his hand draped over my shoulder and enjoy

the moment. The sun is setting over the sea, the warm breeze is blowing salty floral scents into our faces, and we'll be surrounded by people who are a big part of Jack's life here on the island. But we're saying goodbye to my only tie to my prior life, saying goodbye to Suzanne, and I'll miss her being around. I say as much to Jack, even sharing the worries I had earlier about who's taking care of the boys.

"Why don't ya have Suzanne check on your boys when she gets back to Maine?"

"Jack! That's a great idea!" Suzanne could be like an undercover spy and feed me information about how the boys are doing, good or bad.

"Well, ya said she lives in the next town over from where the boys are living, and Frank doesn't know she's friends with ya."

"Frank?"

"Your ex-husband."

"Ben."

"Whatever the guy's name is. It would be the perfect way to get some updates on your boys. Seems like she'll need something to do up there; this will be a perfect mission for her."

I spin around just enough to put my arms around his neck and look into his haint-blue eyes. "It's perfect. A perfect idea." I'm overcome with excitement, and I press my lips hard against Jack's. I'm unprepared when his hands move up to hold my head as he presses his lips back against mine. He keeps me there, unable to escape. I'm pulled between making everyone go away so Jack and I can be alone and for Suzanne to hurry up and get here.

The outside preparations invade my senses when Ramone drops a glass and pulls us out of our cloud. I sit back. "When is everyone getting here?"

"Any minute." He sounds out of breath.

"Finish this later?" I let my hand follow the buttons of his Hawaiian-print linen shirt until I get to his khaki shorts.

He grabs my wrist. "Are ya sure ya wanna stop?"

"Guests," I remind him and kiss his tanned cheek. "We'll have guests any minute."

The doorbell rings, Ringo barks, and soon we have a house full of friends.

Suzanne, of course, is crying. "I don't want to leave." She sips from her mango mimosa between sobs. "I don't have any friends up there."

"Suzanne, we just went through this."

"I know, I know." She takes a bite of the pineapple that garnished her glass. "This. is. so. good." She lets out a sob and plops herself down with me.

"I have a job for you once you get up there."

"A job? What kind?" She sniffles but manages to focus on me.

"I need you to check on things with my boys. Make sure they're okay." I hope she realizes how important this is to me.

"Of course I can do that. I can get all the information you need." She wipes her eyes and hugs me. "Give me the prick's address; I'm on it."

"I'll text what I have." Suzanne looks happy now, maybe because she feels like she has a purpose.

THE PARTY IS a wonderful send-off for Suzanne. I spend most of my time on the outdoor sofa, propped up against Jack with his arm wrapped around me. We listen to the music and watch everyone dance and have a great time. Ringo is curled up at our feet, unbothered by the noise around us.

"How're ya doing?" Jack whispers in my ear.

"I'm going to miss her."

"I know you are." Jack's squeeze makes me feel like everything will be alright. It's amazing to have the support of someone I can trust. Someone I'm falling in love with because of his kindness and generosity. "How about finding a distraction? Something to do with your time?"

"That's a great idea, once my foot heals. I helped at the library back in Maine."

"That's perfect! Once Simon gives ya the all-clear, he can get ya set up as a volunteer."

"Simon?"

"Yeah, we don't just fish together." He winks, and I'm confused, but I set aside my questions as a guest comes over to say hi to Jack.

As more and more people arrive, the party soon reminds me of a middle-aged men's version of a fraternity party. Is this how Jack's parties are all the time? Rowdy frat party after rowdy frat party? I wonder when Jack will ditch me on the couch and go party with his friends.

"Can I ask you something?"

"Sure, anything."

"Why do you have a limbo pole?"

Jack laughs. "I don't know, something fun to do at a Caribbean pool party? It came with the house, by the way."

The limbo pole crowd is in a circle, toasting as they're about to take a group shot of tequila.

"To nipples, because without them, boobs would be pointless," a man with a blue Hawaiian shirt and a chrome dome screams as he holds up his glass.

"Here's to condoms and rattlesnakes, two things I don't fuck with. Cheers!" another man screams, tapping his glass to chrome dome's.

"These are your friends?" I turn around and look at Jack to see his reaction to how offensive his "friends" sound.

"Acquaintances," Jack answers me.

"Good." Returning to watching the zoo, I realize that my moving in has required a 180-degree change in Jack's lifestyle, and I'm unsure he'll be able to sustain it. I settle back in Jack's arms just in time to see Suzanne's latest attempt.

The limbo bar is set the lowest it has been all night. Suzanne downs a shot of tequila, squeezes her breasts together, and yells, "Girls, don't let me down now!"

"Her cheering days are far behind her; she'll be feeling it on the plane." I shake my head.

"You're probably right," Jack says. "And there's no way she's gonna squeeze under there." His eyes are fixed on the main event. "If she does, it'll be a new Lido Deck record."

"Lido Deck?"

"That's what I call my pool deck—the Lido Deck."

"Oh, cute." The band starts playing a familiar limbo song I remember from when I was a little girl in elementary school. "You should write a song about the Lido Deck."

"No." Jack playfully tickles my ribs and makes me jump. "Maybe you should."

Chants from Jack's drunk friends start in. *Blon-die, Blon-die, Blon-die.* Suzanne bends back awkwardly and inches her feet forward. To give herself more clearance, she pulls her breasts to the sides and lets her head fall all the way back so her nose clears the pole too.

Her audience is quiet as though they're watching a golfer tee-off at a golf tournament. And when she breaks the Lido Deck Limbo record, they go wild. "Great form!" "Amazing balance!" and "Limbo Queen" are shouted from Suzanne's smitten fans.

Sarah joins us on the sofa, laughing at the frivolity. "Where have you been?" I ask.

"I was over there." She points across the pool to a man sitting at a table. "I've been talking to Roger, and we're going to go for a walk on the beach."

Jack and I look over at the same time, unable to keep from being obvious. "Did you guys just meet?"

Sarah is all smiles. "Yes! Wish me luck."

"You won't need it," Jack says. "Have fun."

And he has gigantic muscles, Sarah mouths as she gives me and Jack hugs, then spins around and rushes over to Suzanne to tell her goodbye.

Jack catches me yawning, so he gives the band a signal by drawing his finger across his neck. "Let's call it a night," he says into my ear. His hot breath makes me shiver with delight. "Suzanne already won a trophy that doesn't exist."

The head of the band makes an announcement, saying, "It's getting late, and the new Limbo Queen needs to catch a plane tomorrow." This is immediately met with boos from Suzanne's new following. "Thank you all for coming out to the Lido Deck. As always, we'll help you get home safely if you need a ride."

"What does that mean?" I ask Jack.

"Ramone will drive anyone who had too much to drink home. I don't want anyone drinking and driving."

"I like that." It's a great idea to take care of overserved guests. "Suzanne should stay here."

"The Limbo Queen? Yes, she should." Jack moves me forward a little so he can climb out from behind me. "I'm going to thank everyone for coming and then we can go to bed." Jack softly kisses my lips and walks over to a group of his happy, drunk friends.

Suzanne came over and sat with me. Ringo still hasn't moved. "Did you see me?"

"Oh, boy, did I ever." I put my hand out for Suzanne to pull me up.

"I have the record." Suzanne bounces with excitement—and tequila—and hugs me.

"Why don't you stay here tonight?" I hold her close. I don't know when I'll see my newest and dearest friend again. "That way we can have breakfast together and take you to the airport."

"I don't want to go." Suzanne cries and hugs me harder. "I don't want to go back."

What is Suzanne expecting to go back to? Her life can't be as horrible as mine was. She only just got married. Is Henry really that awful of a man? As a husband? I can only wish she had a haint-blue protector of her own. "Come on, let's go inside."

I hardly use Suzanne for a crutch while walking into the house. If Suzanne wasn't so upset, I would make a joke about "taking a step in the right direction." But she isn't in the mood for jokes right now. She's too drunk and sad.

"Thank you for being my friend," Suzanne says before she drifts off to sleep in the guest bedroom. I brush her hair off her face and wipe the tears off her cheeks with my thumb and cover her up, then make sure she has a glass of water on the night-stand. She will need it if she wakes up in the middle of the night. I shut the light off and hobble off to find Jack with Ringo close behind. Moving better has returned some of my independence to me. If I heal too quickly, though, will I have to leave Jack sooner?

THE ALARM on Jack's phone makes an obnoxious noise at six a.m.

"Why?" I mumble into my pillow.

"Good morning, cutie!" Jack combs my hair off my neck and tickles the exposed skin with his soft wake-up kisses. I feel the tingles all the way in my toes, and he is all I need to be instantly alert.

"Why are you awake?" I ask with a groan.

"Morning workout. Zeus will be here soon."

"You work out with a guy named Zeus?"

"Well, I nicknamed him Zeus. His name's really Roger, but Zeus is more fitting."

"Does he carry a lightning bolt or something?"

"Maybe not a lightning bolt, but definitely a barbell." Jack bends over and kisses me. More incentive for me to get up. "What time does Sleeping Beauty need to be at the airport?"

"Not until later afternoon."

"Good, good. We have some time." Jack pulls on a light gray T-shirt and sits on the bed beside where I'm lying. "I'll make you some breakfast."

He kisses my lips and disappears out the bedroom door.

By the time I make it downstairs, a nice breakfast of scrambled eggs with veggies and toast is waiting for me. The handsome chef and I sit down to eat, and I marvel that this is my life. We finish up just as Zeus arrives.

I completely see why Jack calls him Zeus. Well over six feet of perfectly defined muscle capped with long, luscious blond locks. I'm certain I saw him on the cover of a romance novel in the grocery store back in Kennebunk.

"Nice to meet you." I extend my hand to shake his.

"Are you going to join us this morning?" My hand is engulfed in his, which is more than double the size of mine and one hundred times stronger.

"Ah, no. I'll sit this one out." My foot is still healing, and I don't want to make a fool of myself. "Maybe next time."

"I hope so." His overly bleached teeth blind me when he smiles. "I make working out lots of fun."

"Well, you guys go do that." I wave Zeus away, then give Jack a quick kiss on the cheek. "I'm gonna check on Suzanne."

"We'll be on the Banana Deck." Jack points over to the side of the house that includes the bedroom where Suzanne is sleeping. "You can come watch if you want."

Banana Deck? Cute. He names all his outdoor living spaces.

The guys head out for their workout, and I decide to clean up after breakfast.

Gabrielle and Ramone take care of Jack so well. There's no sign that last night's tequila and going-away party ever happened. But I want to familiarize myself with the kitchen. If I'm going to live here, I want to know my way around.

I go through all the drawers and cupboards, learning where the glasses, dishes, and silverware are kept. Everything in this kitchen, from the French porcelain dishes to the All-Clad pans to the La Cornue range screams high quality.

I don't think Jack can cook anything other than eggs. Gabrielle must have outfitted his kitchen for him. She has nice taste.

Once everything is picked up, I head back to the guest room.

Knocking on the doorframe, I poke my head in to see Suzanne, who's spread eagle on the bed, snoring. At least she's alive after all she drank last night. She should be thanking Jack for ending the party before she ended up naked in the pool. I wonder if she will remember anything from the evening.

I close her door and find the Banana Deck.

Outside, a roof with a haint-blue ceiling covers a porch where Jack is running on a weird treadmill—instead of the base being flat, it curves up at both ends. "I know you can run faster than that!" Zeus yells at Jack.

Jack's fresh gray T-shirt he put on this morning is now dark gray and soaked with sweat. "Thirty seconds," Zeus announces. When the thirty seconds are up, Jack hops off and bends over; he's out of breath and his sweat is dripping on the ground.

"Good job." Zeus goes over to a digital stopwatch mounted on the wall and programs it. "Get set up for the AMRAP I wrote on the board."

Now that I'm no longer mesmerized by Jack's movement on the treadmill, I can look around the Banana Deck. A white-board mounted next to the stopwatch contains a list of what I assume are workout instructions.

"Tater Tot"
18 Minutes
AMRAP
6 205-pound Power Clean
6 24-inch Box Jump
6 Toes to Bar

Geeze, I know I don't want to start my morning with Zeus yelling at me. I'm dying to find out what an AMRAP Tater Tot is, though. Is it some treat Zeus gives Jack for finishing his workout?

Jack, still out of breath, loads weights on a metal bar and fastens them on with a clip. He leaves the ensemble on the floor and puts a wooden box next to it.

"Three. Two. One." Zeus starts the wall-mounted stop-watch with a remote, and Jack is off. "Remember, lift with your legs, not with your back," he calls as Jack lifts the weights bar to his neck and drops it to the ground. Even though a thick rubber mat covers the entire area, the weights still make a loud crashing noise with each release.

Then Jack jumps onto the box six times and jumps up on his jungle gym and hangs while he swings his toes up to touch the bar six times. He goes back and starts the weights again.

Zeus is encouraging, but mostly a hard-ass, making sure he does all the moves correctly. If his toes "almost touch," the move doesn't count toward the six needed.

After eighteen minutes, Zeus calls time, and Jack falls to the ground. He rolls over onto his back, soaked in sweat, his chest heaving. Zeus leaves him to die and comes over to me.

"I think you should really give this a try." Zeus flashes his neon whites at me.

"I definitely could not do this."

Suzanne appears, rubbing her eyes like she's adjusting to the daylight, looking like hell. Her hair is tangled, and she's still wearing her clothes from last night.

"Is someone drilling a well or something?" I guess the dropping of the weights woke her up. Still unable to see, she walks into Zeus. Her fists, still at her eyes, are at pec level, and as if by reflex, she opens her hands to feel what she's against. Zeus flexes his pecs, and Suzanne squeaks. "Oh, my God," she says under her breath and turns around and runs back into the house.

"That's our friend, Suzanne," I explain. Jack is still lying on the ground.

"I'd be glad to help her any day." Zeus winks.

"She's leaving today, and by the way, didn't I see you with Sarah last night?" The tanned skin of his cheeks turns dark and he looks away as I walk over to Jack. "Do you need some water?"

"Water..." He reaches straight up with one hand. "I need water." I bring him his water bottle. "Thank you. He makes me get it myself."

"Yes, he should get it himself," Zeus says, back to his arrogant self. "It builds character."

Jack sits up and sips his water. "How'd I do?"

"A little better than the last time you did Tater Tot." Zeus is reading from his iPad. "At least you didn't get worse. Let's go, you have more to do."

Jack gets up from the floor, leaving his outline in sweat, and goes over to turn on a big industrial-size fan.

"Wow!" I say, looking at the wet floor. "You sweat a lot."

"If I don't leave a sweat angel, I didn't work out." Jack gets his phone and takes a picture of his sweaty outline. "Right, Zeus?"

"You're not done yet. Put your phone away," Zeus says.

"I gotta go." Jack gives me a kiss and goes back to his torture.

As I leave the Banana Deck, I notice an open chest freezer full of water and ice tucked in a corner. "Jack? What's that for? Are you having people over for beers?"

"Nah, that's an ice bath for after my workout." I look at him with disbelief. "It helps with recovery."

"You get in there?" I have flashbacks of miserable blizzards, sleet, whiteout conditions. "You get in there with the ice?" I'm probably the only kid in Maine who hated snow days. I greatly preferred to be in school than in the outdoors.

"Yes!" Jack says with way too much enthusiasm. Where is he getting his energy? "No pain, no gain." He jumps up and down in place.

Why would anyone do this to themselves? "What if your body temperature drops and you become hypothermic? Do you have an electric blanket?"

"I only stay in for four minutes. I won't be in long enough to become hypothermic," he says. "It will be okay, Isa. I do this several times a week, and I have yet to become hypothermic."

Why would someone escape the cold and move to the islands only to take a bath full of ice? It just doesn't make sense. I wouldn't willingly subject myself to an ice bath. Maine winters are more than enough for me.

"You can watch me and do the countdown if you want," Jack suggests. "Then, if I get into trouble, you'll be right here to help me."

"You are crazy, but all right." I can't believe I'm going to watch someone willingly get into a tub of ice.

"I'M GOING to go check in on Suzanne. She needs to get herself ready to catch her flight." I give Jack a quick kiss on his sweaty cheek and trace my finger down his chilled abs before heading toward Suzanne's room. I'm really going to miss her. I haven't had a friend in a long time, and even though we're very different, I'm glad that she recognized me and came over to talk at Snorkels. I'll be sad when she leaves later.

I knock softly on her door before pushing it open. There she is, back in bed, her small figure curled up under the sheets. She drank way too much last night and is obviously feeling it this morning. Without thinking, I crawl in beside her, the mattress dipping slightly under my weight. The smell of old tequila on her makes me gag a little.

"You okay?" I ask, my voice barely above a whisper. "Can I get you anything? Some Advil or something?"

Suzanne opens her eyes a tiny bit to look at me and smiles. "I feel fine, just thirsty. A little hungry. And I'm so tired. My head hurts."

"That's what happens when you drink as much as you did last night." Geeze, I don't think I've ever been that drunk, but I don't want to tell her that when she looks like she's feeling this bad. "You need to leave for the airport soon. Do you want me to help you get ready?"

I don't want her to leave, but she's meeting Henry. I'm tempted to help her miss her flight for my own selfish reasons, but instead, I offer the only thing I can: routine. "I'll make you something to eat. Why don't you get showered and come have breakfast?"

"You're my best friend, Isa." Suzanne's eyes are closed, and she sounds like she's on the verge of falling back to sleep. "I don't want to leave yet."

"I don't want you to leave either, but Henry is going to be waiting for you." Has she forgotten she's married? She certainly didn't act married while putting on the limbo show. I don't understand their relationship. I know that when I was married to Ben, we spent a lot of time apart and now I know it was because he had other women. Is that what's going to happen with Suzanne and Henry? Where he "works" all the time and Suzanne is home alone? God, I hope not. I don't want Suzanne to go through what I did when Ben would stay out and screw around with other women. I don't know Henry at all; I hope he isn't like Ben. "He is waiting for you, right?"

"Oh, yes. He's picking me up at Logan and then we're headed up to Maine." Suzanne smiles. Good, she is happy to be seeing him later.

"You know, I don't know much about him. He's good to you?" I want her to have a healthy, thriving marriage, not like mine.

"Yeah, he's very good to me." She struggles to sit up. Once upright, she yawns and stretches her arms up toward the ceiling. "Who is that god? I can't believe I squeezed his pecs. He made them *dance!*"

I chuckle. "Jack calls him Zeus."

"I can see why." She wiggles her eyebrows and laughs.

"Go take a shower, then come eat something." I grab her hands and pull her up to stand with me. "I'll be in the kitchen."

Later, we sit outside on the Lido Deck while Suzanne eats her breakfast, the ocean breeze ruffling her hair as she slowly regains some color. I sip my coffee. "Tell me about Henry. How did you two meet?" They're so different. Henry is much older than Suzanne and acts it, whereas Jack is much older than me but doesn't act it.

"I really haven't told anyone, but he was my teenage crush." She narrows her eyes, as if preparing to defend herself against anything negative I might say. "He was best friends with my father, God rest his soul. I grew up with his kids."

"I'm sorry for your loss," I say automatically. There's another thing Suzanne and I have in common: we've lost our fathers. But the implications of the other things she said hit me, and I blurt, "What? He dated you while you were underage?" The thought of Suzanne sitting in class next to me and being in a relationship with a pervert all that time turns my stomach.

"It wasn't what you think," she snaps. "I was the one who had a crush on him. He had no idea, and if he had, he wouldn't have done anything. He isn't like that."

"You liked him?" I try to picture Henry ten years ago. I doubt he's changed much; he's still old.

"Yes, I did. A lot." Suzanne looks tired, not shocked, by my reaction. She's probably seen it from everyone. "I ran into him when I was in Paris, and we fell in love. The rest is history."

"Oh, Paris. That sounds romantic."

"It really was." Suzanne's smile is wistful. "But reality sucks. His kids don't like me very much anymore. Growing up,

I was friends with them, and now I'm technically their stepmother."

"I can see why they would be upset." Wow, that sounds awkward. I can't imagine my father marrying a friend my age, let alone having a relationship with her.

"But Henry says he loves me and that time will heal, and hopefully soon his kids will come around and we can be friends again."

"I hope they do." Although I can't see how they will. Not from what I've read at the library. "I want you to be happy. I wasted too much time on the wrong person, enough for me to question any future relationship, including one with Jack."

"Jack's a sweetheart. He's nothing like what I've read about him in the magazines."

"That's a good thing."

"Very good. It's obvious he's infatuated with you." Hearing that makes me blush. This is all new to me. A friend who's looking out for me. A man who seems to genuinely like me. It makes me feel good. "And when I get back to Maine," Suzanne says, her voice stronger now, more protective of me, "I'll find out everything I can about Ben and the boys,"

"I know you will." A knot of anxiety twists tighter in my stomach as I'm reminded of my boys. Suzanne is now the only connection I have left to Maine, to the mess I left behind.

"Don't worry," she says, leaning over to me and pulling me into a hug. Her embrace is warm, solid. I squeeze her back, relishing the friendly affection. Zeus yells at Jack from the other side of the house, and the sound jolts us from our thoughts. Suzanne and I pull apart and settle back into our chairs.

"I can't believe he pays someone to do this to him," she says with a laugh.

"Jack?" I shake my head, the absurdity of it all finally

bringing a smile to my lips. "He said that he needs to stay in tip-top shape for his concerts. They're physically demanding."

"And what's with the Greek god drill sergeant?" Suzanne mocks a salute.

"I don't know. He tried to recruit me into his torture sessions this morning." I laugh, imagining myself doing push-ups while Zeus counts loudly. No way am I expending that kind of effort.

We chat quietly, soaking up the morning sun and savoring the last moments we have together. When it's time to take Suzanne to STT, our laughter fades, replaced with the solemnity of an impending farewell. Jack loads her suitcases into the back of the Expedition and drives us to the airport.

"Thanks for the party last night." Suzanne hugs me tight. I cling to her, not wanting to let go. "I'm glad I was a great source of entertainment for everyone."

"You were more than that," I whisper, my throat tight with emotion.

Jack unloads Suzanne's bags at the curb, and the skycap checks them in.

"Oh, you were entertaining, Limbo Queen," Jack teases, joining us in a final group hug.

As Suzanne walks into the terminal, she turns and looks back, her expression serious. "I'll keep you posted on what I find out about the ass." She blows us a kiss, and we wave back.

Jack puts his arm around me as we watch her until she disappears into the crowd. He opens the door to the Expedition for me and I climb in. We catch the car ferry and drive on board.

As we wait for departure, Jack is thoughtful. "To be honest, I really liked not being part of the party last night. I liked just hanging low with ya." Jack reaches over and rests his hand on my knee.

"I like just being with you," I say, content. "This could work, you and me."

"I really want it to." Jack squeezes where his hand is resting. "More than anything."

TEN

May 21

IT SEEMS like the library on St. John is exactly place I should be, I muse while enjoying the gentle morning breeze on Jack's deck. In one of my darkest times, the Kennebunk Library sent me here to St. John via a grand prize raffle ticket. Fast forward three months, I'm living on the island and teaching literacy at the local library. I should send them a thank-you note or maybe an update.

Three days a week the literacy center is open, and I'm there with Simon and two other teachers to tutor the nine children and six adults from the local community who need help learning to read and write.

I love working with the children. But I have learned that my passion is really working with the adults. Whatever the reason is that they missed out on learning how to read when they were children doesn't matter now. They are eager to learn, and I am just as eager to help them.

I was surprised to see Sabastian, the cab driver I met when I first landed on St Thomas, being one of them. He didn't remember me right off but when I told him I was the one he picked up who was by herself, it must have jogged his memory. When I pulled his card out of my wallet with his name and number handwritten on it, he seemed very impressed.

"Ma'am, you never called me!" I'm unsure if he is joking or offended.

"Sebastian." I look directly into his eyes so there is no question how sincere I am. "I didn't need any rides, but you would have been the first person I would have called. Don't you live on St. Thomas?" St. Thomas is where I met him when he drove me from the airport to the ferry.

"No, I live here, with my family," Sebastian says. "There is much more work on the bigger island."

"So you commute to St. Thomas for work."

"Yes, ma'am. My family has lived here for many years."

"Well, believe me, you will be the only person I call if I need to get somewhere." Opening a book that Sebastian has been working on, I say, "Let's get down to business."

He nodded and eagerly took the book. Not only is Sebastian a hard worker and determined, he is just as kind as when I first met him. I like him a lot.

Simon says I'm a natural teacher and have patience and respect. I enjoy helping people learn something that will change their lives for the better.

"Good morning, Isa" interrupts my musing, and I turn back toward the house where Gabrielle has walked through the back door carrying two plates of steaming waffles. Jack's not far behind.

"Oh, yummy! Thanks, Gabrielle. You know just what I was craving."

"When aren't ya craving waffles, darlin'?" Jack teases as he helps me into a chair at the patio table.

"Well, I'm not gonna apologize for it," I say. "Gabrielle makes amazing waffles, and I'll gladly eat them any day—and any time of day."

"I'll keep that in mind," she says, her hands now empty of our breakfast plates, which sit on the table in front of Jack and me. "Enjoy!"

"I love dining al fresco." I pop the first bite of my mango syrup-smothered waffle into my mouth. "It's so beautiful here."

My hair is a mess, just pinned in a bun on top of my head. The loose strands are blowing in the breeze, and I need to brush them away from my face every now and then so they don't get stuck in the syrup. I'm wearing one of Jack's big T-shirts. The one with Reba on it.

Before I can raise my napkin to catch the syrup dripping down my chin, Jack wipes the corner of my lips with his thumb and puts it into his mouth. After briefly sucking on it, he says, "You are so sweet. Messy, but sweet."

He returns his thumb to my lower lip and gently runs it back and forth.

"Do I have something else there?" I feel a little self-conscious, thinking I may have more food on my face.

"You know what makes you so beautiful?" Jack asks as he returns his hand to his lap. Does he really think I have an answer to that question? I shrug and run my fork around my plate, trying to capture all the remaining syrup.

"The fact ya have no idea how beautiful ya are. You're not hung up on yourself when ya very well could be. And you're smokin' hot!" I put my hand up to shield my eyes so I don't have to watch him say this embarrassing stuff. "You're authentic. You don't try to be someone you're not. And when you met me, you didn't act like a fan. You've never even asked me for an autograph."

I take my hand down and look at his haint blues. "Well, I didn't know who you were at first."

"Yeah, and when ya learned, ya still didn't treat me any differently."

"Well, I'm not obsessed with Jack Kendall the country music star. I like Jack Kendall the man who's generous with his hospitality."

"It's easy to be kind to ya, darlin'. You have such a good heart."

"Please stop with the compliments. They make me... uncomfortable."

"Nope." His eyes are on me. "You've been my girl for nine weeks, four days, eight hours, and"—he looks at his watch—"fifty-two minutes. I'd hoped ya'd become accustomed to hearing how great ya are by now. I'm the luckiest man alive, and I want ya to know it."

"Where's this coming from?"

"I have to be in Nashville tonight." He reaches out and takes my hand, playing with my fingers as he continues, "My producer is being a real hard-ass about my retirement. We need to have a conversation face to face."

Jack's going to do it. He's actually going to do it? Scaling down his music career is a big step... and to do it so he can be with me? What if everything goes wrong?

"You're a popular performer. People aren't going to like what you're going to say."

"Oh, probably not." Jack stands and pulls me up. "Follow me, little lady."

Jack leads me into our room and closes the door behind us. Leaning against the closed door, he reels me close to him.

The circulating air from the ceiling fan blows my bangs into my eyes. Jack strokes them out of the way. "I'm gonna hate being away from ya for a few nights."

"I'm going to hate being away from you too." I catch a glimpse of his haint-blue eyes before my lips are on his, my tongue urgent. I press my body against his, reveling in a partner who considers me his equal, who encourages me to take my pleasure. Jack releases my bun and my hair falls, cascading around my shoulders as I hold on to him and surrender to desire.

Any uncertainty from last night is a cloudy memory. I try to catch my breath as I have lost all track of time. "When do you leave?"

"A few hours." We're breathless. "Look what you've done to me."

I run my hand over his hardened bulge. I can't help but feel proud that I do that to him.

As if by mutual agreement, we make our way toward our bed, removing our clothing as we go. I'm left wearing just my white lace bra and Jack his underwear.

"Stop right there," I say, and drop to my knees in front of him. I'm determined to give Jack something to think about while he's on his trip.

"Isa? When did ya become so demanding?" Jack's eyes are dark with want. "I love this new side of ya."

"I need to peel these off you." I strip Jack of his underwear, and then he's standing before me, nude.

My gaze moves from his eyes to his erect cock.

"Isa," Jack says softly, "you don't have to do this."

I don't listen. I don't want to listen. I want to please him at this very moment as much as he's pleased me.

I tighten my fingers around his silky, rigid erection. A drop of wetness forms at the end of his shaft. I tilt forward to kiss the tip and allow my tongue to taste him. He tastes salty like a Maine oyster, only better. He tastes like Jack.

Grabbing his hips for balance, I slide him into my mouth. Jack moans, the voice that has sung for arenas overflowing with people now singing for me alone.

Finding a rhythm I can handle, I take him deeper and deeper, making my eyes water.

"Fuck!" Jack shouts. His hands grip my hair, and his legs begin to tremble. I take that as my cue to suck harder and move a little faster.

"You're gonna make me come in your mouth if ya don't stop, baby doll."

I'm not stopping.

"Isa!" Jack holds my head still as he releases a guttural groan and fills my mouth with his warm, salty come. He steps back and sits on the bed, leaving me still kneeling on the floor.

"Come here," Jack says between breaths and pats his lap.

Staying on my knees, I shuffle over and position myself in front of him, between his legs.

He wipes the corner of my lips with his thumb and puts it into his mouth, briefly sucking on it. "I love that you're a messy eater." He pulls me up to straddle him on the edge of the bed and slides his tongue over and around mine. Kissing me firmly. Holding me tightly.

"Was I okay?"

"Oh, sweetie!" He unhooks my bra and tosses it to the floor. "More than okay." He kisses my breasts with gentle, moist kisses that evaporate in the breeze from the ceiling fan.

I trace my fingers down his CrossFit-inspired abs and reach for his hard cock again. I want him inside me.

But I can't find it. Is he not interested? Did I give too much too fast?

Jack pulls back and admits, "I'm a lot older than you. My recovery time isn't as quick as when I was your age."

The all-time excuse: It's me, not you.

"It's okay." He doesn't act older than me. "No biggie." I wince. I can't believe I just said that. Ben would've taken it as an insult.

"Give him a little bit." He wraps his muscular arms around me. "He'll be back shortly."

"I... I didn't mean to. I'm sorry." I didn't mean to shame him. I didn't even know that this was a thing. I don't remember them talking about this in tenth-grade health class. I can't do anything about how old he is.

"Nothing to be sorry about." Jack scootches back so he can roll over and open the drawer in his nightstand. When he returns to me, he's holding a rather large silicone dildo in its original packaging. "I got you a backup."

"For me?" Jack hands me the package. I've never seen one in real life before. When I was in college, some girls in my dorm held a pleasure party, with all sorts of lingerie and sex toys for sale. But I was dating Ben, and he got sick that night and needed me, so I missed the party. Then when we were married, I learned not to imply anything about his ability in the bedroom; a dildo would've been the ultimate emasculation.

"I've never once let a partner go without being pleasured, and I'm not going to start now," Jack says, pulling me from my thoughts.

I accept the package and inspect its hot pink contents. "Would it be okay with you if we wait until you come home before we break out the artillery?" The dildo is intimidating, with its synthetic veins and fat head. Better to wait to use it when Jack has more time.

"Sure, sweet pea." Jack must sense that I'm uncomfortable. I hand the package back to him and he returns it to the drawer.

"We'll have plenty of time to play with toys." He strokes my arm and sits up to kiss me. "We'll have all the time in the world."

"I like that." I pull back from his embrace. "You have a plane to catch. I'm jumping in the shower. Join me when you're ready?" I leave Jack sated and lethargic on the bed as I saunter to the attached bathroom.

———————

THE STEAM from the shower fills the glassed-in stall when I turn the water on.

"Come on, sleepyhead," I call from the doorway where I'm leaning, nude. Jack has fallen asleep. "You need to get ready!"

He opens his eyes and throws his legs over the side of the bed with a groan. How can he be this tired? I thought his workout was supposed to give him more energy. "You need some help up?"

He winks. "That view sure is getting something up." He looks at his lap, then back up at me. "Or would, if I was younger." He stands and heads toward me, and I duck back into the bathroom and step into the shower.

Jack's shower is a big, glass enclosure with a rain head coming from the ceiling, several handheld sprayers, and multiple wall-mounted body sprayers. The control panel is full of options, so I'm grateful I managed to turn on at least the rain head.

Before he joins me, Jack pushes a few buttons and water comes at me from all directions. I throw my arms above my head and enjoy the massaging sprays, marveling at the luxury and how it almost feels like I'm in the ocean, but safe and secure and protected.

"Want me to wash your hair?" Jack asks as he squirts some shampoo into his palm.

I drop my arms and turn my back to him so he can reach all my hair. He works the shampoo into my waves and massages my scalp.

"That feels so good. Smells good too." With my eyes closed, I could be standing in a tropical rainforest, amid an abundance of flowers and fruit. "I recognize the coconut, but what's the other scent?"

"I believe it's tea tree," Jack says as he continues to trace across my head, generating subtle tingling and warmth. I'm so relaxed, my body feels heavy, languid.

"I like it," I murmur.

He reaches around me and picks up a handheld sprayer and carefully rinses away the shampoo, then replaces the sprayer. "Conditioner?"

When I agree, he repeats the process, but piles my hair on the top of my head to let the conditioner have time to soak in.

"Ya knocked my socks off earlier," he says in my ear, and traces the X-shaped tan line my swimsuit left on my back. "I like this." He repeatedly draws soft X's, and I shiver, ticklish.

"You seem to be an X-Man, but I kinda like the O's," I joke. Jack's chuckle is deep and delicious as he wraps his strong arms around me.

"You surprised me earlier. I really wasn't expecting a send-off like that."

"I surprised myself." I giggle. "Just wait until you get home. I may have some more surprises planned."

"I can't wait." Still holding me, he retrieves the handheld sprayer again. He kisses my shoulder, then rests his chin on it. "Now, my lady," he says as he runs his free hand over my breast and down my torso, "I need ya to spread those pretty legs of yours. Earlier I said I'm not in the habit of leaving my partners unpleasured, and I'm not about to break my promise."

Jack's directions have my arousal flaring, and my belly burns hot. I lean against him for the strength and stability that have escaped me and slowly part my legs. "That's it," he croons, ghosting his fingers across my mound, then delving between my folds. He brings the sprayer up and targets it at my clit. As I bliss out, Jack sings my favorite song into my ear. "Come for me."

ELEVEN

May 25

EVER SINCE JACK arrived in Nashville, his texts have been sporadic. Not surprising. I know he's in a lot of meetings. Every few hours, I get an XOXO or XXX text, reminding me of him tracing my tan line and giving me that amazing orgasm. I respond with multiple kissing-lip emojis or pictures of Ringo in his shark life jacket swimming in the pool.

Ramone or Gabrielle would take me into town, I'm sure, but I'm enjoying their company, and I'm not yet ready to leave this cocoon with its evidence of Jack everywhere. Instead, I shoot a text to Suzanne:

How cold is Maine? Bet it's freezing!

She replies immediately.

I found him

I've been tailing him off and on for a few days

Over

Me: *Ben?*

Suzanne: *Yes, silly! That's who you want me to follow and feed you information about. Right?*

Me: *Yes! Does he know you're following him?*

Suzanne: *No, He's really dumb.*

I can't see you 2 together

Me: *Me either*

Suzanne: *Call you later? In hot pursuit!*

Me: *Yezzz! Be SAFE!*

Suzanne: 10-4

I giggle at Suzanne's trucker lingo. She's really getting into this spy business!

———

THE DOLPHIN STATUES around the pool are spitting water, making a serene background sound as I eat my eggs and toast at the dining table on the Lido Deck. How nice it is to be wearing only a swimsuit with a towel for a skirt. Try doing that in Maine during the month of May.

Gabrielle walks out of the house, carrying a FedEx box. "Miss Isa, this just came for you."

"For me?" It's the first mail or parcel delivery I've received during my vacation here. Who would send me a package? How would they know where to send it? I take the box from Gabrielle. "Thank you."

The Nashville return address answers my questions. Jack.

Using my butter knife, I break the tape and open the box. The card on top says *Isa* and has a hand-drawn heart. A feeling of euphoria sweeps through me, leaving me giddy.

I carefully tear open the envelope and remove the card. The front shows two olives holding hands, with a caption *Olive You.*

Inside, Jack scrawled, *I love you! Happy Birthday Isa XOXOOO ~Jack <3*

I look at the date on my phone; it's my birthday. I've completely forgotten.

Jack's so sweet! But then I'm struck with a horrible thought. How does he know today is my birthday? I don't recall ever telling him when it was. Did he go through my things again? What was he doing in my wallet? All giddiness has fled, and I'm left with suspicion churning in my stomach with my eggs and toast.

My phone chimes, and I pick it up out of habit.

SUZANNE: *Did you see this?*

A *People* magazine article is linked. "In the Mood for Love" is a collage of celebrities with their significant others. Why did she send me this? I'm ready to toss my phone aside, but the flash of familiar sun-bleached hair grabs my eye.

It's Jack, in a restaurant, kissing a woman in a skimpy red dress. She's sitting on his lap, the arms that cradled me in the shower the day he left now wrapped around her svelte body. The caption says this is Lila Sharp, Jack's producer.

My blood runs cold. This photo has to be an old one, from before he met me, right? It can't be recent. Jack said he had to have a face-to-face conversation with his producer. I thought he meant a formal business meeting in a conference room some-where. Not this—I grasp for words, my chest tight as I get my thoughts together—funny business. Is *this* what he meant? They're certainly face to face!

My eyes burn with impending tears as I read the accompa-nying article. It's dated today.

"Jack Kendall getting cozy out and about in Nashville with his new love interest... as he plans for his new tour."

My throat tightens, and it's hard to swallow as I examine the picture closely. Jack said he was going to Nashville to retire.

To tell his team he's cutting back. Why is he out with Lila? I thought he didn't want to leave me and the island and that he would be back in only a few short days. But they're celebrating his new tour?

I rub my chest, where my heart has been ripped into a million pieces. I can't believe I believed him. I can't believe I fell for another man who can't stay faithful to me.

I screenshot the picture.

Me: *What is this?*

Suzanne: *I'm sorry Isa <3*

Me: *He said he loved me*

Suzanne: *I know. If you need me I'm here.*

I wipe at my eyes, where the tears have begun to run silently down my cheeks. The movement jostles the shipping carton on my lap, and I'm reminded that I was unpacking it. I wonder whether Jack sent it before or after he cheated on me.

All joy gone, I pick up one of the two small giftwrapped boxes and peel back the starfish-printed paper. A bottle of perfume. Bobbi Brown's Beach. I take the bottle out of its packaging and spray some on my wrist. It smells like sunscreen, my favorite scent. I won't be able to smell it and think happy thoughts again.

The second box is small and square. The wrapping paper reveals a haint-blue jewelry box. Inside it rests a white-gold chain with a starfish dangling from it. I pick up the necklace and let the delicate chain dangle from my hand, watching sunlight glint off the tiny links.

Ben never gave me birthday gifts—or Christmas gifts, for that matter. After we married, he never once made me feel special. I stopped remembering my birthday because no one else did.

I pick up all the giftwrap and the boxes and pack everything into the FedEx carton. I'll give it to Gabrielle, and she can dispose of its contents. Now what do I do? How did I not see that Jack was just like Ben?

Flipping through my phone, I reread all of Jack's texts. They're sweet and caring, kind and solicitous. And funny! I've laughed more with Jack during these last few weeks than I have in years. I never knew I could feel so connected to a man. Especially someone as gentlemanly as Jack.

Did I think that way about Ben? There were warning signs I should've noticed, signs I ignored. Granted, I haven't seen any of those warning signs with Jack, but we've only been together for a short time. Better that the truth about his character comes out now before I'm too involved. I made bad decisions in my first relationship; I'm not going to make the same mistakes again.

At the bottom of the list, after the last series of X's and O's, I attach the screenshot of him and Lila. Take a deep breath. Send.

Celebrating? I type, then quickly erase it. I don't need to caption the picture. It's self-explanatory.

"Well, it was fun while it lasted" and "This fairy tale romance was just a fairy tale" are the lines I repeat in my head as I prepare myself for the inevitable. Damn it, I enjoyed the fairy tale. There's nothing wrong with that. But once again, I chose the villain. I wasted my time. I allowed myself to think this relationship was different, but it isn't, other than I'm in a warmer place. *Happy birthday to me.*

I have to get out of here. Maybe the villa is vacant so I can go there until I can arrange where to go next. I head into the bedroom to pack my things. I'll be gone before he comes home.

"We'll be fine." I put my hands on my belly and give it a rub as I look for a pair of cutoffs and a shirt to pull on over my suit.

My phone chimes with a text.

JACK: *Isa, it's not what ya think.*

Yeah, I've watched that movie. Not even worthy of a response.

"You send chills, a sweet suspense. Our beginning, I don't want this to end, can't be caught." Jack's voice sings from my phone in his special ringtone.

Not gonna answer.

I'm angrier at myself than at Jack. I knew this was going to happen eventually. Oh, I thought I was growing, with all my library research and self-help reading. But in the end, I just couldn't resist the allure of romance, of being wooed, of being *important* to someone.

I open his contact and block him. I'm not falling for it anymore.

I'll be gone when he gets back. He can compliment whomever he wants, it just isn't going to be me. I should have listened to Sarah. I should have paid attention to the red flags.

I throw all my things into my old duffel bags and set them by the door.

Oh, one more thing. I go into the kitchen and open the junk drawer, grab a Sharpie, and head back to the bedroom.

The hot pink silicone dildo seems to laugh at me in the drawer next to the bed. I pull it out of its package and write "For you to fuck yourself with — I. C." across its length and stick it under his pillow.

So, this is what empowerment feels like.

Ringo barks, startling me. I crouch down and look at his furry face. At least dogs don't lie. I give him a little scratch. "Wish I could bring you with me."

Picking up my bags, I step outside and look up at the haint-blue roof of the porch. So much for warding off negative spirits. I head down the stairs toward the big gates. Haint-blue is no longer my favorite color.

"Isa! Isa, wait!" I stop and turn back toward the house.

Ramone comes running over to me. "Please, let me take you where you need to go."

"You know what? I would appreciate that." I allow him to take my bags from my hands and carry them over to the Expedition. It would be much more dramatic if I walked several miles carrying all my belongings, but I don't need any more drama today.

Once Ramone loads my bags in the rear of the SUV, we climb into the front seats.

"Where can I take you?" Ramone starts the engine.

"Does Jack know you're driving me?"

"Yes." Ramone pauses and looks straight out the windshield. "He wants you to stay."

"Well, I can't." I look straight ahead too as Ramone puts the Expedition into Drive and the air-conditioning starts to blow in my face. "Please take me to Jammin'."

Ramone steers us toward the opening gate, then once through it, down the steep hill. "He told me to tell you he loves you and he understands why you're mad, but he says it's not what you think."

"He doesn't know what I think."

"Please, let him explain," Ramone begs.

"A picture says a thousand words." I smile over at Ramone to let him know I'm not upset at him.

A few minutes later, we pull into the dusty lot of We Be Jammin'. Ramone opens the back and hands me my bags. "I wish you'd stay. Me and Gabrielle liked having you in the house. You're good for Jack."

"But he wasn't good for me." And I walk away, not looking back.

SARAH IS BEHIND THE BAR, and I'm so glad to see a friend. I drop my bags and break down. I can't be strong anymore.

She stops what she's doing and rushes over to me, giving me a big hug.

"How could I be so stupid?" I cry on her shoulder, my tears not making a difference on her sweat-soaked T-shirt.

"Suzanne sent the picture to me too." Sarah squeezes me harder. "I'm so sorry."

"What am I going to do?" I'm not really asking Sarah; I'm asking myself.

"Do you want to stay with me? I have a couch."

"I'll be an inconvenience." My stomach clenches and I feel weak. "I'm gonna go over to see if there are any vacancies at the villas." I need some time to myself to process and plan.

"Well, my door is open." Sarah gives me one last squeeze, then lets me go. "Leave your bags here. I'll watch them."

"Thanks so much, friend."

"For you, always."

I walk over to the villas on the same path that Jack and I took that first night just over a month ago. When I pass villa 8, bathing suits drying on the porch railing signal someone else is staying there. The bell above the door rings as I enter the office, and Sam, the manager, comes out from the back room.

"Hey, stranger. What can we do for you?"

"Would it be possible to rent a villa again?"

"You're in luck. I had a cancelation. It's yours if you want it."

"I'll take it," I say, not caring which villa it is. I'm just glad he can accommodate me.

"Do you know how long you'll be staying?"

I didn't even think about that. How much cash do I have

left? Jack wouldn't let me pay for anything while I stayed with him. "I'm not sure. Maybe a week? I need to make some plans."

"Well, let me know." He hands me a key attached to an aqua keychain. "Number 18. It's one of our nicest ones, but it's all the way at the end of the row. If you can wait about fifteen minutes until Hannah gets back, she can take you there in the golf cart."

"Nah, I don't need a ride." I let out a grateful sigh. "Thank you, Sam. You're a lifesaver."

"Not a problem." Sam walks around the counter and opens the door for me. "Enjoy. Let me know if you need anything."

"I will, thank you."

On my way back to the bar, the white-capped waves capture my attention. I love it here. I love being on the island. Leaving isn't an option. I'll figure things out; I have to.

While I was gone, Sarah moved my bags to the storage room so no one would trip on them.

"Do you want anything to eat?" she calls from where she's sweeping sand out of the building, a Sisyphean task. "You can take your meal with you and have it for dinner later."

"That's actually a great idea. Thanks." I take a seat on the stool I used to sit on when Jack flirted with me, trying to guess my middle name. I give Sarah my food order, then request a juice to sip on while I wait.

"So you're still gonna stay?"

"Well, I can't let my tutoring clients down. They're depending on me."

"I'm glad you're not going." Sarah sets the juicy concoction down in front of me. "Wanna get together tonight?"

"How about tomorrow?" I take a sip. "I just need some time right now. I'm looking forward to a quiet evening alone."

"Yeah, tomorrow's fine. I start at four."

"Can you do me a favor?"

"Of course. Anything."

"If Jack calls or shows up and asks if you saw me, please don't tell him where I am."

Sarah pinches the invisible zipper on her lips and pulls it shut.

"Thanks."

"Your meal should be out soon."

I finish my juice and carry my bags and dinner back to the villa. I don't even bother to unpack, just put my meal in the fridge, fall face-first onto the bed, and sob.

TWELVE

May 25

THE VILLA IS EXCEPTIONALLY NICE. Not only is it updated and fitted with a full kitchen, but there's a small covered porch facing the water where I can sit and watch the sun set. I slide open the glass door and step out. Looking up, I am hit with an overwhelming canopy of haint-blue. Doesn't Sam know this is an ineffective color? It doesn't ward off evil spirits. If anything, it invites them.

The water looks inviting, and I decide to take advantage and float away my worries. Stepping back inside, I slap some sunscreen on, wincing at the fragrance that reminds me of Jack's treachery, grab a towel, and run toward the water, stripping down to my suit and leaving everything on a chaise on the way.

Jack's swimming pool was nice, but nothing beats the warm salty ocean. I love how the waves rock me. It's very soothing. All sounds are muffled by the crashing waves and the strong breeze. It must be what being in a womb is like, muffled, warm, and watery.

I realize I haven't been back in the ocean since the sea urchin incident. I better keep an eye out for those nasty little porcupines.

Running all sorts of scenarios through my head, I ask myself, do I stay? Do I leave?

I've made friends and feel at home here. I have a job here, even though it doesn't pay. I'll need to find something that does —maybe on St. Thomas like Sebastian?—and then find a place to rent. I can have my baby here. And with Jack touring, I won't run into him very much either.

I'm staying. And while I'm here, I not only need to watch out for sea urchins, but I also need to watch out for sharks posing as Olympic swimmers who aren't paying attention to where they're going.

My stomach starts rumbling, telling me it's time to get out of the water and eat some dinner. I'm not arguing. Quite the contrary. After the separation and ensuing divorce, I didn't eat for weeks. I'm not going to do that now. Jack just isn't that important. My baby and I are more important to me. Plus, I've been hurt so much, I can't feel anything anymore.

I trudge through the surf, pulling myself from the froth and onto the beach, then grab my towel and clothes and head up to the villa. At the outdoor shower, I hang my things on a hook and turn on the spray. Still in my bathing suit, I get under the water and stand there, letting the spray massage my head. Letting it wash away the past few months of ups and downs.

"Isa?"

Oh, shit!

"Isa?" The voice is louder, as if the person has moved closer.

I turn the water off and quickly wrap my towel around me.

Thank goodness I kept my suit on. This might be the end villa, but that doesn't mean it's private.

Still dripping, I step out of the wooden stall to see Sam holding the largest bouquet of red roses I've ever seen.

"Sorry to interrupt you." He keeps his gaze trained on the water. I bet he's seen some things in his time here. "I was coming to put these in your villa when I heard you back here." He turns away as I slip my sandals on. "I wanted to get them to you quickly before they started to wilt."

"Those are for me?" There must be five or six dozen roses in that large blue vase.

"Yes, do you want me to put them inside for you?" Sam hitches the vase higher in his straining arms.

"Is there a card?"

"I'm not sure."

Feeling bad for Sam and not wanting to see him struggle to hold them any longer, I make a hasty decision. "We can take them inside."

"You got it." He heads toward the unlocked slider, and I rush to open it for him. In the kitchen, I shift the fruit bowl to the side and he sets the vase in the middle of the table. Then he steps back to stand beside me, and we stare at the riot of roses.

Sam finally breaks the silence. "Someone really likes you. Even our couples who come here to get engaged don't order this many flowers."

If he really liked me, he wouldn't have been seen kissing another woman. I can't say that to Sam, though. It's not his fault Jack is a lying cheater.

"I don't think I've ever seen that many cut flowers together at one time." This is more elegant than the flower selection at Hannaford's.

"How do you like the villa? Is there anything you need?"

"I'm fine, thank you. Everything's great."

"Call if you need anything." Sam leaves through the front door, closing it behind him.

Taking a deep breath, I face the garden of red flowers on the table. Their fragrance has overtaken the villa and seems out of place here on the island. They're beautiful, but I don't think roses are a local flower. Jack must have had these flown in from somewhere else.

I take the card and look at it, certain I already know what it says.

I understand why you're mad. I would be mad at me too.
Please believe I didn't do what you think I did.
I won't bother you.
I am here if you need me.
Love, J

Now I feel bad for two reasons.

Number one, no one has ever apologized to me, and number two, no one has ever sent me flowers, especially so many beautiful roses like these.

How can I go from being so connected to being so disconnected to feeling guilty for something I didn't do and all in one day?

All the decisions I've made have put me in the position I'm in now.

"Well, I'm not going to allow myself to feel guilty about any of this," I announce to the empty room. After opening the front door to the villa, I turn to my attention to the roses. Grunting as I pick up the vase, I remember Zeus yelling at Jack to lift with your legs, not with your back and I follow his instruction. I carry the huge bouquet outside and set it on the small front porch. Back inside, I shut the door behind me and on Jack's apology.

My stomach grumbles. I'm going to eat my dinner in peace, and I hope the iguanas do too. Opening the refrigerator, I pull out the meal I brought over from the bar. I hope the kitchen packed me something yummy.

Jerk chicken salad, with orange slices and a side of french fries. Thank you, Sarah!

Dinner is wonderful, even if the fries are a little chewy, but that's my fault for not taking the time to reheat them properly. Guess it's another opportunity to practice rejecting guilt. I grab a pen and dig my journal out of my pack, then sit out on the haint-blue-covered porch to write a long-overdue entry.

HERE I AM FACING *freedom again. This time, I'm the one who left the relationship.*

I'm not going to let myself be distracted by pretty words. I won't put up with being treated poorly.

Self-discovery? Who knows if that is even a thing? The only discovery I have made is that I am good at making huge mistakes and then trying to correct them by making even bigger mistakes.

I think the term should be "people-discovery." I'm discovering more and more about people. I want to think people are more like me, and I'm shocked when they aren't. When people like Ben or Jack don't treat me the way I treat them, I get hurt—shocker! Lesson learned.

I need to realize that people are different, and that people don't always treat me the way I treat them.

In preschool, I learned life lesson #1: "Treat others how you want to be treated." But it took me twenty-nine years to learn not to expect that other people learned the same lesson.

I was once a girl who rushed into warmth and companionship without considering compatibility or stability, assuming my needs would be looked at as important enough to be met. And now, I'm a woman who needs to realize that my needs are important and need to be met, and I will do that. I will find my own stability.

GLASS BREAKING on the other side of the villa makes me jump. It sounds like someone threw a bottle at my door and then picked up the broken pieces of glass and threw those at the door too. Running inside, I peek through the front window. Three iguanas are feasting on the roses, the vase in pieces around them. I didn't expect the roses to attract the iguanas so fast or that the iguanas would be so noisy and destructive about their meal.

Well, I'm glad someone enjoyed the flowers. Guilt threatens to invade, but I push it away. I'm feeding Jack's apology to the iguanas. The thought tickles my funny bone. What a surreal day.

Note to self: Sweep up the glass in the morning when it's light out and the iguanas are back up in the trees. I don't want anyone stepping on the glass in bare feet.

I return to my seat on the beach-side porch. Watching the sun sink down over the ocean never gets old. It's a sunset I can watch over and over every day of my life, with someone or without.

The bugs emerge and the bats come out to eat the bugs, and I take cover inside.

I brush my teeth and pull on my old T-shirt, then shut off the lights and climb into bed, taking my phone from the night-stand to check my messages before I fall asleep.

Nothing from anyone. If I feel a pang at not having heard from Jack, I ignore it. I blocked his number for just this reason. I don't want to resort to messaging him in a moment of weakness. Instead, I decide to check on Suzanne.

Me: *Hey, how are you doing? Everything OK?*

Suzanne: *Everything's good with Henry. It's you I'm worried about. Are you OK?*

Me: *I'm doing great. I'm staying back at the Villas. I'm gonna stay on the island.*

Suzanne: *That's great! Where's Jack?*

Me: *Don't know. Don't care.*

Suzanne: *Really? Don't care?*

Me: *Really*

Suzanne: *Wow! I thought you two had something.*

Me: *Yeah, well, I shouldn't have expected better from a music star.*

Suzanne: *How are you feeling? Baby and everything?*

Me: *Good, I'm hungry a lot. Eating tons.*

Suzanne: *Have you seen a doctor yet?*

Me: *Funny you should ask. I'm seeing Simon tomorrow.*

Suzanne: *Who's Simon?*

Me: *Dr Easton, the doc at the clinic. He pulled out the spines after my accident.*

Suzanne: *You call him by his first name?*

Me: *Yeah, I work with him at the library. We're tutors.*

Suzanne: *Oh that's cool. Message me tomorrow and tell me about the baby.*

Me: *Will do. Night*

I'm hungry again. Tomorrow I need to stock the refrigerator, so I make a shopping list on my phone of everything I could eat right now. I drift off to sleep thinking about food and for once in a long time, not thinking about the men in my life.

THIRTEEN

June 9

ON MY WAY to my appointment at the clinic, I stop at a little coffee shop and pick up a few muffins and coffees, thinking Simon might like a muffin and some coffee too. Banana muffins with dark chocolate chunks sound absolutely delicious, so if Simon doesn't want his muffin, I'll enjoy it for him. I put the small bag containing the muffins into my pack and sling it over my shoulder so my hands are free to carry the two coffees just a few doors down.

I'm greeted by a nurse sitting at the front desk. "You must be Isa."

"That's me." I toast her with one of the coffees.

"Here, please fill this out. I'll let Dr. Easton know you're here." She hands me a clipboard, which I tuck under my arm, and points to a cup of pens. Behind her, Simon walks out from the same exam room I was in a few months ago.

"Isa! How are you this morning?" Simon greets me in a

jovial voice. "Come on back. You can fill that out back here while we talk."

"Hi, Simon." I hand him one of the cups I'm holding. "I brought you a coffee."

"Thanks!" He takes the cup and holds the door open for me, and we move into the examination room.

"Have a seat." He points toward two chairs against the wall as he sits on the stool with casters. "How's Jack? I haven't seen him out and about lately."

"Last I knew, he was in Nashville." Simon's brow knits in confusion, but before he can say anything, I continue, "We aren't together anymore."

"Really?" The brow returns to neutral and even crinkles a bit as his eyes soften. "He seemed serious about you," he says gently. "As far as I know, you're the only woman who's stayed this long with him, and you're the only love interest who's stepped foot in his house here."

"Well, it seems like I wasn't the only woman in his life, so I moved out. It's for the best." I smile to hide the fact that I miss what we could have had. The picture of Jack and Lila in Nashville flashes into my mind, and I strengthen my resolve. I shrug. "I guess I was wrong about him."

"I'm sorry. I like you both a lot."

"Thank you."

"What's your plan? Are you going to head back to Maine?"

"Actually, no." I sit up straight, proud of the decision I made. "I'm staying right here on the island."

"That's great!" His jovial voice is back. "What will you be doing?"

"I haven't figured that part out yet." I take a deep breath, knowing that I haven't thought everything through. "I need to find a job and a place to live. I love volunteering at the library, but it's not a paying role, as you know."

"Hmm. I'll keep my ears open, see if any of my patients say anything about hiring workers. In the meantime, will you continue at the library?"

"I'm happy to do it."

"There is one thing."

"What's that?"

"Jack's a benefactor. Actually, the only benefactor other than myself."

"Oh." Disappointment deflates my mood.

"But all he really does is write checks. He doesn't do much with the program on a day-to-day basis."

"No, I wouldn't think so." Of course Jack pumps his money into projects on the island. He's a giving person. And if I'm going to stay here, I better get used to it, and he better get used to me.

"Well glad to have you continue with us. So, how are you feeling?"

"I just started feeling hungry all the time." Opening my bag, I pull out the muffins. "I brought you one."

"No, thank you." He laughs. "Sounds like your baby is growing. I'm going to have Amy assist me with the exam." He opens a cabinet and takes out a pink johnny with starfish on it and sets it down on the exam table. "Change into this while I get Amy. She'll come in and help you get your paperwork done and take your vitals. All the good stuff. I'll be back in shortly."

"One thing. You won't tell Jack anything about me being here, will you?"

"HIPAA doesn't apply here, but no, I would never violate a patient's trust, and I never discuss someone's confidential medical information unless they give the clinic explicit permission to do so."

"Oh, thank you. I'm so relieved."

ME: *Baby is super healthy. I can't stop eating*

Suzanne: *Great news! boy or girl?*

Me: *Won't know until next month. I'm due November 2*

Suzanne: *If you go early, you could have a Halloween baby.*

Me: *Scary!* 👻

Me: 😖

Suzanne: *lol*

Me: *Any word on the boys?*

Suzanne: *I don't think Ben works and there is a tent in his parents back yard. I'm still trying to figure it out*

An image file quickly follows, and a photo of a family-size tent with two bikes on the ground in front of it opens in my messaging app.

Me: *That's Luke's big boy bike and Cole's balance bike. Maybe they're playing campout at Grandma's house?*

I can only hope that's the case. Carol wouldn't make her son and grandsons sleep outside all the time, would she? "Charity begins at home" she always said when asked for donations to worthy causes, meaning the folks in need should ask their family for help instead of asking strangers. Well, looks like it's Carol's turn to practice what she preaches.

Suzanne sends another photo, this time a close-up of the tent. An adult-size bike is barely visible on the other side of the tent. Ben has never ridden a bike with our boys, so is that his father's bike? Or is Ben entertaining company? But then where would the boys be?

My mind travels down a dark path before my phone buzzes again.

Suzanne: *You still there?*

Me: *Yeah. Thanks for checking on things, I miss them. I hope they are ok.*

Suzanne: <3

JUNE 10

"You hungry?" Sarah asks me, and I know she knows the answer already as Simon and I sit down at the bar. "Hi, Dr. Easton."

"Hi, Sarah." Simon looks around the bar. The band is not one I've seen here before. It's not Jack's. Not Jack's friends. Such a relief.

"Isa, we have your favorite mahi-mahi tacos tonight." Yum!

"Really? Sign me up! And a large water with lemon."

"Make that two and a Red Stripe," Simon adds.

"You guys got it." Sarah dances over to the computer screen and bounces to the music as she enters our order. Then she opens a cooler to grab Simon's beer.

"I haven't seen you for ages." Sarah skillfully pops the cap off the Red Stripe using a bottle opener affixed to her side of the bar and sets the bottle down in front of Simon. She tosses the cap into the trash, fills a glass with ice and water, and puts the glass in front of me.

"Sarah, I saw you two days ago." She stabs a lemon with a wooden pick and puts it on my water.

"Yeah, but I'm used to seeing you every day. You okay? I'm worried about you. How did your appointment go?"

"Whoa, settle down there, Mother Hen," I tease. "Everything is all right. Baby is fine. Simon, here, gave me a checkup yesterday."

"You'd tell her if she was doing too much, right?" Sarah bites out in Simon's direction.

"Hey, you don't have to be hostile toward me," Simon says, visibly annoyed with Sarah's inner bodyguard. "I'm keeping an eye on Isa, both as a doctor and her boss, and as the friend of her former boyfriend."

"That sounds like you're helping Jack stalk Isa. She doesn't need any more men in her life right now."

"Hello? I'm right here!" I can't believe Sarah's reaction. Did something bad happen to her that I don't know about? Maybe my pregnancy is bringing up hurtful memories for her. "You know I'm volunteering at the literacy center with Simon. We just finished up and came here for something to eat."

Sarah grunts and spins around to check on other customers.

"Geeze, I thought she liked me," Simon says.

"I don't know what's gotten into her."

Simon shrugs. "I don't know either." He picks up his beer. "To another great day as a teacher. You did a good job today." I pick up my water and tap his bottle gently.

"Thanks for the feedback." I take a big sip of my water as he does the same with his beer. "I really enjoy it. Sebastian is so smart."

"All the students are smart; they just lacked the opportunity to learn and now that they have it, they're working hard to capitalize on it."

"I like that." Over Simon's shoulder, the sun is sinking into the ocean. One more beautiful sunset.

Sarah brings out our tacos and sets them down. "Any hot sauce?"

"I'm good," I say, afraid to ask her for anything for fear she'll bite my head off again.

"No, I don't need any. Thanks." Simon is wise to follow my lead.

Three crispy tacos filled with heaps of pan-blackened fish, diced tomatoes, peppers, onion, avocados, pineapple, and mango take up most of my plate. A huge helping of rice and black beans fills the rest of the space.

"This looks so good." I take a big bite and some of the fish goes down the wrong way. When I start coughing uncontrollably, Simon reaches around and rubs my back until I stop coughing.

"You need to slow down." He leaves his hand on my back while I take a sip of water.

"Thanks, Simon." His hand stays there as a familiar scruffy dog comes running over, barking and trying to jump up on me. "Ringo!" I quickly look around, knowing his owner must be somewhere close by.

Jack is standing there, the post-sunset sky a red glow behind him. From his perspective, we must look awfully cozy, sitting here with Simon and his hand on my back. Not that I must explain anything to anyone, especially Jack. Not that I even need to talk to him after seeing the picture in *People*.

He moves fully under the thatched roof, and I can finally see his face. His eyes are haunted and his hair is overgrown. His shirt is wrinkled, and there's a stain down the front. He sees me looking at him and breaks into a tired smile, but it quickly disappears as Simon leans over, oblivious to Jack's arrival, and says, "I'll pick you up again on Friday. I'll bring lunch."

Can this get any more awkward?

Jack comes over to the bar and flags down Sarah. Then he turns to us.

"Simon. Isa." His voice is frigid when he greets his friend, but it breaks when he says mine. He clears his throat. "Moving on already?"

Simon stiffens beside me, and I can hear his puzzlement as he says, "Isa had a coughing fit. That's all. I'm not sure I like what you're implying."

Jack's lips purse as if he's about to speak, but he shakes his head. "You're looking well, Isa," he says. "Ringo, come."

But Ringo circles my feet and sits down beside them, as if to declare his allegiance to me. Jack's shoulders slump, and he sighs. "Even my own dog doesn't want to be with me."

He leaves us and goes over to the stage, where he chats with the band. Turns out they might be his friends after all. Or maybe Jack's just good at socializing, using his Southern charm and "aw, shucks" attitude to get what he wants. That charm worked on me once, but no more.

I lean away from Simon to remove his hand from my back. I don't want it there any longer. And I don't want to be here anymore.

"I'm sorry, Simon. I'm very tired. I'm gonna take this home to eat." I wave to catch Sarah's attention.

"I'll walk you home."

"No, thanks." When Sarah comes over to us, I ask, "Can you pack this to go?" She nods and picks up my mostly untouched meal. I'm sure she guessed why I asked. I take a sip of water and bend down to give Ringo some attention so I don't have to deal with any human males. And because I missed my little buddy.

Sarah brings back my dinner in a bag. "Please give me my bill," I tell her.

"Hold on. I'll print it out for you."

Bill before me, I lay down the cash. I'm not letting Jack or Simon pay for my meal. Grabbing my dinner, I head for the front door so I don't have to walk past the band. Ringo follows me. When I get to the exit, I bend down and scratch the pup behind his ears. "Sorry, little guy, you can't come with me." He whines, but sits down.

Glancing back at the band, I see Jack looking my way. It

doesn't seem possible, but he looks even worse than when he came in. His misery threatens to tug at my heartstrings, but I shore up my resolve and go back to my villa.

FOURTEEN

June 14, morning

THE BUZZING of my phone pulls me from a deep slumber, and I reach out with my eyes still closed, slapping the nightstand several times before finally finding the offending device. I pull it into the bed with me and blink to clear the sleep from my eyes. I hope nothing's wrong with my boys.

The phone shows it's 6 a.m. and a message is waiting from Suzanne. She's never texted me this early, so it must be important.

Suzanne: *This was in the paper this morning.*

I click on the attached link, and the *Portland Forecaster* opens to an article titled "South Portland Man Charged for Drunk Driving with Two Children."

Multiple charges have been filed against Benjamin Cushing, age 30, after he was clocked driving 74 miles per hour on High-land Avenue on Sunday at around 11:30 p.m. Per state law, the default speed limit in residential areas is 25 miles per hour unless otherwise posted.

An on-site breath analysis returned a blood alcohol content of 0.11, nearly 38 percent more than the legal limit of 0.08. Two children, ages 5 and 4, were in the car with Cushing.

Cushing was charged with driving under the influence of intoxicants (OUI) and child endangerment in accordance with section 2411, Criminal OUI, of the Motor Vehicles and Traffic code. If convicted, he will be fined $500 and spend at least forty-eight hours in jail. Additionally, his driver's license will be suspended for 150 days plus an additional 275 days for having minor passengers while committing the offense.

Police said the children were turned over to family members, and the Office of Child and Family Services (OCFS) will be notified of the incident.

Cushing is being held in Cumberland County Jail pending arraignment.

My hands start shaking uncontrollably as I call Suzanne.

She picks up immediately. "What a piece of shit!"

"The boys? Are they okay?"

"I just read the story and sent it to you. I don't know anything more."

"I need to come back. The boys can't stay with that nasty troll. Can you pick me up at the airport?"

"Of course I can. Henry is out of town. Stay with me."

"Thanks. I'll call you back when I book my flight."

I log on to the airline site and use my return voucher to book a flight back to Portland tonight. I'm glad it's off season down here, so there are plenty of seats left.

I text Suzanne my flight information, and she immediately confirms she'll be there.

I don't need be at STT until three. What am I going to do for eight hours? Panic is setting in as I start shaking again. More than a year without a driver's license. Good thing he has a bicycle!

Cue uncontrolled laughter that soon turns into sobs. This isn't how I imagined leaving this island, and I still don't have enough money for an attorney, but I'm going to do what I should've done back in February—fight for my boys.

I throw everything I own into the same duffel bags I showed up to the island with a few months ago. At the Beach perfume Jack gave me for my birthday, I collapse onto the bed and hold the glass bottle close. Jack has access to attorneys who could fix my situation with the snap of his fingers, but I'm not the weak woman who ran away from Maine. I grew up in Cinnamon Bay, and I'm going back to Maine a stronger, more confident person.

There's still time for a swim before I go, so I retrieve my suit from its duffel and pull it on.

I don't want to leave this haven, and who knows if I will ever be back to St. John? I wish I could just take the boys and bring them here. I know they would love it as much as I do.

Floating in the warm saltwater feels good. The sun feels good. It's hard to believe that I will be in Maine in a few hours.

My plan: Get the boys back, then come back to the island and away from the Cushing clan ASAP.

Now I just need to figure out how to go about it with minimal resources.

"YOU'RE LEAVING TODAY?" Sarah, my first friend on the island, comes out from behind the bar and throws her arms around me after I explain about Ben's arrest. "I don't want you to leave. Promise me you'll come back."

"I promise," I say, hugging her tight. "I promise I'll be back. And I'll have the boys with me."

"I'm going to miss you. How're you getting to the airport?" Sarah releases me and returns to her place behind the bar.

"Oh my gosh, thanks for reminding me! I need to call Sebastian." I pull his handwritten card out of my wallet and dial his number.

"Miss Isa! Of course I will drive you to the airport." Sebastian's voice resonates happiness through my phone. He's another person I will miss dearly. "I will meet you at the port for the three-o'clock ferry."

OK. I have my ride to the airport, my bags are packed, and I've said goodbye to Sarah. Let's hope I don't run into Jack.

I order a fish sandwich with fries and a water. Maine has great seafood, but I love how it's prepared here. Pan-blackened mahi with spices and some sort of spicy sauce is so good! It's one of the many things I'll miss.

"I wish we had more time," Sarah says. "I know you'll do great getting the boys back. I can't wait to meet them sometime soon." She leaves her workstation for one more hug, and I have to pull myself back from clinging so long it becomes awkward.

Sarah has seen me grow from a timid divorcée fresh from court to a strong, confident single woman who won't tolerate being yanked around by a man. "Thank you for being a friend when I needed one," I tell her. Then I pick up my bags and leave We Be Jammin' for the last time.

Saying goodbye to Sam and checking out of the Villas also hurts my heart. This has been my home off and on for the past few months. "Thank you for everything," I say. "I'm flying out later today. How much do I owe you?" It occurs to me I never signed anything or gave him a credit card when I checked back in.

"It's all been taken care of," Sam replies. "Jack wanted to

make sure you had a place to go. He took care of your bill for as long as you wanted to stay here."

"I didn't know he did that." No wonder Sam gave me that nice villa. My stomach twists with doubt that I'm doing the right thing. But I've promised myself I won't fall for a man's schemes again, no matter how nice they seem. I pull out my wallet, bracing myself for an astronomical bill. "Well, I'd like to pay for it myself."

"I'm sorry, I didn't know he wasn't supposed to pay." Sam makes a gesture of helplessness. "He paid up front, so you have no outstanding bill."

"It's okay." I feel bad for Sam. Jack shouldn't have put him in the middle like this. "Thank you for everything."

"Goodbye, Isa." Sam forces an uncomfortable smile. "Please come back soon."

"That's my plan."

THE FERRY CROSSING IS UNEVENTFUL. After several months in St. John, the close quarters on the watercraft don't bother me like they did on my arrival. When the ferry docks and I make my way onto land, Sebastian's waving arm grabs my attention. As I walk over to his van, I realize that I've made friends at nearly every step on this journey. I might've said farewell to Sarah on St. John, but here in St. Thomas is another friend to bid me well. How lucky am I!

"You won't be gone long, will you?" Sebastian asks as he loads my bags into the vehicle.

"I'm not sure." I feel sad letting Sebastian down. I really like working with him. "I have some personal business I need to attend to. Then I will hopefully be back."

"Sooner than later, Miss Isa."

"I'll certainly try! And hey, maybe by the time I come back, you'll have moved on to writing stories, not just reading them."

"No promises, ma'am, but I'll consider it." His laugh is ebullient, and I join in willingly.

We arrive at STT too soon, and I pull out my wallet for the fourth time today. "How much do I owe you?"

"I can't take money from you." Sebastian looks offended that I am trying to pay him. "I will help you whenever you need me." He unloads my bags and carries them over to the skycap. After the two men greet each other and ask about their respective families, Sebastian says, "Take good care of my friend Miss Isa."

"Absolutely." The skycap sketches a salute toward Sebastian and smiles at me, then takes my bags into the terminal to check them in for my flight.

I throw my arms around Sebastian. "Thank you so much! I will miss you."

"Have a safe trip. I will see you very soon."

I wave as he gets in his van and drives away. I've made more friends here in the short time I have been on the island than I have in the past five years living in Kennebunk. One way or another, I'll be back. I know it.

Inside the terminal, I buy a drink and a book to read and sit at the gate to charge my phone. I keep looking around, thinking I might see Jack. By now someone must have said something to him about my leaving. But he doesn't show up. There is no dramatic "goodbye for now" scene. I'm still mad at him. Is he mad at me too? I thumb my phone, switching his contact info from blocked to unblocked and back again. Argh! Why am I stressing out over a silly man? I should be plotting my strategy for getting my boys back.

My mind is a jumbled mess that only settles down when my group is called for boarding. On the aircraft, I take my seat next to the window. Sitting in front of me is an older lady. She's complaining that the woman sitting next to her has a cat in a carrier. The flight attendant keeps coming over and asking if she would like to move her seat.

"I hope she calms down soon," the man sitting next to me says. "I don't want to listen to her the entire flight."

I just smile to acknowledge him. I don't want to have any part of the commotion. I just want to take off. I look outside, half expecting my own commotion and to see Jack walking toward the plane. But he isn't there.

"Ladies and gentlemen, I'm sorry. We are going to be delayed a few minutes, but not to worry, we will make the time up in the air," the pilot announces over the intercom.

I keep staring out the window. It's a tiny airport, so if Jack were to show up now, I'd see him right away. My eyes burn as I focus on the tarmac, hoping my fierce wishing will make him appear.

The woman in front of me starts screaming. "I'm not going to move! I was here first. Make her move. I'm allergic to cats."

"Ma'am. She doesn't have a problem sitting here, you do." The flight attendant's voice is calm, but a thread of steel runs through it. "You have two choices. You can change your seat, or you can get off the plane."

"I'm not moving! This is my seat!" The woman is screaming now.

"Unbelievable," I say to my row mate. "She's being ridiculous." I check the time on my phone. We're behind schedule, but it will give Jack a chance to get here. I check my phone, flipping it off airplane mode to see if there are any messages. None. Should I text him? What would I say? "Leaving St. John for the indefinite future. It was good while it lasted." No, that's harsh, and this new, grown-up me isn't harsh.

A shadow looms in the aisle, and my heart stops. It's Jack!

But when I look up, two members of the St. Thomas police force are standing there, speaking with the screaming woman. They get her things out of the overhead compartment and escort her off the plane. Passengers clap as she leaves, and the cat owner speaks soothingly to her pet, who hasn't made a sound during the entire kerfuffle.

The flight attendant closes the exterior door, then picks up a handset. "Cabin secure."

I turn back to the window, giving the airport one last thorough scan. If Jack were to make a grand appearance, sweep me off my feet, and tell me "don't go," now is the time. But he's not here.

We pull away from the gate and take off. The beautiful blues and greens of my adopted home get farther and farther away.

FIFTEEN

June 14, afternoon

OUR LOW APPROACH is up the Fore River with Portland to the right and South Portland to the left. The roof of Ben's parents' house is easy to locate by counting the roofs from the elementary school. I look hard to see if I can catch a glimpse of Luke and Cole outside, but we're too far away and at the wrong angle. I can't believe I'm so close to seeing my sons again. How much have they grown? Will they still remember me? Will they want to spend time with me? How can I even begin to make up the time we've lost?

Our landing is uneventful, and Suzanne is waiting for me at the bottom of the escalator.

"Hey, stranger!" She greets me with her arms open wide. "Welcome back!"

I gladly fall into her hug; it does my heart good. "Thanks for picking me up. I have a few bags to wait for." I wish I could say I'm glad to be home, but I'm not. I want to get my boys and go back to St. John.

"How were your flights?" Suzanne and I walk over to the baggage carousel and wait for the bags from my flight to come out.

"Interesting. I wasn't sure we'd ever get to leave St. Thomas. I learned that the airline has zero tolerance when it comes to unruly passengers."

Suzanne gasped. "What did you do?"

"No, not me! The woman in front of me." I hope she's only kidding. I've learned it's OK to put myself first, but I'd never go so far as to be selfish. She can't actually believe I could be unruly.

"No! Of course not. But you never know with pregnant women."

"Thanks for the vote of confidence." I laugh; it's good to see Suzanne again.

"I've written down all the contact numbers for you to call tomorrow to find out what's going on," Suzanne says as I watch the belt for my bags. "I still can't believe that prick is that irresponsible, putting his own children in danger, not to mention everyone else on the road."

"I know." Both of my bags are on the belt and headed our way. "I have to get the boys away from him before he causes them any more harm."

"And his parents, especially his mother."

"Her too."

We each carry a bag out to the parking garage. "This is a pretty classy ride," I comment as Suzanne pops open the back of her Land Rover Defender.

"Henry gave it to me for my birthday." Suzanne takes a deep breath and lets it out. "He's in New York this week."

Does Henry buys Suzanne expensive gifts to make up for not being around?

"Well, thank you for staying here to meet me."

"Oh, I don't go on Henry's work trips. I would just slow him down."

"But he's twice your age. Shouldn't it be the other way around?"

"Haha." Suzanne's laugh is dry, but she doesn't say anything more, just starts the engine. Then she pauses. "I know he loves me. I just wish..."

"Wish what?"

"I wish he was around more." Suzanne backs out of the space and drives carefully through the garage to the exit. "I wish he was more of a husband."

"I'm sorry." It's the only thing I can say. I really don't know anything about Henry other than he's a lot older than Suzanne and he's never home. At least Jack spent a lot of time with me. Well, at first he did. And then he left me. Is this a pattern? Are Suzanne and I just unlucky in love? Our hearts are stolen by older men who leave us?

"There's nothing for you to feel sorry about." She glances over to me before inserting her credit card to pay for parking. "We'll figure it out." The bar swings open, and she steers the Land Rover out onto the road that takes us away from the airport.

"If you love each other, you will." I pat her shoulder as we stop at the intersection of International Parkway and Jetport Boulevard.

"So, our house is in Prouts Neck, to the left, or we could take the long way through South Portland if you want to take a chance on the boys playing outside today."

"Do you really have to ask?"

"No," Suzanne says as she signals and makes a right turn, "but I wanted to give you the choice."

I nod. I want to see the boys. I want to know they're okay. My fingers find my necklace and start to twirl the starfish between my fingers.

"I like your necklace. Is that Tiffany's?"

"I think so? Jack gave it to me for my birthday."

"I thought you were done with Jack. Why are you wearing a necklace he gave you?"

I shrug. I don't know why. Maybe I wear it because it's the only birthday present I've received since my parents died. Maybe I love the necklace because someone took the time to learn I love starfish.

Suzanne turns down the Cushings' road and slows when we come to their house. It's a typical Cape Cod with some deferred maintenance. It needs paint, and the landscaping is overgrown; a pile of debris outside the garage needs to be taken away. That's not safe for the boys to play around.

Why isn't Ben helping his parents? If he's staying with them, I would think that he'd be helping them take care of the house. I hope they care for Luke and Cole better than they care for their house.

Suzanne pulls over just past the house so I can get a better look into the back yard. There's a green tent set up on the grass. Does Ben camp out in the backyard sometimes with the boys?

I don't see any activity. I don't think anyone is home.

"Have you seen enough?" Suzanne asks as I take a few pictures with my phone to look at later. Maybe that pile of rubbish in the driveway will help a judge see this isn't the place for my sons to live.

"Yeah, I guess." I'm disappointed I didn't see the boys. Suzanne pulls away and points the Land Rover to Prouts Neck.

"Thank you for the detour. I really appreciate all you're doing for me."

"I don't mind. Really." Suzanne turns onto a small dirt road that resembles a driveway. Along the road, I count six large houses, all of which look historic. "I can use the company."

I smile. I can use the company too.

The Land Rover bounces as we hit holes left over from the cold and snowy winter that recently ended.

"The potholes are traffic deterrents. They help keep sight-seers away," Suzanne explains after she carefully navigates one that stretches across the driveway. I can imagine getting stuck during mud season without four-wheel drive; it's easy to see why Suzanne would need the Land Rover Defender.

"Sightseers?" I ask but before Suzanne answers, I see the answer to my question: the ocean. The road dead-ends at a pile of sharp-edged boulders. Beyond that, the land falls away, and below that, strong waves crash into the rocky shore. It's a much harsher landscape than the one I enjoyed on St. John.

"That's Winslow Homer's studio." Suzanne points at a small red-trimmed gray-shingled dwelling with a large wrap-around balcony on one corner. "The art museum owns it now and gives tours." She laughs. "By appointment only."

I remember learning about Winslow Homer in high school. He painted scenes of the Civil War, but he also focused on seascapes. This must've been a great place to watch the tide change.

Suzanne pulls into the driveway across from the studio. This is the last house on the road and the one closest to the water.

"This is beautiful." The large shingle-style house looks like it has been here forever. We get out, and my nostrils fill with the salt spray tossed up when the waves hit the weathered rocks. The wind off the ocean is constant. Even though it's the middle of June, the air here on Prouts Neck is chilly.

"Henry and I just had it restored before we moved in." We take my bags out of the back of the Land Rover and start toward the house. "It's a John Calvin Stevens."

"Hah. Paying attention in art class is really paying off now. He's the guy who designed a thousand buildings in Maine, right? He was a popular architect in the early 1900s."

"Yep. That's him. He did the redesign on the studio." Suzanne points her thumb over her shoulder, then unlocks her front door, and we step into the foyer. "I know more about him now than I want to."

Inside, it's like stepping back in time a hundred years. "It's still very nice."

"The restorers did a good job." We drop our bags on the floor, and Suzanne turns to me. "You hungry?"

"Famished!"

"Let's find something to eat."

WHY DO I wake up in the middle of the night? I'm so tired when I go to bed that I fall asleep immediately. Now it's three in the morning and I can't sleep. The nearby lighthouse reminds me with two blasts that a minute has gone by. Lighthouse? Foghouse. I giggle. Wow, I am punchy. Instead of counting sheep, I can count the fog horn blasts to fall asleep.

But between writing a script in my head about what I'm going to say to the state about Ben and trying to figure out the best way to see my boys, counting every minute the lighthouse sounds its warning won't put me back to sleep tonight. Way too much is going on in my head.

I watch the sun come up over the water. I'd forgotten how

early the sun rises in Maine. It's 4:30 a.m., and it's already getting light outside. It will be "one of those days" if I don't get some coffee into me.

Using the light on my phone, I find my way through the dark hallway and down the stairs to the kitchen and start a pot of coffee. Bonus that it's Dunkin's French vanilla. Thank you, Suzanne!

I go through my phone as I sip on my coffee. I know I shouldn't do it, but I I'm a glutton for punishment. I open Jack's text messages to reread some of our conversations.

At the bottom of the text screen are the words "Jack unsent a message." Not once, not twice, but five times. I didn't even know you could unsend a text message.

Jack texted me and then unsent it? Why would he do that? Was he was thinking about me? Does he know I left and he wanted to say goodbye but then hit unsend to be respectful of my wishes? Or did he write something mean and then he took it back?

I think about texting him something and then unsending it just so he knows what it feels like to have to guess. But I'm better than that, and I don't want to open the door for him to start communicating with me again. I have too much on my plate right now with trying to get the boys back.

I close out of Jack's text messages and open up a game app. Sipping my coffee and playing solitaire will pass the time until Suzanne gets up.

NINE A.M. ON THE DOT, I dial the number to the state and ask what's going on with Ben Cushing's case.

"Apparently, nothing," The woman's voice on the other end says. "No one has been assigned."

I explain everything I knew about the arrest and how the boys were in the car with him when he was drinking. When I say that I don't have custody but would love to more than anything, she asks me to send over the custody arrangement and any other information that might be important.

"Absolutely! As soon as I hang up." I give the woman my phone number and my email so she can reach me with any questions or updates. She promises to keep me updated on her investigation, but she warns me this could be a slow process.

Hope fills my heart. Finally, someone who cared enough to listen to me. That's more than I can say about my first interaction with the court.

Using Suzanne's all-in-one printer, I scan the copy of my divorce decree along with copies of the boys' birth certificates and my driver's license.

"Suzanne, thank you." I hug her, tears flowing from my eyes. "Thank you so much!"

"For what? Inviting you to stay with me?" Suzanne returns my embrace.

"That, and for coming across the article."

"That's what friends are for. You would do the same for me."

We weren't close when we went to school together, but that has changed. What are the chances that we would be in the same restaurant at the same time in St. John? Our running into each other was the universe knowing we needed each other's friendship. It feels good to have Suzanne as my friend.

SIXTEEN

June 17

"YOU'RE JUST WHO I NEED," Jeff says, shaking my hand. "When can you start?"

My new boss is a kind, fatherly man. At least, he's been kind so far. Other bar owners, when they saw I have no recent work experience, offered me a free beverage to thank me for coming in and excused themselves.

"I can start immediately."

After my previous attempts at landing a local job, I'm surprised Jeff gave me the time of day, let alone hired me. I'm jumping for joy inside but trying to stay calm on the outside. I don't want him to rescind his offer.

"Perfect!" Jeff's eyes are sparkling, his cheeks are rosy, and together with his round belly, I'm reminded of a beardless Santa Claus. "Let me show you around."

We walk back to the small kitchen, and Jeff introduces me to the on-duty cook, an older man named Andy.

"Nice to have you on board." Andy flips some burgers on the griddle. "It's nice that Jeff finally hired someone who isn't a regular."

"Alright, get back to work," Jeff jokingly snarls.

Our next stop is the office to fill out paperwork. "So didja get too cold in Canada and decide to move somewhere warmer?"

"Canada?" I'm confused.

"Yeah. Up north." He jerks his chin into the air as if to indicate the direction. "St. John, New Brunswick."

"Oh! I forgot about that one. No, I was in St. John Virgin Islands, the Caribbean. That's real warmth." I sign the last piece of documentation and hand over a voided check to set up direct deposit. For the first time since I opened my checking account before I left for the island, money will be flowing into it instead of out.

"And yet you came back here. Well, their loss is my gain." Jeff takes the stack of paperwork and puts it in a file. "Why don't you come in at noon on Wednesday?" Standing up to walk me out, he says, "It's slower then, and you can learn the ropes before the busy weekend."

"Works for me." I shake Jeff's hand even though I want to give him a hug. "Thank you so much. Looking forward to working here."

I have a job. I can't wait to tell Suzanne and Sarah.

Once in the car, an older BMW sedan Suzanne said I can use until I'm back on my feet, I text them in a group chat:

I did it! I have a job!

No one responds.

I flick to my messages with Jack and type out the same message, but before I send it, I reconsider.

He would really be excited, but he would also be sad that

I'm not on the island with him anymore. That I'm not with him anymore. I better not send it.

I'm so excited when I pull out of the lot that I forget where I'm headed. It's like I'm on autopilot and instead of turning left to go to Suzanne's carriage house, I turn right as though I'm headed to Kennebunk. I don't even catch myself until I'm about to go through the tollbooth on the turnpike. What am I doing?

When I make it back to Suzanne's, I knock on her door. She doesn't answer, so I let myself in.

"Suzanne?" Where could she be?

"Hold on!" she shouts from upstairs.

"I'll wait right here." I make myself comfy at the kitchen table, and a few minutes later, Suzanne drags in, hair messed up and still in her pajamas.

"Suzanne? Are you alright?" My fingers find my starfish pendant and twirl it between my thumb and index finger.

"Yeah, I'm fine." She yawns and walks over to the coffee maker and picks up the empty pot, sighs, and puts it back down.

"Are you sure? It's three in the afternoon and you're acting like you just woke up. Were you sleeping?"

"I didn't get to sleep until seven this morning."

"Why? What happened?" Now I'm getting really concerned. She isn't her normal bouncy self with her perfect hair and perfect outfit.

"Nothing. I was up helping Henry get something done."

"Henry's back?"

"Oh, no, no." Suzanne yawns again and fills the coffee maker with grounds and water, then switches it on to brew. "He's in Italy, looking for a chef for his new restaurant on Beacon Hill."

"Really?" I didn't know she was involved with his business.

"Yes, Isa. I try to help out when I can." She sounds annoyed with my questions. I definitely think something more is going on with her. She's always in a good mood.

She picks up a large envelope from the counter and tucks it out of sight into a drawer.

"Well, I have some great news." My eyes don't stray from the drawer she just closed. "I got a bartending job at the Aqua Oyster over on Preble Street. You know, across from the water."

Suzanne leans against the counter and looks exhausted. "Isn't that a dive bar?"

"I like dive bars. We Be Jammin' was practically my home away from home." And I like to pay my bills. "Jeff said it will be good for business to get some new blood in there."

"Jeff is your boss? Jeff at the Aqua Oyster?" Suzanne retrieves a mug from the cabinet above the coffee maker. "Just be careful."

"Why? Why does everyone warn me about the men I meet? First Sarah warned me about Jack, and now you're warning me about my freaking boss. Why does no one trust me?" I throw my hands into the air with a huff.

"Everyone has a history." Her voice carries a sharp edge of caution.

"What?" Oh, no, here it comes. The first job offer I get is from a serial killer.

"Jeff may seem like a nice guy, but he has had a lot of trouble with women," Suzanne continues. "I know he used to hit on women at his bar. He was sued for sexual harassment. That was when his business started tanking."

I can't see Jeff mistreating anyone. He was really nice to me. But I've been wrong before. I've been very wrong.

I've ignored red flags my whole life, but Suzanne seems to see one being raised on the flagpole right in front of me, illuminating it with bright lights. Why *would* Jeff hire someone with no experience? Is it to prey on me? Or does he see me as a naive young woman who desperately needs a job?

"He's my boss. I'm not a patron." Suzanne turns away and starts filling her mug with coffee. Is she even hearing the excuses I'm making for my new employer? "I figure I can learn some of the drinks from the island. Maybe people will like the Caribbean thing?"

"Just be careful." She adds creamer and sugar, then brings her mug over to the table and sinks into the chair across from me. "Do you even know anything about tending a bar?"

"Well, I have plenty of experience meeting the every whim of a demanding man, so I should be fine."

When Suzanne just blinks at my joke, I roll my eyes. "I told Jeff I didn't, and he still hired me." I shrug. "He wants to train me. I told him I learn fast."

"That's great!" She toasts me with her mug, then takes a big sip. I wince. How can she drink coffee that hot? "You should let Sarah know; I bet she can help you."

"I texted both of you." I raise my phone to see if Sarah got back to me, and her message greets me.

Yay! And I mean Yay!

Smiling, I text her back.

I'm going to need all the help I can get!

Sarah quickly responds.

You'll do great! But I will be on standby if you need me! YAY!

I have a job. I can't imagine working at a bar will be as fulfilling as volunteering with the literacy program was, but the money I'll earn will help me make a home for my boys. That's an entirely different kind of fulfillment.

Suzanne yawns and finishes her coffee. I want to ask her about the envelope. I want to make sure she is okay. I know how lonely it feels when you face something alone, and I don't want

her to go through that. She's here for me, and as much as I can,
I'll be here for her too.

———

JUNE *19*

"TWELVE O'CLOCK ON THE BUTTON! I can't
remember when someone showed up here on time." Jeff's
cheeks are rosy as he welcomes me.

"Hi, Jeff." I follow him behind the bar, where he shows me
how to use the register and enter a food order so the kitchen
will make it, and then he gives me a quick lesson on pulling
beers. As long as I tilt the glass away from me and grasp the tap
handle by the base, I should be okay.

"I'm sure I don't have to tell you, because you seem to
always smile, but customers like pleasant bartenders."

Pleasant? How about ecstatic? I've been so happy since Jeff
told me I have the job, my cheeks have been getting a workout
from smiling so much.

"Alright, I'll be out back doing paperwork if you need me.
It's all yours."

After Jeff disappears into his office, I take a closer look at
my new domain. All the different kinds of liquors and beers
overwhelm me. I don't know if I will ever manage to memorize
their names. I pick up the bottle of Black Velvet and recall Ben
reeking of it when he came home after being gone for three or
four days. I hate this stuff! I hope no one orders it.

A familiar upbeat tune with beachy vibes suddenly comes
through the speakers, and I'm swept back to St. John. The song
starts in, and an ache fills my chest. "Palm Trees and Pickup
Trucks." Of course it's one of Jack's songs. I don't know all of

them, but the good thing is they average about two and a half minutes. The bad thing is, he has a lot of hits.

The door opens and my very first customer walks in. He's older, maybe in his sixties, and his skin is weathered like he's spent years on a fishing vessel. I hope he orders something easy.

"Welcome to the Aqua Oyster," I call as he takes the seat at the end of the bar.

He grumbles something I can't make out.

I walk over and stand in front of him, making sure to put on my best smile. "Are you here for lunch? What can I get for you?"

"Who are you?" The man's motor oil-stained blue work shirt has the name Jerry embroidered on a patch over his left pocket.

"Isa. I just started." I'm as hospitable as I can be. "What can I get you to drink, Jerry?"

Jerry looks down at his name on his shirt and snorts.

"Vodka soda, no fruit," he grumbles. "Short glass."

I grab a short glass, fill it with ice and pour the well vodka in as I count to five like Jeff told me. Then I top it off with soda water from the soda gun. "Would you like to see a menu?" I set his drink down on a napkin in front of him.

"No," Jerry growls, then adds "thank you" in a softer tone.

Two more men come in—they're about my age, maybe a little older—and sit down at the bar. I greet them and ask what they want to drink.

"Jeff just hire you?" one asks. "I'll take a rum and Coke."

"Where're you from?" the younger-looking of the two asks as he gives me a once-over. I cringe inside but keep my smile. "Great tan."

"Yes, and I'm from Kennebunk originally, but I was living down in the Caribbean for a little bit."

"Really?" the second says. "Make me a Caribbean drink."

I'm unsure what to do. "Alright."

I stall for time, looking around the backbar and paying closer attention to the names on the bottles. On the shelf two levels above the Black Velvet, a swashbuckling face leers out at me. Captain Morgan! He's Caribbean, right? Grabbing that bottle, I pour a five-count into a fancy glass, then replace it on the shelf. What's next? Something fruity?

I poke around, finally finding a dusty bottle of banana liqueur. Banana and rum? There are worse combinations. And I bet these men have never spent a day in their lives away from South Portland, let alone visited a Caribbean island. How will they know any different?

I add a two-count of the liqueur and am about to serve the drink when I remember how much I enjoyed the fresh fruit garnishes on my drinks in St. John. I look at the options in the well, but lemon, maraschino cherries, and olives don't sounds appetizing with banana. Oh, well. Here goes nothing.

The glass slides across the bar when I give it a gentle shove, and the customer catches it. Lifting the glass to eye level, he gives it a close look before taking a sip. "This isn't bad!"

I breathe out, relieved he likes my concoction. I might be able to do this job after all.

"SUZANNE! THAT'S TOO MUCH!" I can't believe she's offering me her carriage house to live in.

"Isa, there are hardly any apartments for rent, and the ones that are available are way out of your budget. Especially two- and three-bedroom apartments." She shows me her phone where a browser window is open to the Rentals section of the online *Forecaster*. The list of available units is short, and the prices make me sick to my stomach. She's right. There's no way a bartender with two children can afford these. "And you would need to sign a year's lease. Who knows where you'll end up in a year."

"True. I don't know where I'll be or what I'll be doing."

"Besides, I talked to Henry about it. We didn't want to rent out the carriage house because he didn't want me to have to deal with tenants while he's not here. But he doesn't want me to be by myself either." She walks toward the front door, and I trail after her. "If you stayed in the carriage house, I won't be alone when he isn't here and I won't have to deal with strangers renting from us." She opens the door, and we step out into the humid summer. "Come on, let me show it to you before you say no again."

Following Suzanne across the drive to the carriage house, I look over to the studio across the street. Too bad I don't know how to paint. I could channel my inner Homer if I were to live here.

The carriage house is closer to the water than the main house. The first floor is a three-car garage with an extra bay for storage. Suzanne and I climb the stairs to the apartment.

"It's only a two-bedroom, but it's partially furnished. The electric isn't separated from ours, so you don't have to worry about setting up an account. Oh, and we can extend the wifi to reach out here too."

"That's so generous, Suzanne. You really don't mind me staying here?"

"I want you to stay here," she insists. "We can have coffee together in the morning and dinner together at night." I didn't realize how starved for company she really is. "When you have your baby, I can help you. We can set up a nursery in here." We walk into the smaller bedroom. "Henry will feel much better about not being around if you're right next door."

She bumps my shoulder with hers. "And just think about it:

This way, you'll have your own apartment. To a judge, you'll look better than Ben, who lives with his parents. Besides, it gets lonely here, and it's a great way to keep my best friend nearby."

I look around. She's right. This would be the perfect situation for everyone, my baby included. The boys can have the larger room, and their new sibling and I'll take the smaller one.

"Oh, friend, thank you. Thank you for everything!" I can't believe how much she's doing for me. Tears overflow my eyelids and roll down my cheeks.

"Does that mean you'll move in?"

"We'll be neighbors!" I embrace my friend. "Thank you!"

I can't believe she's moving me into her carriage house. Suzanne is very generous. And she's right. Having my own place will look good in the state's eyes when it comes to custody of the boys. It will also give me a nice place to bring my baby home to.

SEVENTEEN

September 6

NEARLY FOUR LONG months have passed since I left the island. I'm almost seven months pregnant, and the Aqua Oyster is now an up-and-coming restaurant with great food, fun drinks, and live music. Jeff has really made an effort to rebrand the bar with a Caribbean flair, and it's paid off. In addition to typical bar food, burgers, and chicken tenders, he's added spicy coconut shrimp and crispy fish tacos using Maine seafood.

Labor Day was this week, which means the tourists are gone and we're back to just the locals. Surprisingly, the vibe has stayed the same; there's more of a family atmosphere now. All our regulars now bring their wives. Maybe they think it's cheaper than actually taking them on island vacations. Whatever it is, the Aqua Oyster has become *the* place to be.

As I'm setting up the bar to open, Jeff stands in the kitchen opening, staring at me.

"Do you need something?" I've caught him staring more

than once. Has he never seen a pregnant woman before? I force a smile to make sure my job is secure.

"Why did you come back to Maine?" His voice is low and not animated like it normally is. "You're too pretty to be working in this place."

Screwing the lid on the jar of cherries I'd partially emptied into the garnish tray, I say, "I had to come back."

"You could go anywhere, but you came here."

"You're the only one who gave me a job.." I don't want to let my messed-up personal life interfere with the only job I could get. I twirl the starfish pendant with my fingers.

"But you're so pretty. Why didn't they see how pretty you are?" I wish he would stop saying that. Is he drunk? Concussed?

Jeff leans against the door jamb and drops his eyes to my feet then slowly moves them up my body, never making eye contact. I feel like a piece of meat being obsessed by a customer at the butcher shop next door.

"I'm just trying to support myself." I turn away so he can't see the revulsion on my face. Maybe this is what Suzanne had tried to tell me back when I was hired? "Thank you for the opportunity."

"I'm glad you came to see me when you needed a job." He's right behind me. The hair on the back of my neck stands up when his warm breath hits my collar. "I hope you know you can come to me if you need anything." His voice drops to a rumble as he leans in closer, speaking almost directly into my ear.

The screen door in the kitchen slams. Jeff steps back and regains a professional demeanor just before Andy joins us behind the bar.

"Hi, guys!" Andy has great timing, whether he knows it or not. If I didn't need this job to try to get custody of the boys, I would be long gone.

"It's a great day at the Aqua Oyster," I cheese, trying to use my smile and my eyebrows to send him thanks for saving me. But he looks at me like I'm being weird.

"Jeff, did our meat order come in yet?" he asks instead. Maybe Jeff can stare at that instead of me.

"It came in this morning." Jeff looks me up and down again, winks, and takes a deep breath before he turns to follow Andy back into the kitchen.

It takes both hands to hold onto the bar to steady myself once Jeff is out of sight. I need to find something else to do, but there are no other jobs out there. Too bad Jeff turned out to be such a creeper, because I love working here.

THE BAR IS busy for a Wednesday afternoon. I have at least one customer at all times, and although that keeps my aching body moving, it takes my mind off the uncomfortable situation from earlier. I rub my lower back, then reach for a bottle on a higher shelf. I'm grateful for the stretch.

Later, as I restock the beer cooler, Jack's voice starts singing on the radio, except it isn't a song I recognize as one of the many in rotation on our local station.

Maybe I should have held you closer and never let you go
Now I'm stranded on this beach alone
Writing messages in a bottle
Sending prayers in the waves
Hoping they find you

I stop what I'm doing and move closer to the speaker to hear the words.

Sandy fingers can't hold you tight
Wishin' on seashells, under the moonlight.
Echoes of your laugh in the warm ocean breeze
But without you, baby, this beach ain't home.
Every starlit sky brings back our love so fast.
Missin' your touch, missin' all of you.
So here's my heart, bare by the sea
Wishin' on stars, hopin' for one more try.
Wishin' on stars, hopin' you'll come back to me

Oh, shit! This is about us. Sandy fingers? Our hands were all sandy at the beach, and he made the comment he would have a hard time holding on to me. He wrote about our sandy fingers and now they're on the radio?

I'm stuck in the tide getting pulled from the shore
Sunset memories, they're haunting me,
I need you here, back by the sea.
This beach ain't paradise when you're not here with me

He misses me. Looking back on that whole thing around my birthday and his trip to Nashville, I've realized I overreacted. I should've given Jack the time to explain. Given him the chance to show that he's trustworthy instead of assuming the worst. It seems so obvious now: Jack wouldn't do anything to hurt me. *I miss you too, Jack,* I think as I blow a kiss toward the speaker.

"That kiss for me?" Jeff asks with a leer as he comes around the corner. I can't stop the full-body shiver that comes over me. He makes me feel disgusting. "I'll watch the bar so you can go on break."

"Thanks." Perfect timing, Creepo-O Jeff. I grab my phone and my bag and go sit in the car to eat.

There are several texts from Suzanne, including a link to a *People* magazine article.

Country music icon Jack Kendall surprised his fans this week by revealing plans for a farewell tour through a heartfelt message shared on his official Facebook page.

In the announcement, the 48-year-old star conveyed his decision to gradually conclude his touring career within the year. Reflecting on his incredible journey that began over three decades ago, Jack reminisced about the early days when music was distributed on vinyl records and cassettes.

The Tennessee-born artist shot to fame with the success of his 1992 hit "Not Your Average Tan Line," which soared to the top of the Hot Country Songs chart. His remarkable talent earned him the prestigious Country Music Association's New Horizons Award in 1993, solidifying his position as a prominent figure in country music. Kendall went on to tour the globe fifteen times, first as an opening act for the likes of Loretta Lynn, Garth Brooks, and Diamond Rio, and then as the headliner.

Expressing his awe at the enduring support of his fans, Kendall invited them to join him on this scaled-down final tour, bidding adieu to the touring life that has been his passion for so many years.

While Kendall hasn't explicitly stated the reason behind his retirement from touring, speculation has arisen, especially considering his recent heartfelt track, "This Beach Ain't Paradise (When You're Not Here With Me)." The song's emotional depth and poignant lyrics hint at themes of longing and loss, suggesting a personal narrative. Fans and music enthusiasts have begun speculating that Kendall's decision to step back from touring might indeed be connected to a significant relationship hinted at in his latest song. This possibility adds a layer of emotional resonance to his farewell tour.

Kendall's retirement marks the end of an era for his devoted fans. His legacy as a country music fan favorite is a testament to his enduring talent and the lasting connection he's forged with his audience.

He did it. He announced he's done.

I text Suzanne back: *Holy shit! He retired!*

Suzanne: *I thought you might want to know.*

Me: *Thanks <3*

I open Jack's texts.

Me: *Congratulations on your retirement. I hope you are doing well.*

I send the message.

Then I think better of it. What am I doing? I'm just causing more pain all around. I unsend immediately.

I need to stop obsessing over Jack Kendall. I eat my sandwich, then head back into the Aqua Oyster and finish my shift.

I can't stop missing Jack.

———

THE EVENTS of the day are swept down the drain with the warm water as I stand under the shower. I always feel gross when I leave my shift, but today I'm extra gross because of my boss's inappropriate comments. Shampooing the smell of stale beer out of my hair makes me feel human again and helps me forget about Creep-O Jeff.

But the release of the day leaves room for Jack's new song, which plays on repeat in my mind.

"Missin' your touch, missin' all of you. So here's my heart, bare by the sea," I sing and think about the island... and Jack.

I shut my eyes, allowing myself to drift back to Jack's shower, when we were happy being with each other. The gentle spray prickles my skin, sending tingles through me similar to the tingles I got when Jack touched me.

I haven't been touched by a man since I left the island. Jack introduced me to enjoyable sex. He showed me what it's like having a partner who cares that I have fun too.

Leaning my back against the shower wall, my mind drifts to memories of Jack touching me. Taking the handheld shower-head off its cradle, I turn the outer rim to the massage setting and run the concentrated stream below my rounded belly. The feeling takes me back to Jack's home and when I was in his shower with him.

I can almost feel Jack kissing my abdomen and lower as I part my legs, using my free hand to open my folds, allowing him access. I angle the shower head so it's pointing up and direct the hard stream of water so it massages my clit. Surprised by the intense sensation, I move the spray away, then find a rhythm: in and out, back and forth, and occasionally up and down.

"Come for me!" Memory Jack whispers in my ear. My body shakes with an intense orgasm and I cling to the wall for support. Warmth and peace and pleasure wash over me.

I come back to the present breathing hard. Dazed, I open my eyes and watch the water hit the shower floor. I'm light-headed and my legs rubbery. My body feels good, but my soul feels empty. I miss Jack's touch.

Opening the steamy glass door, I step out and towel off. Completely relaxed and in my oversized T-shirt, I climb into bed. Looking at my phone, I open Jack's text messages to read them again. There's another unsent message from him. I smile to myself. Looks like he misses me too.

EIGHTEEN

September 7

"THANKS, Isa. Business sure has picked up since you started here." The register rings as Jeff closes out the cash drawer. "Let me walk you out to your car."

"You don't have to do that. I'm a big girl." Even though Jeff wasn't as much of a creep today as he was yesterday, I don't want to be alone with him.

"I'd feel better if I made sure you got to your car okay. I don't want any of your new fans lurking around, wanting autographs or anything. I want to make sure you come back to work tomorrow; you're good for business."

Wanting an autograph? My stomach clenches at thoughts of raving fans calling for Jack's attention. This final tour of his will be unlike any other.

"I'm a bartender; no one wants a bartender's autograph, just their alcohol. But if it makes you feel better..." I pull on my rain jacket and give in to Jeff. I'll get out of here and home sooner if we don't argue. Besides I'm already alone with him, so if he were to try anything, it would be inside where no one can see, not out in a parking lot.

Jeff walks with me to my car through the nearly empty lot. I recognize his trusty old beater, and there's an unfamiliar pickup parked in the corner. Jeff opens the door for me. "See you tomorrow?"

"Wouldn't miss it. Thanks, Jeff." He nods and shuts my door. I chalk up his chivalry to his wanting to protect his new moneymaker.

As I'm pulling out, I look in my rearview mirror. He's standing, watching as I turn onto the road. Thank you, Jeff, for not trying to molest me tonight.

It's about a fifteen-minute ride out to Prouts Neck. There aren't many streetlights, and as I get closer to Henry and Suzanne's carriage house, the rain relentlessly drums on the roof of my car, the only sound on this desolate, pitch-black road. Each raindrop adds to the growing tension holding my chest in a vice as I grip the steering wheel, my knuckles turning white. I can barely see the headlights of the car far behind me. I'm glad they're keeping their distance.

When I come up to the turn on Prouts Neck, I almost miss it and make the turn without using my signal. I let out a big sigh and loosen my grip on the wheel a little, knowing I am almost home.

Just as I let my guard down, the car is slammed into from behind. The impact is like a thunderclap on this stormy night. My body's thrown violently forward, abruptly stopped by the seat belt, and then tossed back. The crunch of metal fills the air, mixing with the sounds of the rain and my own labored breathing.

The other driver must not have seen me take the turn. *Stupid, foolish Isa. Too lazy to use your signal.* Ben's voice is suddenly loud in my head. I thought I'd silenced the vile beast, but the crash must've shaken it loose. I answer back just as loudly, my voice harsh in the crumpled car.

"Well, Ben, guess what? You're the lazy one, who couldn't keep a job, who couldn't take care of yourself, let alone your family. And you know what? I don't think I've ever seen you use a signal whenever I was in a car with you."

I hope no one in the other car is hurt. I should get out and check on them, but I'm still too stunned to move enough to get out or find my phone. Instead, I rub my belly and whisper calming words even as I try to calm myself.

"Breathe, Isa. Take deep breaths," I say aloud. My baby hiccups, and I wonder whether they're trying to take deep breaths too. I grin. I can't wait to greet this little person, even though they'll always remind me of Ben. I won't allow him to ruin our mother-child relationship, however. I'm going to do things differen—

An ear-splitting crash sends me lurching forward, then snapping back against the seat. The jolt is like a physical punch to the gut, and I gasp for breath.

Raindrops blur the view through the windshield, and the inside of my car fills with the smell of burning rubber and gasoline. There's an odd shuddering, as if it were in the throes of some mechanical agony, and then it dies.

"What the...? Oh my god!" I exclaim, my voice trembling with fear and disbelief.

The second hit is enough to push me into action. My hands shake as I fumble for my phone, then struggle to dial 911.

"Cumberland County dispatch, what's your emergency?" The voice on the other end is in and out because of the poor cell service in this area, but it's still a lifeline in the darkness. I start to explain my situation, and I'm stunned by the chilling realization that someone intentionally crashed into me on this dark, rain-soaked road.

As I try to convey where I'm located, the car's interior lights flicker and my car door opens. Terror washes over me. A shadow, a man. He lunges toward me, his hand snatching my phone. Creep-O Jeff has finally snapped and come after me, and I burst into tears.

But it isn't Jeff. It's worse.

"Ben!" Fear clenches my throat. A litany of thoughts scream through my mind. How did he find me? Why did he come after me? Is he going to kill me?!

The dispatcher's voice crackles and distorts and fades into the background, replaced by the sickening realization that I'm utterly defenseless. Ben stomps on my phone, and the crunch echoes in the rainy night as the screen, the last flicker of connection to the outside world, shatters under his heel.

The car's interior, once a sanctuary, now feels like a trap. Ben's eyes bore into mine, and in this moment, I'm acutely aware of my vulnerability.

"Get out of the car." I recognize his tone and know what comes next. "Get out of the fucking car!"

I struggle to unbuckle my seat belt. My shoulder's hurt, and I'm unable to obey.

"I can't," I say meekly.

He leans in to roughly unbuckle me, maneuvering around my protruding belly. "Always were a fat fuck," he says with a curse.

Once I'm free, Ben grabs my ponytail and yanks me out of the car and into the rain. The familiar smell of Black Velvet is on his breath. My stomach lurches, and bile fills my throat. Even the baby thinks Black Velvet is vile.

"You ruined my fucking life, you fucking piece of shit!" Spittle flies as he shouts at me. I listen, paralyzed with fear. He knots his hand in my hair. My head is now under his control, forced to follow his every movement.

"I've lost everything because of you!" His grip tightens and pulls downward, forcing my face up toward his. "You called the state on me? They're taking the boys!" Suddenly, he gets quiet and looks at my chest where I'm worrying with the starfish. "What's this? You've never worn jewelry. Where'd you get it? Did you buy it with my money?" His voice rises with each question.

"Someone gave it to me," I manage to say before I'm shaken so hard my jaws are forced together, catching my tongue between my teeth. The pain is like none I've ever felt. Even the urchin's sting wasn't this bad. Oh, to be back in St. John and away from this misery!

"It was a man, wasn't it?" Ben asks in a lethally quiet voice. My silence must be answer enough because he rips the starfish necklace from me and throws it into a puddle. "Whore. You'll spread your legs for anyone."

He punches my head, and I sag. My knees have given out, and Ben is keeping me upright with only his hold on my hair. I want to sleep so when I wake up, this nightmare will be over.

Headlights pull in behind our cars, and he wrenches my head up as he turns to face the new arrival.

A car door slams, and footsteps splash toward us.

"Isa! Isa!" I can't see the man's face, but I recognize the voice, the shape of his body. I'm so relieved, my tears start all over again.

Ben leans over and shoves his filthy tongue into my bloody mouth, then pulls away. "Hey, buddy, we're kinda busy right now!" he shouts at the newcomer.

"No, you aren't," Jack says and punches Ben in the face,

driving him to the ground and me with him. I land hard, but on my backside. My baby is still safe. My tongue is still bleeding.

The pressure of Ben's hold relaxes slightly, and I take my chance to pull away. But as I stand up, so does Ben, his hand still caught in my hair. "Nobody punches me and gets away with it," he growls out and takes a step toward Jack.

I can't let him get away with this!

I clear my throat and gather all the blood in my mouth, then spit it at Ben. I watch in horror as the mess of blood and mucus slides down the side of his face.

Now I've done it.

Ben's wrath is back on me, and his eyes are wide, the blood-shot sclera looking red in the rain-dimmed headlights. I brace myself for impact, but the next hit doesn't come. Instead, Ben's eyes roll back and he falls to the ground.

He doesn't move.

"Ben?" I croak.

Nothing.

I toe his body, but he lies still.

Is he dead? Did Jack and I somehow kill him? I crouch and put my hand under Ben's nose. He's breathing. If I could feel anything, it would be relief.

"Darlin' girl! Let me help ya up." Jack bends down and, gently gripping my elbows, guides me to my feet. I sway when he releases me. "Hey, now," he says, appearing in front of me. "You're okay. You're okay." He wipes my hair back from my face and runs a hand over my forehead. "I'm real proud of ya. Real proud."

My stomach lurches, and I retch. Jack quickly steers me away from Ben, and once again my hair is held by a man. But this one holds it with tenderness as I fold practically in half and lose my dinner onto the shoulder of the road.

"...not that he wouldn't deserve it," Jack says, and I realize he's been talking quietly the whole time I've been puking up my guts. "But even I draw the line at vomiting on an unconscious guy."

"Now come on, darlin'. You're clammy and breathin' hard. Think you're going into shock. Come lay down in the back seat, out of the rain. Let's get you warmed up."

NINETEEN

September 8

I DON'T REMEMBER MUCH about what happened last night, but Jack explained everything when I woke up in a strange bed this morning.

No, I wasn't in Jack's hotel room. Last night's attack sent me into shock, so emergency services took me to the hospital, where I was treated with oxygen and fluids and then monitored while I slept overnight.

"Thank you, Dr. Grillo," Jack is saying now. He awkwardly shakes her hand with his left. His right hand—the one that punched Ben—is wrapped in bandages.

"Isa, you take care. Everything looks good." She puts her hand on my good knee. "Just remember, for the grade one whiplash, ice and Advil for the next week, then switch to heat and stop the Advil. Take Tylenol for pain. You'll be sore, and you need more rest. But"—she squeezes and I jump—"given time, you should be good as new."

"And my baby?" I ask.

"She's doing great! Exactly where I would expect her to be."

She? I'm having a girl? Since I don't have the best insurance, I declined the optional gender scan at 20 weeks.

"Are you sure?"

"Yes. The sonogram tech didn't tell you?" Dr. Grillo looks through my records. "Oh, yes. Definitely a girl."

"Wow!" After two boys, I'm having a girl. I wonder if raising her will be different from raising her brothers? My mind is a whirl as Dr. Grillo congratulates me, then excuses herself from the room.

Kissing my forehead carefully and tucking my now-dry, matted hair behind my ear, Jack looks into my eyes, "I never should have let you leave. I'm so sorry."

"Jack, why are you here?" I reach for my necklace, for the reassurance of my starfish. But my neck is empty.

"I couldn't spend another day on the island without you—"

"What are you staring at?"

Jack is looking hard at my neck, as if to see something that isn't there. I look down too, and comprehension dawns.

"The necklace you gave me—it's gone. Ben tore it off me." I fold my hands in my lap to keep my fingers from twitching. I love that necklace; it really means a lot to me. But that's Ben, always destroying what I care about.

Someone knocks at the door and pushes it open. A police officer pokes his head into the room. "May I come in?"

"Yeah." I want to get this over with so I can go home. "We'll talk later," I whisper to Jack.

"Ms. Cushing. I'm Officer Anderson with the Scarborough Police Department. How are you feeling?"

"Better, thank you." I shift my weight in the bed and pull the sheet up a little higher. "What happened to Ben?"

"Your ex-husband?" he asks, like there's another person who tried to kill me and then passed out after I spit on him. "Oh, yes. He's been admitted. When he regains consciousness, we'll arraign him, and the court will decide where we go from there."

"Regains consciousness? But he tried to go after Jack after Jack punched him. He only dropped after I stopped him." My cheeks burn with embarrassment. I've never spit on anyone in my life, and I hope I never have to again.

"I take it Mr. Cushing liked his alcohol." I nod as the officer continues his explanation. "From what the ER doc could tell, between the effects of alcoholism on his cardiovascular system and the intense anger Mr. Kendall reported him experiencing, Mr. Cushing had an"—he studies his notes—"intracerebral hemorrhagic stroke."

"Wow," I breathe.

"The ER doc also informed me that patients with this kind of incident usually recover in four weeks or less."

"Four weeks?!" Jack sounds as gobsmacked as I feel.

"How, how did you find us?" I ask, suddenly curious. "I didn't have a good cell signal."

"You were able to get a call out to 911, and they were able to pinpoint your location. The signal wasn't strong enough to carry your voice, but it broadcast your location loud and clear."

I shiver. Suzanne's not gonna believe this when I tell her.

Suzanne! I turn toward the bedside table automatically, but it's empty. "My phone! What happened to my phone?"

"We found your cell phone near your car," Officer Anderson says. "Unfortunately, the screen is shattered, and the device won't turn on."

"Suzanne must be worried sick! We have coffee together every morning."

Jack reaches over from his seat beside the bed and squeezes

my hand. "We'll go back to Suzanne's house as soon as they release you." He looks to the policeman. "Is there anything more you need from us?"

"No, not today. You get some rest." Officer Anderson steps out into the hallway, where he pauses to speak with a woman dressed in a blue blazer and matching skirt. She keeps looking in at me and Jack. Probably some reporter wanting a story for the six-o'clock news, and now it's even juicer that Jack is involved.

The woman knocks on the door jamb. "Hi, Isa? May I come in?"

Jack must sense my uneasiness because he says, "I would rather you respect her privacy. She isn't ready to speak to the press."

"I'm a social worker with Maine OCFS. My name's Eliza Bennett. I'd like to speak to you about Cole and Luke." My blood runs cold as she steps closer. My boys! I hope Ben's actions haven't put them in danger. "How are you feeling?"

"I—I—I'm doing okay, but how are my boys?" Jack squeezes my hand, and I cling to it like a limpet.

"I was called in because your ex-husband has been arrested. Again." I watch her lips move; I didn't think anyone real actually worked at OCFS, yet here someone is. "I wanted to come in person to speak with you." She gives me a kind smile. "You didn't answer your phone when I called earlier, but now I understand why."

"Where are my boys? Are they with Ben's mother? He thinks I reported him to you."

"First, we were closely monitoring the situation because of his arrest for intoxicated driving with the children in his car. And second, we have them. One of my colleagues has taken them out for breakfast. Your in-laws didn't want responsibility for two young boys while they're waiting for their son to awake from a coma.

"First thing tomorrow, I'll ask the court to grant an emergency custody order giving you full custody of the boys. Considering what Mr. Cushing did to you and his previous arrest, the judge will almost certainly grant you custody. With our recommendation, of course."

"What?" I can't get air into my lungs. "I can have my boys back?" An alarm going off on the machine next to my bed startles me, and I'm suddenly able to breathe again. I look at Jack and burst into tears. He stands up and pushes the chair away so he can lean in and hug me, oh so carefully.

"Yes, darlin'. Ya have your boys back." Jack rubs my back as I cry into his shirt.

"Of course, there will be a hearing in the next week or so to make this a permanent order," Anne says. "I'll testify on your behalf and give my recommendations in person."

"Thank you." The tears rolling down my face are happy tears. Very happy tears. "Thank you. When will you bring them?"

"Once you're back home and settled, one of you can call me on this number"—she hands me a business card—"and I'll bring them over."

I clap my hands and thank the universe that the terrible event last night led to something amazing.

"I hope you feel better," Anne says. "Hopefully this news helps."

"Oh, it does! I'll see you soon."

I'm overjoyed. First Jack is back in my life—and boy, does he have questions to answer—and now the boys are coming home.

ONCE DR. GRILLO gives the all-clear, Jack drives me back to the carriage house. Suzanne runs out when we pull up the driveway.

"Isa! Oh my God! Are you alright?" Suzanne launches herself at Jack's rental car as soon as he parks. "Let me look at you!" She throws the door open and stops, waiting for me to unbuckle myself. Once I've swung around and put my feet on the ground, she takes my hands in hers and pulls me up to stand in front of her. She hugs me gently, then steps back to get a good look at the physical signs of trauma. "I heard it was Ben. And he's been stalking you for a while?"

"Who told you that?" Jack asks since neither one of us could have told her what happened.

"Remember Darin Walker from school? He likes to listen to the emergency radio scanner. He heard the hullabaloo last night and knows I live out this way, so he messaged me to let me know what happened. Wow! When Ben wakes up, he's gonna be in a lot of trouble!" Suzanne almost sings the last word, breaking it into two long syllables.

"You can't even get beat up by your ex-husband without the whole town knowing," I grumble.

"More like the whole state because you-know-who saved you." With every syllable, Suzanne points at Jack with one finger, then the other.

"Wonderful," I mutter as I start toward the carriage house, but Jack interrupts before I can take another step.

"Isa saved herself." I've never heard Jack so serious. His Southern drawl is gone, his consonants crisp, vowels short. "Isa is strong and determined and every bit the hero the media is trying to make me out to be. I might sing and play a little guitar, but Isa here is the real star."

"Oh!" Suzanne gasps. When I look over, her eyes are bright

and shining, her hands clasped under her chin. If I didn't know better, I'd think she was watching the latest Hallmark romance.

I don't know how to handle this Jack, so I deflect. "Luke and Cole will be here soon. Well, they will if I can borrow your phone. May I?"

"They're coming today? Now?" Suzanne squeals and bounces on her toes. "Of course you can borrow my phone, silly." She pulls the device from her pocket, unlocks it, and hands it to me. "You call and get those precious babies home."

AFTER I'VE CALLED Eliza Bennett and arranged for the boys to be delivered after morning naps, I wearily climb the stairs to my apartment above the garage. Jack shadows me up the steps. I guess this is what we do now.

My muscles are stiffening up, and a shower will feel so good. I say as much to Jack, and he's kind enough not to remind me of Dr. Grillo's instructions. I can do ice packs on my neck later. Right now, the rest of me needs hot water.

"May I help?" he asks.

"Sure."

In the bathroom, I unbutton my blouse and slide it off, revealing more black-and-blue marks than I initially counted. The bruises will get uglier before they get better. The pain will fade too. Before we left, Dr. Grillo suggested I see a therapist to help me deal with the trauma of the attack. My mind is protecting me by withholding the memories, she said, so it would be ideal to put some coping skills in place now for when they return.

Therapy is a good idea. Seeking professional help is a theme that came up often in the divorce recovery books I read in St. John. Now that I'll be parenting the boys again, though, I won't have any money for extras like counseling. Maybe I can find some helpful books in the Kennebunk Library. It's high time I went back and thanked Martha Sullivan and the other members of the Friends group. They need to know how much that raffle prize changed my life.

Jack joins me in the bathroom after raiding the kitchen for plastic wrap. I help him wrap his hand so moisture can't get into his bandages, then he tunes the water to the perfect temperature and undresses down to his boxers. He helps me into the shower, then steps in after me, holding me by the shoulders as I adjust to the spray.

At first, the water feels like needles stabbing my skin, but it soon feels good. Eventually, I relax enough to melt into Jack's arms. He's quiet as he gently washes my hair—I poured the shampoo into his palm—and then runs my bath pouf over my body, finishing by rinsing me off.

When I'm ready to get out, Jack jumps out and manages to wrap a towel around his waist before holding one up for me to step into. He softly pats me dry and helps me step into panties and then pull on an oversized sweatshirt. He holds the hair dryer while I wield the brush until my hair is mostly dry.

"You look exhausted." Jack says as he shuts off the appliance. "I'll be on your couch."

"No," I sleepily protest. "I want you here with me."

"Are you sure?"

"Uh-huh."

"Okay. Let me finish drying off and put on some dry clothes, and then I'll join you." He walks me over to the bed and tucks me into my flannel sheets. I snuggle in, so cozy, so loved. I want to stay awake until he comes to bed, but my body is demanding I sleep.

I'm fading quickly as I hear him say, "I've set an alarm for noon."

What a thoughtful, thoughtful man.

"I missed you so much. I should have come sooner." Jack's voice is soft, and his breath is warm on the nape of my neck as he presses his lips against my skin.

"You're here now. That's all that matters."

And then I sleep.

JACK'S ALARM pulls me from a deep sleep.

"Good mornin', sunshine." His drawl is back, I realize as he kisses my neck, picking up where he left off last night. "Can I make you some coffee and lunch?"

"Lunch, yes, but no coffee. I usually have that with Suzanne at her house, so I don't have any here."

Jack jumps up. "Lunch, it is!"

"I have sandwich fixings, and that's about it," I holler as I hear his rustles in the kitchen. "And how are you gonna manage with one hand bandaged?"

He doesn't answer, and I shake my head as I sit up very slowly. Or, I intend to shake my head, but my neck reminds me it was thrown around only yesterday and screams at me. I need to scrounge up some painkillers.

Moving my feet from under the covers takes effort, and I grunt as I stand. I'm so stiff, I feel like I was hit by a truck. Maybe because I was. I laugh out loud when I make the real-life connection to the cliché, then wince. Alright, so laughing is out for the time being.

In the bathroom, I ease my sweatshirt over my head and examine myself in the mirror again. I look like hell. It might be my imagination, but my bruises seem to have darkened even in the few hours I slept. I don't want to scare the boys, so I pat a little makeup on the visible bruises. Thank goodness my face doesn't look like my chest, all covered with blacks and blues. I get dressed and go out to see Jack, who has somehow managed to make two passable-looking sandwiches.

"The boys will be here soon."

"I can't wait to meet them." He holds out his arms, and I cuddle close, careful of my sore spots.

"We're still due a very long talk, mister," I say. "Don't you forget."

JACK and I wait with Suzanne on her front porch. My body might be the picture of chill in the luxury patio set, but my mind is racing a mile a minute. I wish my phone wasn't broken. What if Anne changed her mind and decided not to bring my boys back because it's Sunday and she doesn't have official permission to return them to me? What if Ben's parents decided they want to keep the boys after all?

My worries are interrupted when a car slowly drives by the house and turns up the driveway. I can see two little blond heads in the back seat. I wonder if she told the boys they were coming to see me.

"I hope they still like me." I start shaking, I'm so nervous. "It's been almost nine months since I've seen them." I rub my belly where their sister is kicking. "They've changed so much, and I've changed too."

Jack takes my hand as the three of us stand up and walk down to the car.

The boys are watching us as we draw closer. "Momma? It's Momma!" Their little voices are muffled by the closed window. I don't know what to do. I don't know if I'm supposed to go to them.

Eliza Bennett gets out of the car. "Would you like to get Luke out? I'll get Cole."

My injuries are forgotten as I run up to the car and open the door, tears flowing down my face. "Luke! Oh, Luke!" My fingers tremble as I undo the buckle on his booster seat.

Luke throws his arms around me. "Momma! Where have you been? I've been looking all over for you."

"I looked for you too, little buddy. I missed you so much." I hold him in my arms, never wanting to let him go again. The pain from the previous night is gone, overshadowed by the joy I feel right now.

Cole runs into me and grabs my leg. "Momma!"

I set Luke down on the ground and kneel so I'm at their level. I hug both of them together, one in each arm. "I love you guys so much."

I pull back and inspect them. "Let me look at you! You're both all grown up."

"Momma, where've you been?" Cole asks. "You missed my birthday."

"I've had to take care of a few things. I've missed you something terrible."

Luke pokes at my tears. "Don't cry, Momma." He hugs me again and pats my back the way I used to calm him down when he cried. "Don't cry. Everything will be okay."

I hug him back. "It's okay to cry, Luke. Don't let anyone make you feel bad for crying. Besides, these are happy tears."

I stand up and take one little hand in each of mine. "I want you two to meet some very special friends. This is Suzanne, and this is Jack."

"Hi, Suzanne!" Cole shouts. "Hi, Jack!" I smile. Cole has always been the loud one.

"Hi." Luke sticks close to me, but waves at Suzanne and Jack. My older son tends to be the quiet, observant one. I wonder how my daughter will fit in. What will her personality be like?

Eliza joins us on the passenger side of the car. She hands me a folder, and I let go of Luke's hand to tuck it under my arm. He's quick to put his hand back in mine when I offer it. "You have two very charming little boys."

"Thank you so much for everything you have done to help us."

"You're very welcome. I'll be in touch." She returns to the driver's seat and backs out of the driveway, leaving my family unit of one suddenly tripled in size.

The boys are attached to me, one on each side. No one will ever take them from me again. Ever.

SEPT. *12*

"Granted!" With a flourish, the judge signs off on the paperwork in front of him. "Good luck, Ms. Cushing, to you and your boys."

"Thank you, Your Honor." It's done! It's over! Ben's still in a coma, and his parents didn't show up. Suzanne stayed home to watch the children so Jack and I could see the judge. Her support has been invaluable. I don't know what I'd do without her.

I hope that someday Ben will love himself and his family enough to be part of his sons' lives again. He's hurt all of us, and we all have a lot of healing to do, but people can change. I hope for all our sakes' he does.

The ride back to Prouts Neck seems longer than usual, and I tense as we drive past the place where Ben attacked me. I don't let go of Jack's hand the whole drive. "Thank you for being here. I don't think I could have been this strong without your support."

"Isa, you're a lot stronger than ya give yourself credit for." He squeezes my hand. "Remember, ya saved yourself."

I think on that, and we ride in a comfortable silence for the rest of the drive.

Suzanne is waiting for us as we pull into the driveway. "How did it go?"

"As planned. All done," Jack calls as he emerges from his side of the vehicle.

"Well, that's a relief. If Ben could've been there, the judge probably would have asked him, 'Why are you such a piece of shit?'" Suzanne laughs. "That would have sent him into a rage and he would've been thrown in jail for contempt."

I laugh too, even though it's sad that the boys' father has put us through all this pain. I really hopes he figures his life out.

"Speaking of, where are the boys?" I rub my fingers over the nonexistent starfish and look around the yard. I'm suddenly tense, and my heart beats wildly. I'm frantic. Where are the boys? Where are they?

"Isa, it's okay," Suzanne says soothingly. "They're taking a nap upstairs in the main house. Do you want me to wake them?"

"No, no. Let them sleep." I make myself take slow and deliberate breaths. The papers sent home with me from the hospital explained that anxiety and mood changes are side effects of going into shock. In, hold, out. In, hold, out.

I press the code to unlock the door to my apartment stairs and pull it open. "Thank you, Suzanne. You're the best!"

Suzanne smiles. Her bubbles are back. "I'll take care of the little cherubs. You guys get some rest. Have a little alone time while they nap."

She turns and runs into her house.

"I don't know what I'd do without her," I say as we climb the stairs. "She really is an angel in disguise."

Inside the apartment, we get comfortable on the sofa. "Thank you for going with me today, and thank you for coming back to me," I tell Jack.

"I came to ask your forgiveness, not ride in on a white horse."

"Well, I'm glad you were there. And I do forgive you. I shouldn't have been upset over some tabloid pictures. I should have done the mature thing and talked to you about it." I think about the magazine layout that include pictures of Jack and his producer.

"Isa, there is nothing between me and Lila." He looks down. "She is rude and obnoxious and is only looking out for herself." My heart clenches as he stumbles over his words. "When she caught wind that I might be retiring, she saw that as a hit to her financial future."

"Continue." I wave him on.

"She told me my retirement didn't fit in with her financial planning, and she knew I wanted a future with ya. I think she saw it in her best interest to have ya removed, out of my future."

"So she staged photos with you knowing they would be published?" I ask, putting two and two together.

"She knows all the paparazzi. I'm sure she probably made some sort of deal with the person who took the ones ya saw."

"That makes sense."

I look at him with new understanding. Our situations, although very, very different, have some strong similarities. Both of us were controlled by selfish people, and both of us were able to find the courage to call it quits. Well, I found my courage after the divorce, but it still counts.

"I swear to you, I don't have anything going on with Lila or with anyone else for that matter," Jack continues, solemn. "The only person I want something going on with is you."

"Sounds like you should write a song about that."

"Maybe someday." He leans over as if to kiss me, but I put a hand on his chest to hold him at bay.

"Hey, you never told me—how *did* you happen to come along right when I needed you?"

"Do ya know how many Caribbean bars are located in Kennebunk?"

I rack my brain. "None that I'm aware of."

"Right. I tried to get Sarah to tell me where ya were, but she wouldn't budge, so I started hanging around the bar more often, hopin' I could change her mind. I just so happened to catch a conversation one day that gave me a clue.

"Some sleazeball had bellied up to the bar and demanded that Sarah make him something that wasn't on the menu. Something *unique.*" Jack rolls his eyes. "So she pulls out a bottle of rum and a bottle of banana liqueur and splashes them into a glass. 'There,' she says, as she shoves it across the bar, 'enjoy your Mainer's Banana.'

"Well, that got me thinking. I know someone from Maine. Actually two someones. Maybe Sarah knows the same people. So one night, late, I was futzin' around on the internet and looked up the Mainer's Banana. I searched it with Kennebunk, but nothin' popped. Then I tried South Portland, and you'll never guess what happened."

I groan. "You found the Aqua Oyster's website."

"Yep." Jack grins, proud of his research. "And what do I see, but copycats of some of the very same meals I enjoyed in Sarah's bar. And cocktails that looked just like the ones Sarah had served me." He turns a sharp eye on me. "And the very ones she'd served you."

"Guilty as charged." I hold my hands up as I shrug. "The

Aqua Oyster was the only place that would hire me, and I didn't know any drink recipes, so I tried combining stuff." I drop my hands into my lap. "The Mainer's Banana was one of the good ones. After one too many flops, I asked Sarah for help, and she filled me in."

"That explains it." Jack nods sagely. "Well, when I got into town, I knew I needed to start my search at the Oyster, but I got there after closing. It was too late to go inside, and if ya were working late, I didn't want to scare ya in the parking lot, so I parked on the street and waited to see if ya'd come out."

He reaches over and takes my hand in his. The bandages have come off, and the redness in his knuckles has subsided. He'll go back to the doctor to get his stitches out in a few days.

"Sweetheart, that first look I had of ya took my breath away." He raises my hand and strokes his lips over my fingers, one at a time, capping each stroke with a kiss. Now I'm the one with stolen breath. My senses are on high alert, and my panties are becoming wet.

"Ya stood there under that awful yella light that could make Dolly herself look ugly, and to my eye, ya were the most beautiful thing I'd ever seen. From straight on, I couldn't see your belly, but then ya turned, and oh!" He kisses the back of my hand. "Absolutely gorgeous."

With my other hand, I rub my belly self-consciously, remembering Ben's harsh words when he unbuckled my seat belt. "I've gained some weight with this pregnancy."

"Honey, you'll always be beautiful to me." Jack turns my hand over and kisses the inside of my wrist, flicking out his tongue to trace the tender flesh. He blows softly on the wet spot, and I shiver, arousal flooding my panties now.

"I couldn't pull myself away, even after ya left. The guy you'd come out with left in a pickup truck, and then the last car in the parking lot drove off. The driver was all over the place, so

I followed to see if he'd need help. And voilà! He led me right to ya."

Jack surprises me by kneeling in front of me and taking both hands in his. "I hate to think what would have happened if your ex had succeeded in hurting ya. I don't ever want us to be apart again. Come back to St. John with me—you and the boys. Come home."

I lean forward and throw my arms around his neck. "Of course, Jack. Of course I'll come home!"

TWENTY

September 14

CLOUDS AND FOG fill the sky, and puddles are scattered across the driveway, leftovers from all the rain over the past few days. But at least the weather is clearing. Kind of like my bruises. They're still noticeable remnants from the storm a week ago, but they're healing. I feel better both physically and emotionally, and I know there are better days to come.

I have my boys. My baby girl is healthy and will be here before Thanksgiving. I have Suzanne and Sarah. And I have Jack, who hasn't left my side.

Jack has proven how much he really cares about me. He was here, even if it was by chance, to help me fight back against Ben. From what the police have told me, not only was Ben very drunk, but he had also taken pain medications not prescribed to him.

I turn back to the dresser in the carriage house that has been my temporary home all summer. Most of my things have been packed in suitcases. I sweep my hand through the bottom drawer and my fingers stumble against a hard, smooth surface. My journal.

"Jack." Looking down at my journal, I extend the book to him. "I want you to have this."

A few moments pass and my arm starts to get heavy before Jack finally takes the book. "Isa, I don't want your journal. These are your private thoughts." Jack tries to hand it back to me. "Keep them private."

"Jack." I look up into his haint blues and step close. "I'm not this person anymore. I don't even know who the person in this book is now." I put my hands around his neck and bring my face close to his. A deep inhale fills my lungs with his scent before I exhale slowly. God, I missed being close to him.

"I understand, but without this person"—Jack indicates the journal—"ya wouldn't be who ya are today. And I think you're someone pretty amazing."

I put my head on his shoulder. I want him to know that all is forgiven, that I never should have been mad at him. I should have sat down and talked with him. "I still want you to have it. Really. I want you to keep it." I press myself as close as I can with a baby belly in the way. "That book is my past, but you're my future." I wink. "You can use it to write some songs."

"I love you, Isa." Jack returns my embrace, making me feel safe. Cherished. "Thank you for this. It really means a lot to me."

"Write something good." I smile, hoping the song isn't about corn harvesters and coconuts. "I love you too, Jack." Knotting my fingers in his hair, I pull his head down for a kiss. I nibble along his lips, trying a technique Suzanne showed me in one of her magazines. He groans and pushes his thigh between my legs. I rock against his leg, the friction feeling good on my clit.

And then the leg is gone and I'm nibbling on air.

"Wait! I have something for you too." I open my eyes to see Jack reaching into his pocket. I release his hair and step back, giving him room to pull out...

"My necklace!" The starfish glitters as it swings from Jack's hand. He undoes the clasp and reaches around my neck to connect the ends.

"I went for a walk this morning and found it where Ben tore it off you."

"Thank you!" I rub the cool metal, feeling something settle in me I hadn't realized was still disturbed. "I didn't think I would see it again."

"Luckily, he didn't break the chain. It looks like the clasp released when he yanked it off." Jack brushes my cheek gently. "I still want to have a jeweler take a look at it, but it seems okay."

"Thank you for finding it." I survey the apartment. "I have everything I need. Can we get out of Maine now?"

"Oh, yes we can!" He kisses me quickly. "Let's get out of here."

———

JACK IS LOADING our last bags into the SUV. Cole is jumping in a puddle on the driveway, splashing water on Suzanne, who is standing too close. She seems too sad to say anything, just sidesteps to avoid getting drenched.

"I can't believe you're leaving." Suzanne can't hold back her tears anymore. When Cole sees her start to cry, he runs over and attaches himself to her leg.

"It's okay." Cole taps his little fingers on Suzanne's leg to reassure her. My heart swells at witnessing his empathy. Cole will be okay too.

"Thank you so much, Suzanne. You're a true friend." I hug her tight. Cole squeezes her leg tighter too. Bits of blue break up the clouds. The weather is changing for the better. "I'm going to miss you. Please come down whenever you want. We certainly have plenty of room."

"I'll take you up on that."

The clouds break quickly, and the sun casts our shadow on the wet pavement.

"When does Henry get home?"

Suzanne releases her grasp on me a little. "I think the end of the week?" She sighs, and I'm not sure whether it's a good way or a bad way. "I don't know; it always changes."

"I'm sorry, Suzanne."

"It's okay." Suzanne gives me a fake smile. "I'm getting used to it."

Jack loads the last bag and slams the liftgate closed. "You guys ready to head out?"

Cole is still attached to Suzanne's leg, and Suzanne is still attached to me.

"We have to go," I say softly.

"I know." Suzanne lets go of me and bends down to pick up Cole. "Come on, sweet boy. Let's get you buckled in. You get to ride on an airplane today."

Cole releases Suzanne's leg and allows her to pick him up.

"I'm gonna miss you too, cutie." Suzanne presses her nose to his.

Jack buckles Luke into his car seat as Suzanne fastens Cole into his.

Jack comes over and hugs Suzanne.

"Take care of her, or else," Suzanne threatens as she squeezes Jack tight.

"That's my intention," Jack says.

Our goodbyes said, we leave for the airport. The sun has

come out and all the clouds are gone. Everything is perfect. If ever there is a foreshadowing moment, this is it, and I love it.

We pull up to a gate at the airport. Not the regular terminal gate where you would check in for Southwest or United, but what looks like a maintenance entrance. Maybe where snowplows enter and exit the runways.

Jack rolls the window down when a security guard comes over. As soon as the guard sees who it is, he opens the gate and waves us through.

We drive over to a sleek jet with a palm tree-wrapped tail and the name of one of Jack's hit songs—"Not Your Average Tan Line"—written across the belly of the plane.

"Yours?" I ask, just to confirm.

Jack nods.

Of course it is.

A handsome man, his skin nicely tanned, walks over as Jack gets out of his rental car.

"Hey there, Pilot Pete," Jack says as he shakes the pilot's hand.

I get out and join my boyfriend. "Pete, this is Isa. She's flying with us today. So are those young men in the back seat."

Pete walks over to the open window and bends down to peer in at Cole and Luke. "Hi, guys! Are you ready to go up in the plane?"

Cole squeals and kicks his legs, and Luke hops out of his booster after unbuckling his seat belt. He pushes in front of Cole to get closer to Pete, who talks to the boys while another crew member unloads our luggage and stows it in the belly of the plane.

Jack holds my hand as he walks me around the outside, pointing out different features of the Embraer ERJ145. When we're finished with the tour, we return to the car and release the boys. Once out of the car, Luke and Cole take off, racing to the plane. I laugh, enjoying their enthusiasm and excitement. Joy bubbles up inside me, light and effervescent. It's a new experience—one I hope I never forget.

We climb the short flight of stairs into the jet. Cole insists on taking each step on his own. It's easy to forget he's had a birthday and he's no longer my little toddler. But then I look at him and see all the time we were apart. Those bubbles aren't so full anymore.

Inside the jet, we're greeted with luxury. Palm trees are embossed into the rich brown leather headrests on the over-sized swivel recliner-style seating. A large leather sofa faces a movie screen. Plush white carpeting covers the floor from wall to wall, even under tables with place settings and napkins folded into starfish. This is just what I see walking on, and I'm sure there's a lot more. I've been on a commercial jet only twice, and never a private one.

Pete pops his head in and asks the boys if they would like to sit in the cockpit. "I may need some more copilots," he explains. They jump at the chance. I'm shocked they're not shy around anyone.

Jack and I are alone. "The boys are great. They'll love the island," Jack says as we watch the boys soak up knowledge about dials and gauges and whatever else Pete requires to fly the jet.

"Thank you again." I turn and wrap my arms around his neck. "I want this to work. I want us to work."

Jack's hands on my waist pull me close to him. "Thank you for giving me a chance." He leans forward and brushes his lips across my forehead.

"That's it? That's all I get?" I stick my lower lip out like a little girl who's been denied the toy she wants.

"Stop doing that. Ya still look adorable." He grazes the edge of my lip with his thumb.

"Not gonna."

Jack shakes his head and lets out a deep, resonant groan. "Why do you do this to me?"

He draws me closer, aligning our bodies while tenderly cradling my face in his hands. He guides my lips to his—a sweet mingling of tastes, the softness of lips, the warmth of our embrace and the cadence of our racing hearts—I'm melting; this is where I'm supposed to be. This is where we are supposed to be.

"Excuse me, Mr. Kendall." One of the crew members has brought the car seats back to where we'll sit. "I need to install these before we get going."

Jack pulls away, but keeps his eyes locked on mine. "Thank ya, Austin."

Austin clips the boys' car seats in and disappears out the door again.

As he leaves, Luke and Cole come barreling in from the cockpit and almost knock us over with hugs. They're followed by a grinning Pilot Pete. I wonder whether he has kids, or perhaps he's a doting uncle.

"Are ya guys pilots now?" Jack asks Luke. "Do I need to put ya on my payroll?"

"They sure like to push buttons! And there are a lot of buttons to push up there." Pete messes up Luke's hair, indicating Luke may have pushed a few. "We should be ready to depart in about twenty minutes. Annie should be here in a few minutes."

"Did someone say my name?" A gorgeous blond flight attendant takes the final step into the plane and joins us. Her starched uniform is so stiff and crisp, it looks as though she'd break if she fell over. "Hello, Mr. Kendall."

"Hi, Annie. Did ya have a nice time visiting Maine?"

"I sure did!" Her Southern twang emphasizes *did*. Annie

introduces herself to me and then busies herself preparing the cabin for takeoff.

Jack and I buckle the boys into their seats. I double-check to make sure the boys' seats are in fact fastened securely, and once I'm satisfied, buckle myself in next to Jack. I can finally rest. I have everything I want now. Everyone is safe and we can all heal. Together.

"Thank you." The words come out as barely a whisper. "Thank you for all of this."

"You're welcome," Jack says. He gives a gentle squeeze to my hand, and I snuggle close for the four-hour flight to St. Thomas.

The boys fall asleep almost immediately, and Annie keeps us adults fed and hydrated. Finally, Pete uses the intercom to announce we we'll be landing in a half hour.

"I can't believe the boys slept the whole flight," Jack remarks. They're sleeping without a care in the world.

"He did us a favor, you know?"

"Who did?"

"Ben. He did us a favor."

"How? By beating ya?

"Jack, I would have taken a bullet for these boys if I had to. Think about the big picture. This couldn't have happened any differently and had a better, faster outcome." I raise my palm toward Jack's look of skepticism. "You and I didn't get seriously hurt, Ben is indefinitely incapacitated, everyone sees him for who he really is, and I have the boys back.

"My baby is healthy. You and I are together. We're leaving Maine to start a life together." Jack reaches up and touches one of my fading bruises. "I know there are a few loose ends and I'll need to come back and finish dealing with them, but all in all, everything has worked out just fine."

Jack becomes serious, and the haint-blue strengthens in his irises. "No one will ever lay a finger on you again."

"Once I have the baby, I'd like to take lessons with Zeus. Do you think he could teach me how to defend myself? It just so happened that I bit my tongue when Ben attacked; otherwise, my mouth was dry. I can't promise to bite my tongue the next time I'm scared."

"Yeah, sure. That's a great idea. What do ya think about having Zeus teach the boys a martial art? It's good for self-regulation, but who knows when they might need to defend themselves too."

"Thanks. I'll feel better if I know that they know how to be safe."

"Me too. I love your children, Isa, because I love their mother."

The joy bubbles take flight again, as effervescent as ever. I throw myself into Jack's arms and cuddle there, trading grins with him until Pete reminds us to buckle our seat belts, and then we're banking for the approach to St. Thomas.

The sky is clear, so no clouds obstruct my view of the shimmering waters of the Caribbean Sea. I'm yearning to get off the plane, to take the ferry to St. John, and to finally be where I belong.

Our landing on St. Thomas is smooth. Jack and I wake the boys and got them into the Expedition that's waiting for us. "I'll send someone for the rest of our things," he says. "Let's take our family home."

***

"I HAD the staff set up a room for the boys." Jack opens the large door across the hall from where we sleep. We step into the beautiful room with views of the ocean. "I hope this is okay."

I just walked into a Pottery Barn Kids catalog. "This is a little too much."

"I told Gabrielle to get two bunks because I know that eventually each boy might want the top."

Two sets of navy blue bunks. Toys neatly organized and displayed throughout the space. A large sea-themed rug in in the middle of the room to play on. Framed sea-animal prints lining the walls. The linens on the beds are cheerful and covered with starfish and sharks. I would have loved to have a room like this while growing up.

I call the boys, who were flinging themselves onto the huge couches in the living room and giggling up a storm, and they come racing into the room. Where they stop in their tracks.

"This is your room," Jack says in his serious voice, his drawl gone without a trace. "Do you think the two of you will be okay in here?"

"Oh, yes," Luke says, nodding his head vigorously. "This is all for me and my brother?"

"For now," Jack answers. "In a few years down the road, when you're old like us, we'll see about getting you each your own room. How about that?"

"Uh, no," Luke sings, drawing out the second word as if he's having to correct silly children. "Cole and I won't stay until we're old. We've got important things to do."

"Oh?" This is news to me.

"Uh-huh. I'm gonna go to school and learn to read so I can make a million trillion dollars so me and Cole don't have to go away again."

"My boy!" Tears are flowing down my cheeks as I sink to the floor in front of my son. Even in the toxic environment that was the Cushing household, Luke has managed to maintain his purity of spirit. I throw my arms around him and hold him close. Eventually, he squirms, and I release him.

"Come on, Cole! Let's play aliens and monster trucks."

As my two oldest children scamper around the room, inspecting all the nooks, crannies, and closets in their hunt for invaders, I join Jack in the hallway. His arm slides around my waist and he whispers in my ear, "I can get used to this."

"The boys?"

"Having a family. Being happy." His soft lips brush against my cheek. "We all deserve to be happy."

"Thank you." His stubble scratches the top of my head as I nuzzle under his chin and watch the boys explore their new room.

"For what?"

"For everything. For not giving up on me."

"Never."

TWENTY-ONE

September 16

"LOOK AT YOU GO!" Jack swims over to Luke and adjusts his blue goggles and bright red Coast Guard-approved life vest. "You're like a shark."

"I'm a megalodon!" Luke shouts over the splashing water. "Watch me, Mr. Jack." And he jumps off the submerged ledge that runs the length of the pool and paddles his way toward a floating ball in the middle. Ringo treads water along with him, the shark fin of his life jacket bobbing with his movements.

Cole and I are in the big flat shallow area of the pool. He has a bucket that he enjoys filling and dumping on my head. The water is warmer in the shallow end, but it's still feels good under the bright morning sun. It also feels good to see the boys happy. They seem to really love it here. They especially love not needing to put on socks and shoes before leaving the house. I make a note to buy a pair of sandals for each child. I don't want them stepping on anything in their bare feet.

The boys are getting along so well. All three of them. It's fun to see Jack interact with my sons. Maybe it's because deep down he always wanted kids, and now, here they are, so he's going to make every minute count.

The weird thing is, neither Luke nor Cole have mentioned Ben or his family once. Good or bad. I don't know what to think about that, but I hope that once the novelty of being in a new house in a new environment geared toward them wears off, they'll start to talk. Maybe one day, Ben will get the help he needs and he can be a healthy part of their lives.

But for now, Luke and Cole are happy and healthy and safe, and that's all I can ask for.

"I think it's almost time for lunch," I call over to Jack and Luke as another bucket of pool water runs down my face and back.

"No! Ten more minutes, Mom," Luke yells. "I'm about to race Mr. Jack!"

The racer in question is standing in the water, and he looks at me and shrugs. "We have one more race; this is the tie breaker. You could be the referee."

"I'll be the referee, but then we can have some lunch." I stand up and look down at Cole. "Are you going to be my co-referee?"

"Yep." He extends a hand to me, and I pull him up. Stepping out onto the pool deck, we take our places across from where Jack and Luke are. "Ready. Set. Go!"

Luke swims, splashing, and not in a straight line, but in the right direction. Jack stays right behind him, touching off the bottom and pushing himself toward me; he looks up and meets my smile.

Luke touches the edge, and Cole announces, "Luke won!"

"Yay! Luke won!" I grab a towel and help the little champion out of the pool. He's coughing from swallowing water. "Great job. You too, Jack."

Luke turns around to congratulate Jack, and my heart melts. I have such dear, sweet children.

"Good job, buddy!" Jack grabs the side of the pool and straightens his arms to pull himself up, water sluicing off his sleek body.

I fan myself, and Jack catches my eye, then winks. My face burns red with my blush. I grab a towel off the nearest lounge chair and throw it to Jack. He dries his hair and wraps the towel around his waist. Yep, he looks good in a towel too, even with his damp hair standing straight up. I lean in and smooth his hair down as I give him a quick kiss.

When I pull back, Luke and Cole are fighting over the bucket in the shallow end. It's definitely time for lunch.

"You guys want peanut butter and jelly?" I ask as I pull towels from the lounger for them.

"Yes! Yes! Yes!" they chant as they run past me and into the house, still dripping.

"They have a lot of energy," Jack says, his observation almost bordering on a whine. "I'm not complaining, mind, but even with my training with Zeus and doing my shows, I'm beat." He stretches and yawns, and I take that as a hint.

"You can take a nap if you want," I tease with faux sympathy, then dry myself off. We're still laughing as we head inside behind the boys.

Gabrielle, Jack's cook, has the boys dried off and sitting at the island with a glass of milk in front of each of them. "Hello, Isa. I'll have sandwiches for you and Jack too," she says as she spreads what looks like mango preserves on a piece of bread. I wonder whether strawberry jam is available in the islands. If not, that might be the only thing I'll ever miss about Maine.

Cole takes a sip from his glass. "This isn't milk!" he

screams. I'm unsure if he's still using his outside voice or if he's not happy with the milk.

"What's wrong with the milk?" I examine the milk carton. It's whole milk, and only bought yesterday. Did Ben gave them skim milk?

"Cole, that's the milk we have. It may taste a little different, but it's still very yummy and it will help you build strong bones." Cole sets the milk down and doesn't say another word about it. But, he doesn't drink it either. It's strange behavior for him.

Gabrielle bustles over to the table, a plate in each hand. She sets a plate in front of each boy, and that's when I can see she used a star-shaped cookie cutter to cut their sandwiches into stars. "They are starfish," she says.

"Momma, do megalodons eat starfish?" Luke shouts.

"Please use your inside voice. And yes, I believe they would if they came across them." But of course I have no idea what megalodons eat and whether they would eat peanut butter and jelly starfish.

Luke eats an arm off the his sandwich. "I think they would eat them too if they could," he says in a moderated tone.

"And here are yours." Gabrielle hands me a plate with two starfish.

"Thank you, Gabrielle. I'll share with Jack." I pick up my plate and join Jack at the table. The boys are busy thinking up what else megalodons would eat for lunch as Jack and I munch on our starfish.

"I thought you were a better swimmer than that?" I poke him on his hard chest, and he pretends to be hurt.

"We all have our off days. Besides, he's good." Jack looks over toward Luke. "Hard to beat."

"Well, I think he adores you." I move my chair closer to his so I can lean against him and watch the boys. "Did I tell you how wonderful you are today yet?"

"Nope, not yet." Jack looks a little smug. He's attractive when's he's smug too.

"Thank you, again."

"Please stop thanking me." Jack puts an arm around me and uses his other hand to lift my chin. He bends down to kiss me, but stops a few millimeters away. His breath ghosts across my lips, and I shudder. "I told you I would do anything for you," he whispers, then closes the distance too slowly. I can't stand the tension, so I meet him, our mouths melding like the bread in our sandwiches. He tastes like peanuts and mangos.

"Momma, can I have some more starfish?" Luke loudly interrupts.

"I will make some more," Gabrielle says. "You too, Cole?"

"Yes, please. I'll take another." Cole is much quieter. It's funny how their personalities have switched now that they're in a safe place. I'm glad they feel they can be themselves.

Gabrielle gets busy making starfish.

"What are we going to do the rest of the day?" Jack asks. "They'll be all fueled up and ready to go. We could take them for a walk down on the beach or something."

"That would be fun. They need naps, though. And some guy"—I poke his side, and he squeals before wrapping his arms around me so I can no longer poke him—"got tired out while playing in the pool. I wish, however, that we knew someone with some kids their age that they could play with."

"Remember that school I showed ya when I took ya on a tour of the island?"

I remember that day in the dangerous Jolene. The school was very nice. I eye him. What is he getting at? "Yeah..."

"The Gifft Hill School. They have a little preschool." Jack

points his chin at the boys. "We can go check it out. If you like it, let's send them a few days a week."

"You mean, enroll them in preschool?" I haven't given much thought to them going to school. I was focused so hard on getting the boys back that I didn't think about what would happen if I succeeded.

"Yep. Preschool's where I made friends and learned my letters. Send the boys to Gifft Hill, and they'll meet some other kids and learn new things."

Jack has a point. Going to school would give the boys structure, a routine. And as I get further into my pregnancy and then have the baby, I might need the downtime preschool would give me. Sure, Gabrielle will be here, but she's not hired to play nurse. "Well, looks we're going on a ride after we get cleaned up."

"Great!" Jack is all smiles. "I'll call ahead to let them know we'll be making a visit."

———

WHEN WE ARRIVE at the Gifft Hill School, the preschool students are out on their dedicated playground surrounded by a brick fence. It reminds me of the fence on the cover of *The Secret Garden* that I read as a little girl. The bricks form an archway at the gate, and next to it is a bronze bell. I am enchanted.

Jack rings the bell, and a tall brunette woman comes to the gate and lets us in.

"Good afternoon! You must be Jack and Isa." She says, all smiles. "And you must be Luke and Cole. I'm Mrs. Stackpole, and I'm very pleased to meet you." She shakes our hands, but when she offers hers to Luke and Cole, they hide behind me.

"I think they're a little nervous." I'm nervous too.

"I'd like to show you around," Mrs. Stackpole says. "Obviously, this is the playground. We have three teaching assistants" —she points out each one—"who supervise the children when they play. We have about twenty-five children and five teachers and paraprofessionals in the preschool program. We like to keep the ratio small so we can give a lot of one-on-one attention."

We follow Mrs. Stackpole indoors, where the first thing I notice is that everything is spotless. She points out the restrooms and the school's other facilities. "We have a kitchen here where we make nutritious lunches and snacks."

Then we follow her into a large room that's filled with child-height activity centers, almost like the displays at the old Bed Bath & Beyond in South Portland. "We have a pretend-play area in this section," she says, pointing to a group of wooden appliances. "There's a water table in the center that we change out with a sand table every few weeks. Yes, it can get a little messy, so we have oilcloth aprons for each child. They're hanging on the wall over there.

"And next we have dress-up in that section." We dutifully follow her finger with our gazes to see a cheval mirror and a wardrobe bursting with colorful clothing.

We leave the play room, and Mrs. Stackpole shepherds us to a soundproofed room. "This is our music room," she explains as we look around. A grand piano sits in one corner, and guitars in a range of sizes hang on the wall. Luke's eyes light up when he sees the instruments.

"We have some of the high school kids, who are very talented musicians, come down and work with the younger kids. Help teach them the basics."

"We get to use all these?" Luke asks from beside me.

"Yes, Luke. You will learn how to properly treat the instruments and play if you are interested in learning more about them."

"Oh, I am." I'm so glad something here is interesting Luke. "Mr. Jack plays music."

"He does? What does he play?" Mrs. Stackpole doesn't know who Jack is? Weird. I thought everyone on the island knew who he was.

"Jack plays guitar," Luke says proudly. "Play a song!" Luke claps his hands. "Please play a song for Mrs. Stackpole."

"I don't mind if you do or don't." Mrs. Stackpole smiles and shrugs. Cole clings tighter to my leg.

"All right. Just a quick one." Jack picks up the biggest acoustic guitar and quickly tunes it. "I am retired, you know."

"Yay, Jack!" Luke looks up at Mrs. Stackpole. "This is going to be so good." She nods, and I'm certain she's just patronizing him. I bet she gets lots of experience with that during the school day.

"This is an oldie but a goody," Jack says when the guitar is fully tuned.

None of his songs are appropriate for a preschool. They're primarily about women and drinking. I can't imagine what song he'll sing.

Then he starts picking away and sings the first verse of "House at Pooh Corner." A perfect choice for a preschool.

"That was wonderful, Jack!" Mrs. Stackpole applauds. "Bravo!"

"See! I told you! I told you Mr. Jack can play the guitar." Luke is jumping up and down. "I want to play guitar like Mr. Jack!"

"Luke! Inside voice." Holding my open hands palms down, I signal him to lower his volume.

Cole laughs at his brother, and we follow Mrs. Stackpole out of the room and into a library. It's bright and full of short book-cases packed with picture books. Cubbies and nooks built in all over the room enable the students to spend time alone to read.

"This is beautiful," I say, looking around at all the framed posters of illustrated book covers. "If I had gone to school here when I was the boys' age, I would have never left this room."

"The kids make use of the art room in the main school as well as the gym when the weather isn't very nice. We also have a professional counselor on staff should your children need help with their transition to a new school."

I think back to the boys' odd behavior around milk. And they've been away from their father for a week, but they've never mentioned him or his parents. We might be making an appointment with the counselor sooner than Mrs. Stackpole expects.

"This is all very nice," I say as Luke takes my hand. "What do you think? Would you like to go to school here?"

Luke looks up at me and then Jack. And then Mrs. Stack-pole. "Yeah, that would be good."

Cole, who has been hiding behind me the whole time we've been on the tour, suddenly pipes up. "I want to go here too." He stays concealed, but I can tell from his voice he is happy. He will go wherever his brother goes.

"I'll leave you here to talk while I call over to the admissions office. They can answer any more questions you may have." Mrs. Stackpole extends her hand again to shake ours. "It was very nice to meet you."

"See you in class," Luke says to her as he takes her hand.

"I hope so." She laughs. "Goodbye, Cole. Nice meeting you."

"Bye!" Cole waves at Mrs. Stackpole as she leaves the library.

"This is beautiful. What do you think, Jack?"

"I want you to feel comfortable where you send these guys. I think they'll be very well taken care of here."

"Me too. Maybe trial basis?"

"Trial basis, it is."

"I can't believe I'm doing this. Giving the boys away when I just got them back."

"Sweetie, you aren't giving them away," Jack consoles me. "You're giving them the beginning of a great future. You're giving them the opportunity to meet friends. Didn't you have friends when you went to school?"

This comment makes me think. Of course I had friends. And I even had classmates who later became friends—Suzanne has been a lifeline this year. Jack is right. The boys need friends too. They need people other than me in their life. "Yes. You're right." I smile wistfully when I realize that my little boys are growing up—fast. "You are absolutely right."

A few minutes later, a petite woman who is maybe in her late fifties enters the library and escorts us to the administrative office.

We sit together at a big conference table. The woman, who introduces herself as school administrator Dr. Regina Maarten, gives Luke and Cole a few sheets of looseleaf paper and some colored pencils, and they set to scribbling. Once we're finished filling out the stacks of enrollment paperwork for both boys, she carefully clips the papers into the folders she made for each boy.

"Welcome to The Gifft Hill School. We look forward to seeing you both on Monday," she says to the boys. Then she turns to Jack. "Mr. Kendall"—her eyelashes flutter—"I am a huge fan."

"Oh, well, thank ya." Jack sounds like he's caught off guard.

"If it's not too much to ask, can you sign my..." She gets up and goes over to her desk, where she roots around, finally grabbing a red inhaler and a Sharpie and returning to the table. "Can you sign this for me?"

"Your inhaler?" Jack raises an eyebrow. When she nods vigorously, he takes the items out of her hands, scribbles his signature on the case, and hands the marker and inhaler back to her.

"Thank you so much!"

"Now you'll think of me when you're having an asthma attack." Jack makes it sound like a joke, but I somehow don't think it is. "Are we all set here?"

"Yes, other than the payment. Will you be paying in full or doing a payment plan?"

"I don't do payments. I'll have my accountant get in touch with you this afternoon."

"Very well. Thank you again. Welcome to The Gifft Hill School family." She goes over to a filing cabinet, takes out some school T-shirts, and hands each of us one.

"Thank you," Luke says and puts his new shirt on immediately.

On our ride home, I hold Jack's hand tight. "I know you don't want me to say thank you anymore. But thank you." I reach across the wide console of the Expedition and give him a kiss on his cheek. "You really did a lot for these boys today."

"I think they'll do well there." He smirks. "As long as they don't need an inhaler."

"Oh my gosh, that was so awkward. Are all your fans like that?"

"No, some are even worse."

I grimace and look into the back seat. The boys are looking out the windows and don't appear to be listening to us, but I don't want to risk it. But sometime soon I need to ask Jack to tell me about his wild fans.

With a flick of his signal, Jack turns off the main road and we start climbing the long curving driveway up to the house.

"I think you should record a children's album." I sit back in my seat, waiting for him to say something, and when he doesn't, I keep talking. "I love that Kenny Loggins song you sang today. That was so appropriate."

"Loggins wrote it, but Loggins and Messina sang it."

"Sorry, Loggins and Messina. It was still a perfect song, and the way you sang it was so sweet."

"Thanks." Jack takes my hand as the Expedition climbs the drive.

When he parks, no noise comes from the back seat, so he checks his mirror. "Boys are asleep. Ya want to go on a quiet ride and let them nap?"

"It's a nice day. Why not?"

He uses the turn-a-round before the gate to point the SUV in the opposite direction, and we head back down the hill. A comfortable silence settles in the vehicle as we take a ride around the island enjoying the views. I don't want to get ahead of myself, but I could get used to this new version of family.

TWENTY-TWO

October 10

"YOU GUYS READY to go to school?" Jack asks as he buckles Cole into his car seat in the back of the Expedition. I'm buckling Luke into his.

The boys nearly deafen us with their affirmative responses. And then begin to tell us all about coral reefs, starfish, and conchs.

At the school, we repeat the process but in reverse and then walk into the schoolyard, Cole holding Jack's hand and Luke holding mine. Mrs. Stackpole is waiting for al the kids to arrive. "Good morning, Luke. Good morning, Cole," she says. The boys respond by running to her and hugging her legs.

I wince; they ran to her too quickly, and the ache of loss strikes anew. I go through this every time I drop them off. Even though they've been with me for a month now, it feels like I just got them back.

Mrs. Stackpole looks up at me. "They are adjusting very nicely."

"I can see that." Jack puts his arm around my waist. I wonder if he feels as proud as I do right now.

Mrs. Stackpole bends down and quietly says to Luke, "I think Mitchell is over by the swings." She points in the direction his friend is playing.

And without any hesitation, Luke releases Mrs. Stackpole's leg and runs toward the swings. Cole is right behind him, following every move his big brother makes.

"You have two very sweet little boys," Mrs. Stackpole says.

"Thank you." My response is somewhat distracted, as I'm engrossed in watching my sons play with a new friend. It's been a long time since I've seen them with other children, and my sadness shifts to make room for joy.

More children and parents arrive, so I wave goodbye to the boys, but they are so busy, they don't notice. Leaving my babies behind, Jack and I walk back to the Expedition.

"When are ya gonna learn how to drive on the left side?" Jack asks.

"I'm not."

"What do you mean, you're not?" Jack laughs.

"Jack. I don't want to hurt anybody."

"Ya really think you'll hurt someone?"

"Yeah."

"Okay." Jack pulls me into his side. "I think ya are too hard on yourself." He kisses my temple. "So I'll take it easy. If ya ever do want to learn to drive here, though, all you gotta do is ask."

GLIMPSES of the haint-blue of Jack's porch are visible through the foliage as we make our way up the long driveway. The gate opens and Jack parks the Expedition in front of the steps leading up to the entry.

I close the door behind us after we go in. "Hey, beautiful!" Jack croons as he grabs me by the waist and pulls me close to himself. We sway as he starts singing one of his songs to me while one hand plays with my long ponytail.

"I don't dance." I laugh, knowing I'm getting clumsier every day, any attempts at dancing will result in a broken *something*— either a bone or a vase.

"That's okay. We aren't really dancing," Jack sings. "I like it. Could be a new song? 'We Ain't Really Dancin'.'"

"If it's about me, it will be a flop." I stick my lower lip out to pout, and he swoops in to snatch it between his teeth. He sucks gently as his tongue darts in to caress the sensitive skin just inside my mouth. And then he's gone, his face a respectable distance from mine, and I'm left with arousal growing below my belly.

I'm sure I'm doing an accurate representation of a fish as I gape at him. How does he do that? His touches, his kisses, his... bites... I make a mental note to research fun ways to pleasure my partner one of these days when the boys are at school and Jack is out of the house. I'd be absolutely mortified if he found me in our room doing facial calisthenics!

"If it's about you, it will be a hit," Jack is saying now. He continues to sway me, guiding us over to the couch where we fall on it together, still holding on to each other. He's very nice to hold on to.

My baby must not have enjoyed the fall because she punches me. Or maybe it was a kick. But the taut skin over my uterus definitely rippled from the blow.

"Did you feel that?"

"Feel what? An earthquake? We don't get those down here."

"No, nothing outside the house. Inside here. Me." I take Jack's hand and put it on my tummy where I felt her. It doesn't take long before—"There! Did you feel it?"

Jack looks up at me with a huge grin and happy eyes. "She's kickboxing! Wait until I tell Zeus!"

"She can join me on my self-defense workouts," I joke.

"I wonder whether Zeus would let me lift her instead of weights?" He smirks. "She'll get increasingly heavier as she grows, and I'll keep building my strength right along with her."

But then he sobers. "Sweetness, things are going well with me and the boys, but that's 'cause they can talk and we understand each other. I don't know anything about raising babies from scratch. Are ya sure ya want me around for this?"

I reach out and rub the deep groove between Jack's eyebrows, trying to smooth it out. "I've been through this twice, essentially on my own. If you continue to be kind and thoughtful like you are now, I don't think we'll have a problem. And, I'm sure we can find a book in the library that will help you. We can also practice changing diapers on a doll."

"I'd like that. All of it. Every time I think of you and the baby, I feel this deep sense of anxiety." Jack's drawl is gone, so I know he's especially serious. "I don't want to screw up like Ben did. I want to do right by you and the three kids, no matter that I'm not their biological father."

My dear, sweet love! Deep down, I wish this was his baby. I can't help but hug him. "Jack, your concern is precious. Let's make a pact: If I see you doing anything harmful with any of the children, I'll tell you so you can change. And you'll accept my input and do your best to adjust. We'll be a team. Work for you?" He leaves his hand right there on my bump as I kiss his cheek.

"Works for me. You're an amazing woman, Isa Marie."

I chuckle. It's been a while since we've played this game. "Nope, still not my middle name."

"Jack, Isa, I am going to the market," Gabrielle says as she comes into the living room. "Would you like anything? Do you have a list of what you would like me to get for the house? For the children?"

"Actually, I do need some things." I push myself up off Jack. "Hold on a minute." I get up off the sofa and head over to the island to sit and write out a list.

"Oh, yes, no problem." Gabrielle smiles, reading over the list I gave her. "A doll baby and disposable diapers to match its size. Is this for the boys to play with, or...?"

Jacks ducks his head, sheepish. "It's for me. So I can practice before Isa has her baby."

"That's wise, Jack." Gabrielle looks proud. "I can share some links to websites that helped me prepare for my children."

Gabrielle and Ramone having children never occurred to me. Am I becoming selfish and self-centered living in this luxury? I'll have to do better about looking out for more than just my tiny family. Starting by texting Suzanne. It's been too long since we talked.

After Gabrielle leaves for her errands, I go into the bedroom and retrieve my phone from the charger. I thumb the screen awake, and freeze.

Suzanne has sent me a link. This time it's the obituary section of the *Portland Forecaster*. Benjamin Cushing died of his injuries on Oct. 2. We're free.

I slump to the bed and just stare at my phone.

We're free.

The boys are mine; their father will never try to come after them.

My daughter is mine; I can put Jack's name on her birth certificate without any hassle.

The connection with the Cushings is completely severed. If they want to play doting grandparents, they'll have to take me to court. I'd have to ask a lawyer, but I don't think it looks too good that Ben's parents sent their children back to OCFS in favor of sitting by their comatose son's bedside.

We're free.

I MUST SIT THERE in a daze long enough that Jack gets worried and comes to find me. When he sees me on the bed, staring at the wall, he rushes over and sits down beside me. He wraps his arm around me and brusquely rubs my upper arm.

"What's wrong?" he asks, his voice warm and caring. I never heard that tone of voice from Ben. I never will.

Clumsily, I open my phone again so Jack can read the obituary. When he's done, he blows out a heavy breath.

"I was not prepared for that outcome," he says. "Never even crossed my mind. Most people wake up from comas, right?" He runs his hand through his hair, messing up the sun-bleached strands. The thought that he's in dire need of a haircut flits through my mind.

"Yeah, I wasn't expecting it either."

"What will ya tell the boys? *Will* ya tell them?"

"I probably should. They don't seem too concerned about him, but they also might be compartmentalizing. We could talk to the school counselor, see if she can give us some advice about breaking the news to the boys."

Jack hugs me to him. "We should also see about getting ya in to see a counselor too."

I pull back so I can see his face. "I've been putting it off. Hadn't figured out how I'd pay for it."

"Darlin', don't ya worry about the cost. You have so much to deal with, and I want to support ya. First the trauma of your abusive marriage"—he holds up one finger—"then the trauma of losing your children in the divorce"—another finger—"then the trauma of the attack, and now the trauma of him dying." He holds up four fingers, then wiggles them. "That's a lot of trauma. And I want my best girl to have all the resources she needs to work through the world of hurt she's been through."

"Oh, Jack!" I throw myself at him, and he moves with my momentum, tumbling back onto the bed with me on top of him. He reaches up and pets my hair, dragging his fingers through the strands, then tucking my hair behind my ears.

"Ramone's in town too, so we have the house all to ourselves," he says with a waggle of his eyebrows. "Wanna get up to something fun?"

I need the distraction, so I say yes.

In one quick, unexpected movement, Jack rolls me to the side and hops up. Then he leans down and scoops me into his arms. I squeak at the fast changes in positions and cling to him, wrapping my legs around his waist and holding on to him for dear life. By the time he's carried me out to the kitchen and deposited me on the edge of the marble-topped island, we're both breathing heavily.

Finished with my impression of a four-limbed octopus, I release my hold on Jack. He picks up my hands and puts them on his shoulders, then I hold on for balance as he expertly unfastens the shorts that I can still wear just below my baby bump. I wiggle to help him slide them and my maternity panties off my body.

"Much better access," Jack says with a wink.

The marble is cool under my ass as he steps in closer to give me a kiss. I move my hands from his shoulders to his neck, where I stroke the soft skin. He shivers, and I let out a peal of laughter. I have Jack all to myself. And he wants me. No one else. Just me. And that is very, very sexy.

TWENTY-THREE

October 10

JACK'S LIPS move down to my collarbone, and I take in scents of the sea from his hair.

Sliding his hands down my sides, he takes hold of the hem of my shirt and helps me pull the garment over my head. It lands with a quiet thud after I toss it away.

Jack pulls my attention back to him when he cups each of my breasts. His thumb teasing one nipple, he brings his mouth to the other and takes the nub into its warm, humid heat. He sucks on my nipple, then lets go. He blows on the wet skin, and my nipple pebbles impossibly harder. His grin is wicked as he replaces his mouth with his thumb and fingers and repeats his oral ministrations on the other nipple.

My head falls back as an electric line hums to life between my nipples and my clit, and I felt a wetness begin to gather. I squirm, the yearning to have his attention on that southernmost nub almost more than I can bear.

"Patience, darlin'," Jack drawls, his accent the thickest I've ever heard it, after pulling off my breast. He gives each nipple a tiny kiss, then slowly moves down my body.

He leaves feather-light kisses over my abdomen, circling my navel, before placing a hand on each of my knees. Pushing them apart gives him a full view of my post private place.

"You're so beautiful," he coos. I lean back, resting on my elbows, to watch what he's doing. He bends, caressing and kissing the insides of my knees. Slowly, he works his way upward.

He touches me gently at first, then inserts one finger while his thumb circles my clit, making me gasp.

The shockwaves from his touch are too much, and my arms shake, so I lie back on the countertop. My shift in position gives Jack more room to work, so his tongue takes over for his thumb. He licks and sucks as a second finger joins the first. I'm writing on his fingers now, as he scraps the tips against the roof of my channel. It doesn't take long for the perfect synchronization of Jack's tongue with his curled fingers to call forth a tsunami of energy. The wave engulfs my body, and my back arches as I cry out uncontrollably.

The kitchen island resembles an altar on which Jack just worshiped me. The marble remains cold in contrast to how hot my body feels. I have chills even though I feel like I'm on fire.

My heels involuntarily come together on the edge of the counter, my knees closing tight to keep Jack from touching me anymore. I'm too sensitive to let him continue.

"You have a lovely voice," Jack says. Lying there, staring out the open porch doors at the boats on the harbor, I try to catch my breath. Jack strokes the lengths of my calves, bringing life back to them with his damp fingers. He starts at the knee and ends at the ankle, reversing his touch from how he started. Calming.

"How did you know how to do that? That was so..." I try to catch my breath. "So p—perfect." Giggling, I'm unable to move.

"I watched you." Jack is rubbing my leg and kissing my knee. "I watched how you responded to me." I cock my head so I can see him better as he speaks. "You responded very nicely." He grins.

"I did. Didn't I?" I giggle more until my ebullience subsides and I regain my composure. Sitting up, I let my feet swing free, keeping Jack between my knees. "Thank you." The scruff on his cheek rasps against my palm. "That was really nice." With my free hand, I grab his waistband and pull him close, then unbutton his shorts, letting them fall to the ground.

"Get out of these too." I help him get out of his boxer shorts with their pink flamingo print, pushing them far enough down so they, too, drop.

Jack slides his hands beneath my ass and tugs me close to the edge of the marble. Encircling him with my arms and legs, I take my time exploring his lips, noticing how sensuous they are. I love the feeling of my naked breasts against his smooth, muscular chest.

I trace his hairline from his forehead to his earlobes with my fingers. My lips press against his throat, and I suck on his Adam's apple until it vibrates beneath my tongue. I crave his noises. Low, carnal growls that resonate deep in my pelvis, making me tingly and warm.

I follow down his sides, following every bump of every toned muscle. I love touching him. Every inch of him.

At his groin, I begin stroking his erection softly, leaving my lips close to his throat, enjoying the vibrations coming from there. I'm doing something right!

With one hand on my thigh, Jack reaches around me and braces himself against the countertop. "I need to be inside you," he says, his eyes begging for permission. I grant it, letting my legs fall open so he can wedge himself close.

He lifts my thigh and delicately enters me, a look of euphoria washing over his face. "You are so wet. You're so ready for me."

"You made me ready," I whisper. My mouth and eyes are curved in smiles, but my whole body is beaming. I wrap my legs over his hips, crossing my ankles against his back.

He shifts us so I'm pleasantly held between Jack and the marble counter. Closing my eyes allows me to take in all the sounds and smells of our intimacy, and most of all, I take in all of Jack.

His back becomes slippery with sweat and difficult for me to hold on to as he moves feverishly inside me. Having already reached orgasm once, I'm caught off guard when I begin to melt around him as he pushes deeper and harder.

But I'm over the edge of pleasure and falling, and I can't hold on any longer. I come hard. My body feels weightless, and Jack holds me down, keeping me from floating away.

He leans me back, lying over me as he continues thrusting into me. As he climaxes, he cries out my name. And when he wraps himself around me, he too is out of breath.

Jack's arm pillows my head me as we lie naked on the island, sweaty and silent. Staring out at the water and watching the boats sail around the harbor, we are at peace. Everyone is where they need to be. Everything is perfect.

"Marry me," Jack says, breaking the silence, breaking the perfection of the moment. He squeezes me tighter. "Be my wife."

"Hmmm?" I ask, not sure I've heard him correctly. I'm in a dreamlike state, a haze like a veil cloaking reality. "What? What did you say?"

"Marry me," Jack whispers again, but this time I hear him clearly. My eyes open wide as his grip around me releases and his hand follows the curve of my body from my breast to my hip.

"I—I—I'm not sure what to say. I'm stunned." Marriage? I never want to go through that pain again. I never want to put the boys through the pain again. I never want to...

"It's okay. You don't have to give me an answer now, but if you're alright with it, I'll keep asking." The breeze from the ocean picks up and carries in the intoxicating smells of the crushed nutmeg shells the garden paths are laid with.

It feels like a lifetime ago when I was married to Ben. I was a different person then. The person I am now wouldn't give a guy like Ben a second look, let alone marry him. What was I thinking? I shake my head, and Jack gasps, then gets himself together and stands up.

"Thank you for giving me the best summer of my life," he says. "I know I can't go through another day without you by my side. When you left for Maine, it almost killed me. I didn't know what to do without you. I couldn't concentrate on anything. All I wanted was to get on a plane and chase after you." He pauses. The tone in his voice sounds as though he's remembering something painful as he chokes back his words. "But... but I didn't. I know you needed time."

I listen to him intently. Ben never cared about my feelings. Ben never cared if he hurt me. Jack is a man who will defend me to the end, who will fight for me and my children, who loves us.

"Finally, I gave in. Against what I told myself I wasn't going to do, I went to find you. To try to convince you to come back to the island. To come back to me."

"And instead you saved me," I say, finishing what he is saying.

"You saved yourself. But you also saved me."

"You do seem to have good timing. It must be a musician thing." I shut my eyes and listen to Jack, feeling the fresh air on my face and his warm breath on the back of my neck. I imagine us married. Husband and wife. He's never been mean, not to one person. Ben was mean to everyone.

Jack's a good man. A good person. I'm glad he showed up in Maine when he did. Not only because he distracted Ben, giving me a chance to get away, and then helping me to get my boys back, but because I really missed him too. Every time one of his songs came on at the Aqua Oyster, no matter how silly I told myself the song was, deep down, I loved it. Every word of it. Because Jack wrote it. Those songs made me think of him when I tried to forget him.

So, we both tortured ourselves by being apart. I guess that's a good thing. At least I know that we missed each other. A lot.

"I'm not going to get into everything that I can offer you, but look at it this way. If I lost everything tomorrow and I had nothing but my love for you, would you love me back?"

"Wow." I take a very slow deep breath and exhale just as slowly. That is a heavy question. But I know the answer right away. "When I first met you, I had no idea who you were. I had no idea you were Jack Kendall. And when I found out you were Jack Kendall, I had no idea that you have what you have." I laugh, thinking back to when he picked me up in a Jeep that was falling apart. "I knew when I first met you that you were someone special and could be someone special to me."

"I had potential?" Jack squeezes me. "I knew it! You liked me the whole time."

I roll over and spot the huge grin on his face. "Jack, be serious for a minute." He needs to come down off this cloud he's on, but I guess I'm putting him up there. "I fought falling in love with you before I left to go north. I didn't want to fall in love with you. I wouldn't let myself believe it." I place my hand on his cheek. I love feeling his scruff. "But I did fall in love with you. Hard.

"Whenever one of your songs came on the radio, whenever I heard someone at the bar talk about one of your concerts..." My hand moves to brush his unruly hair back behind his ear. "Whenever I saw waffles on a menu, I thought of us." A feeling of emptiness washes through me as I remember how I felt when I thought I would never see him again. But that emptiness has been filled, and those memories serve a purpose. They helped me admit to myself that I do love Jack. "I missed the island. I missed us. My whole world is together right here. and I don't want anything to tear it apart."

"If it's within my ability, I won't let anything or anybody tear our world apart," Jack says. "I couldn't be more happier than I am right now." Jack's smile is gone, and he looks serious. "Isa, I love you. Marry me. Together, we can accomplish anything we want." Jack kisses my nose and then moves down to my lips.

I pull away; I'm going back and forth with an answer for him. I know what I would like to say, but there are other people involved. Three other people. "It's not a yes, but it's not a no. Get back to me in a few days?"

Then I snap back to reality. "What time is it?" The afternoon has slipped away.

"It's okay. It's almost two. We have some time." He jumps down off the island and helps me to my feet. "Let's go jump in the shower." Jack grabs our clothes and we run into our bedroom. "I really enjoyed that."

I look back at him as he follows me into the bathroom. "I did too." A lot.

THE BOYS BOUND through the door and come running toward me and Jack.

"Hi, guys!" When I put my arms out to hug them, they both jump at me at the same time, almost knocking me over. "How was school?"

Chattering excitedly, they relay every detail over cookies and two-percent milk, which Gabrielle was kind enough to pick up for Cole. He doesn't think twice about it today and drinks his whole glass of milk while telling me about his new friend, Isaac, and how his mommy died purple.

"I'm so sorry to hear that, Cole." I pet his hair as he eats his cookie. It's horrible that a little boy saw his mother in that state. He will remember her that way forever. I'm so glad the boys didn't see Ben after the attack.

"No, Cole. Isaac's mom dyes her *hair* purple; she didn't die," Luke says his brother.

"Momma, don't ever dye yours purple. I like your color." I give Cole a big hug. He's so sweet.

"I won't," I say as he inspects my hair. "I promise."

I release Cole and give Luke a hug too. "I'm so glad you guys had a great day."

"I can't wait until tomorrow," Luke says.

"Do you guys want to get a swim in before dinner?" They don't even answer my question, just take off to their room. A few minutes later, they come running back with their trunks on. "Give me a second, you guys are too fast for me. I need to change too."

When I come back out, Jack is sitting on the couch with the boys, his guitar in his lap. He's teaching them a few chords and letting them try to play them.

"There ya go, Luke. I think ya got it!" Jack hands his guitar over to Cole and sits next to him so he can position his tiny fingers. "Good job, Cole! Ya did it!"

"Mr. Jack? Will you teach me to play like you?" Luke asks quietly.

"Luke." Jack puts his hand on my five-year-old's head and looks at him sincerely. "I would like nothing more than to teach ya. I'm so glad ya guys are here! Your mom and I are happier than pigs in mud!" Jack takes the guitar back from Cole and sets it in the stand.

Cole holds his belly and laughs uncontrollably. "Pigs in mud! You're funny, Mr. Jack!"

"You guys ready to go swimming?" Jack stands up, but Cole and Luke are already out the door and on the Lido Deck.

"Stop at the edge of the deck!" I call after them. "No going into the pool without an adult."

"I'll get a company out here to put a safety fence around the pool," Jack tells me. "I want to keep our kiddos safe."

Our kiddos. The phrase warms my heart. "And you're worried about being a good dad. You're already thinking like one."

I can't help but notice how naturally Jack and the boys interact. It's almost like my sons have been craving attention for so long and now they have it, they're eating it up. They're enjoying every second of being with us as much as we're enjoying every second of being with them.

Jack and I change into our suits, then head out to the pool. I help Cole into his life vest, Jack puts Ringo in his shark jacket, and then we release the kraken. Luke hops in from the side, and Cole splashes into the shallow end. Jack takes off his shirt and jumps into the pool, tucking his body into the classic cannon-ball position and making a huge splash. The wave soaks me and splashes over the boys.

"Whoa! That was so cool!" Luke shouts. "Do that again!"

"Yeah! Do it again! Do it again!" Cole shouts too.

"Guys, if I do that too much," Jack explains, "there won't be any water left in the pool to swim in. You wouldn't want that would you?"

"No!" they chorus.

———

AFTER DINNER and with the boys tucked in their beds, Jack and I go into his study to talk. I rarely spend any time here. It has the same dark wood floors that are throughout the house.

Jack sits in a big leather office chair behind his heavy desk with carved legs. I relax in a red leather wing-backed chair trimmed with hobnails.

While Jack is shuffling through papers on his desk, I look around and count fifteen dark-framed platinum albums. "Are these all yours?"

Jack looks up from his papers and slides his wire-framed glasses down to the tip of his nose so he can peer at me over them. I didn't know he wears glasses; he looks really good in them. "Yep." Then he follow the direction of my gaze to the walls and lets out a deep sigh. "Never in a million years did I ever think I would sell enough to earn one of these, let alone fifteen."

"Well, that's quite an accomplishment. You should be very proud."

"Thanks," Jack says, then looks back down and continues what he was doing.

Built-in shelves around the room display an array of trophies. I slide out of the smooth leather of the chair and quietly take a closer look. I start at the top: Grammys, AMA's, Billboard Music Awards. "You won Entertainer of the Year?"

Jack turns to me and pushes away from his desk. I see an

opportunity and sit in his lap. He puts an arm around the small of my back and rests his other hand on my thigh. "I should have kept up on pop culture a little more," I say. He actually looks really, really hot in his glasses. "You look very"—I pause to kiss him tenderly on his neck and listen for his moan of approval— "handsome with those glasses."

Using both hands so I don't bend them out of shape, I remove the glasses from Jack's face and take care to put them carefully on his desk. Then I lean in and trace my tongue across his lips until they part.

Jack pushes his papers and glasses out of the way, then lifts me up and places me on his desk, kissing me deeply and feverishly. Jack steps into me as I hug him with my legs. I don't want to take my mouth off his. He groans low with approval. I've never had sex on a desk before.

"Momma?" A little voice from the doorway startles us, and Jack and I jump away from each other. "I had a bad dream."

I mouth "Finish later?" and Jack responds with a smile and a nod.

"Oh, sweetheart." I run over to Cole and pick him up, then we get comfy in the red leather chair. "What was your dream about?"

"The pool was empty and we couldn't get it to fill up." Cole yawns and curls around my belly before shutting his eyes. He's quickly back asleep in my arms.

"I'll be right back." I move to stand up, but Jack is there, scooping Cole out of my arms.

"You sit there," he instructs. "I'll carry Cole into his room and tuck him back into bed."

Heeding Jack's instruction, I relax in the chair and tip my head back. I must doze because I startle slightly when he brushes a kiss across my forehead.

"I'm sorry," he says. He rubs my shoulders, and I practically melt. "Our spontaneous moment was ruined. Raincheck?"

"Of course. Anytime." I try to flirt by fluttering my eyelids. I don't know whether it works or if I look like I have something in my eyes.

He bends down and kisses my ear. "I love you."

I love you too, Jack. But am I brave enough to marry you?

TWENTY-FOUR

October 15

AT SNORKELS FOR BREAKFAST, Amelia seats us at a different table than usual. This one is much more private.

"Thank ya kindly, Amelia," Jack says as he helps me shift my chair up to the table. My belly is heavy, and I'm in that awkward stage where my body isn't ready to give birth, but my mind is so done already.

"Why are we sitting here? We never sit here." I slap my hand over my mouth as soon as the words escape. I'm not a whiner—I never whine—but that was definitely a whine.

"I guess they weren't expecting us." Jack is so gracious to overlook my complaining. "Or maybe they promised our table to someone else?"

"Yeah? Probably." The waterfall provides nice background noises. I like this table better anyway.

"Sorry I fell asleep on you last night." I pout to let Jack know I'm disappointed in myself. "Were you able to get everything you needed to get done, done?" Jack rubs my protruding lip with his fingertip, and I snap my teeth. He pulls away with a laugh.

"Yep. Done and sent back." Jack laces his fingers together and stretches his arms way over his head. "One step closer to retirement!"

"Are you sure that's what you want?"

Before Jack can answer, a new member of the wait staff interrupts us. "Good morning, I'm Emerson. I'll be assisting you today." He fills our water glasses. "How are you doing on this beautiful day?" Emerson is casual but confident. Nothing like I was when I started at the Aqua Oyster. This is obviously not his first wait staff job.

"We are great, thank you," Jack says as Emerson sets down a couple menus.

"Can I start you off with something to drink?" he asks, no pen to write anything down. He's very smooth.

"I would like a cup of coffee, please," I say.

"I'll take the same."

"I'll be right back for your breakfast order."

And then we're alone. I open my napkin and put my silverware on the table, placing my napkin in my lap.

Jack stands up. "I'll be right back. Need to use the restroom." He leans forward and kisses me before heading into the main building.

Emerson comes back with our coffees. "Cream and sugar?" he offers.

"Just cream." He sets down a little carafe of cream and a plate with a large dollop of fresh whipped cream and a couple of Pirouette cookies. What a cute display! I get busy making our coffees, topping them off with whipped cream.

"That looks good." Jack drops a kiss on top of my head before he sits down. "Thanks for making mine."

"Anytime." I smile and take a sip of my coffee. The whipped cream tickles my nose, and I quickly lick away the mustache it left behind.

"What would you like this morning?" Jack asks as he peruses the menu.

"Seriously?" I don't even bother to look at the menu. "I haven't had waffles in what feels like months."

Laughing, Jack shuts his menu and sets it beside his plate. "I thought you might say that. It's kind of our thing."

I roll my eyes, but he's right. We have a thing; waffles are our thing. I let out a great big smile. I love being here with Jack.

When Emerson comes over, Jack orders the waffles with bacon and sausage and plenty of fruit.

"Nice job," I compliment.

"I aim to please." Jack sits back, and he looks a little... nervous.

"Are you okay?" I hope Jack isn't getting sick. He seemed to be fine before he went to the restroom.

"Oh, yeah." Jack coughs, clearing his throat. "I'm fine."

Soon Emerson and a helper bring our breakfast out and set the plates in front of us. They run off, leaving me to just stare.

My waffles aren't their usual square shape. Instead, they're cut in a heart shape, as is the mango. But what really catches my attention is on the rim of the plate. Written in mango syrup are the words "Please Marry Me." Next to the waffle plate is a smaller dish covered in fresh flowers, with a haint-blue box in the middle.

I look up at Jack, whose face is a mixture of yearning and nervousness. He rises from his chair, takes the haint-blue box, and gets down on one knee beside me. He opens the box, revealing a rather large sparkling diamond above a platinum band. "Please. Please marry me."

My mouth falls open, and I gaze into his eyes. The truth is,

I have been debating his question since he asked it. The pros and cons. All the mistakes from the first go-round and how not to make them again.

But the cons don't outweigh the pros with Jack. The mistakes were with Ben, not with Jack. I could spend all day comparing Jack and Ben and never find one similarity, because that is what they are—complete opposites. The boys love Jack, and Jack loves the boys. He loves my daughter. And, even though it took me a while to believe it, Jack loves me, and I love Jack, very dearly.

"I know I've asked you several times. But I wanted to ask you officially. What do you think? Will you marry me?" Jack is filling in the silence while I come up with the right words to say to him where he obviously spent a lot of time and effort planning this proposal.

"You came into my life at its lowest point. And with your help, you watched me come back to life." I reach out and take his free hand in mine. "You've stuck with me through a violent ex-husband, a controlling producer, and a combative sea urchin, a pregnancy with a baby that isn't yours, *and* you've welcomed two rambunctious boys into your house, only for you to love them and help take care of them. Am I forgetting anything?"

Jack shakes his head.

"What's the phrase? Distance makes the heart grow fonder, or something like that?" I ask. "Well, it's true. I missed you so much while I was gone. I started thinking I was the one who made the mistake." I slide from my chair and carefully kneel with him. "I did make a mistake, and I'm not going to make it again." I nod my head emphatically and take a deep breath. Peace suffuses my soul. "Yes, I will marry you."

Jack's face goes slack, and then he breaks into the largest

smile I've seen. "Really? You want to marry me?" He helps me to my feet and pulls me into his arms.

"I love you," I say into his chest. "I don't want another day to pass where we aren't together as one. And, if it's not too much to ask, I'd like to get married soon, so our daughter can have your last name, just like her mother."

Jack holds me tight and kisses me. He rolls his chin away so our foreheads are touching, using his hand behind my head to hold us together. "You just made me so happy, Isa. Can we see if this fits?"

He releases me and steps back so he can take the ring out of the haint-blue box, then slides it onto my left hand. Perfect.

"It's so pretty." I wiggle my fingers, and the diamond sparkles. "It's quite the attention-getter."

"It looks beautiful on you." Jack takes my left hand and raises it to his lips. He kisses the back of my hand before turning it over and kissing my palm. His eyes darken with desire. "We'll seal the deal properly at home. Thank you for saying yes."

"When should we tell the boys?" I want them involved; I don't ever want them to feel left out.

"Speaking of, they're so excited. They helped pick out the ring. I'm surprised they haven't spilled the beans."

"What? They did?" Looking down at my new ring, I realize I've been ambushed by the *men* in my life; at least they have great taste.

My stomach growls, and we laugh. I'd forgotten about my waffles, but now my mouth is salivating. "I'm famished."

"Let's eat, then, *fiancée*."

"I love all the hearts, *fiancé*." But I love yours the most.

EPILOGUE

November 2

THE BEACH at the Westin is dreamy. The sun is going down over the water, giving everything white or cream-colored a bluish hue, including our dresses and the sand. The beach reminds me of one of the romantic bridal magazine shoots I've been looking at for the last few weeks. From the paper luminarias partially buried in the sand to all the white peonies and blue hydrangeas decorating the chairs and the arbor where Jack and I will shortly exchange vows, everything looks perfect. The wedding planner at the Westin thought of everything, and she pulled it all together in two weeks.

Yes, it's a risk to have the wedding on my due date, but it's the only time the Westin had an opening. Besides, I went late with the boys. I'm hoping I'll go late with their sister too.

"You both look fabulous!" I'm so grateful Suzanne and Sarah are here. "Thank you, thank you, for being here." The three of us embrace in a group hug. "I can't believe I'm doing this! I hope I don't fall walking down the aisle."

"You won't fall. If you trip, we'll catch you," Sarah says as she pulls away and looks me over. "Your dress is stunning. I love that this is a 'shoes optional' event. And your 'tan lines as accessory' aesthetic is so cool."

Twirling on the balls of my bare feet, I show them my simple linen strapless dress that falls loosely over my very pregnant belly to end above my knees. I want my tan lines to show. They're for Jack. "I'm kinda going for the full 'barefoot and pregnant' theme."

"Oh my god, Isa." Sarah laughs as she fixes the straps on her airy linen dress.

"What? It's true!"

Our laughter is interrupted by Cole and Luke, who come running up with big smiles. "People are coming!" they shout. They look so adorable in their untucked white button-down shirts and khaki shorts. I flatten their cowlicks with my hand, but they spring back up.

"Have you seen Jack?" I ask the boys.

"Yep, he's inside," Cole says loudly, pointing up the sandy path.

"Are you guys excited?" Suzanne squats down to the boys' level to talk to them and tries to fix the cowlick I couldn't.

"Very!" The boys jump up and down and then run toward Jack's location.

We didn't invite many people. Just a few of Jack's employees, his friends, and his mom. The only people I knew to invite are Suzanne and Sarah, my matron and maid of honor, and Sebastian and his wife. Surprisingly, Henry arrived with Suzanne. I'm glad, of course, but we didn't know until the last minute whether he'd actually show up.

"Jack invited Lila," I inform the girls. "Or maybe the studio sent her. But I'm not worried. Jack proposed to me, and it's me he's marrying today."

"You go, girl," Sarah cheers.

"I'll take care of her if she gets too friendly with Jack," Suzanne adds. She holds her hands out to inspect her nails.

The visual of Suzanne using her manicure to defend me is simultaneously hilarious and horrifying. "I think this wedding is enough to rub her nose in, don't you think? Besides, you don't want blood all over your dress; it will ruin it."

"Yeah, I guess you're right." Suzanne huffs but puts her claws away as music starts to play and people take their seats. "We better get inside. We don't want to keep your hunk waiting."

———

WATCHING the boys walk with Ringo toward Jack standing under the flower-covered arbor, I get weepy. "I'm a little nervous," I admit. I turn to the girls on each side of me. Suzanne removes a tissue from her cleavage and fixes my eye makeup before I ruin it with tears. "I love you guys." Seeing her pull a tissue out of her cleavage makes me laugh enough for a second to forget about why I'm weepy.

"We got you," Sarah says, smiling. "It's our turn."

The string quartet begins to play a beautiful version of the wedding march. The three of us walk between the chairs set up on the beach to join Jack, the boys, and Ringo.

As soon as I'm close enough to see Jack's smiling haint-blue eyes, I immediately feel better, and I know this is right.

Jack, dressed in a white shirt and khakis like the boys, takes my hands as Sarah and Suzanne step to their places at the side. "You're beautiful, darlin'. I love the tan lines!" His words make me giggle.

Luke and Cole give me hugs. "Hi, Momma!" Cole says, then goes back to patting Ringo.

"I'm glad you showed up," I whisper to Jack. I'm still in disbelief that tonight is happening.

"There was no chance I wouldn't." Jack squeezes my hands, and the feeling of his rough fingers reminds me that I'm alive and marrying a hard-working man who loves me and my children wholeheartedly.

The officiant, Marco, clears his throat as the music stops at the end of the verse. He's wearing a light blue button-down shirt and khaki shorts, no shoes. The blue should contrast nicely with our whites, I think nonsensically.

"On this beautiful evening on St. John, we gather to witness the marriage of Isabelle Finley and Jack Avery." Jack winks while he mouths my middle name. I smile wider. He never did figure out what my middle name is.

Marco continues, but I am in such a daze, staring at Jack as the ocean reflects the sunset, that I don't hear what he's saying. I'm just staring at Jack and wondering how we got to this point. Jack squeezes my hand to bring me back to the ceremony and we say our "I do's."

"Jack, you have something you would like to say?"

Jack coughs and clears his throat. "Luke and Cole, I'd also like to say a vow to the both of you, and this comes from my heart. I promise that I will always be here for you, to support you in every step you take. I promise to always love you as my own sons because to me you are. I love you guys."

Luke jumps on Jack and hugs him. "I love you too, Jack, I mean Dad!" Jack holds him and hugs him tight. I hear a collective "aw!" from our guests.

Cole hugs Jack's leg. "I love you, Dad." Jack bends down and scoops Cole up too. The boys wrap their arms around Jack's neck, and he sniffs.

Cole lets go with one arm and taps Jack's back to soothe him. "It's okay to cry, Dad. Tears are good for you."

I didn't think I could cry more than I already was, but now I'm all-out sobbing. The love shared by these three men makes me so happy. Jack and I aren't building just a marriage—we're forming a family.

Finally, with a last set of sniffles, Jack sets the boys on their feet and they run over to Ringo.

"Do you have your rings?" Marco asks Jack. He nods and helps Luke and Cole unpack the rings from Ringo's special wedding harness, then stands back up and hands me one of the rings.

My turn to speak. I'm sure my lack of public speaking skills will become evident to everyone tonight. "I, Isabelle, take you, Jack, as my lawfully wedded husband, to have and to hold from this day forward, for better or for worse, for richer or for poorer, in sickness and in health, to love and to cherish, till death do us part, and with this ring, I pledge my love, my faithfulness, and my devotion."

I slide the platinum band onto his left ring finger and look back up to his eyes. I made it through without stumbling over the words. Now if I can just make it through the rest of the night without stumbling!

Jack makes his vow to me and then slides a platinum band onto my finger. My face hurts from smiling as Marco pronounces us legally married. My husband pulls my hand toward him while he leans to meet me. "I love you, Isa Finley Kendall," he whispers.

"I love you too, Jack Avery Kendall," I whisper back, and he kisses me in front of everyone. Our guests cheer and whistle.

I shut my eyes, blocking out everything and focusing on me and Jack in this moment. Jack's hand is at my nape, his other on the small of my back. He holds me securely as he leans me back with care and kisses me tenderly.

"Mr. and Mrs. Kendall. Kinda has a nice ring to it, huh?" Jack whispers in my ear.

"I love it," I whisper back, feeling like the corners of my mouth are at my ears.

"Forever." He kisses me again before helping me stand up.

The string quartet plays as Jack and I, hand in hand, lead everyone to the pool deck where the Westin staff members await us.

"How are ya doing?" Jack asks when he sees me cradling my stomach.

"I'm fine. She's not used to all this excitement." I give my hard belly a rub and hold on to Jack's hand. I felt tightness in my back this morning and occasionally throughout the day, but I've done my best to ignore it. This baby isn't coming today. The more I say that, the more it will be true, right?

Jack helps me into my chair, and a steaming plate is set in front of me. The chef used a maple glaze on the fish and beef, and a heart-shaped waffle accompanies each entrée. Glee at the thoughtful touch fills me, and I look up from my plate to smile at Jack. "Did you tell them to do this? Maine maple syrup and all?"

"Waffles are where it all sort of started." Jack shrugs and cuts into his waffle, then feeds me the first bite.

"Very true." I cut into my own pastry and dip the golden square into syrup before I hold it out to him. He leans in and sensuously drags the waffle from the fork. A drop of maple syrup catches on his lip, and I wipe it up with my fingertip. I pop my finger in my mouth and suck off the sweet liquid. Jack groans and shifts in his seat.

"You can get syrup all over me anytime you want." Jack winks, then bends toward me and leisurely peppers my mouth with kisses. My laugh bubbles out of me. Tonight is magical.

"I'd love to get out of here and have my way with my wife, but our guests would be disappointed," Jack says.

"I wouldn't be opposed to leaving either, but I haven't had a chance to talk with your mom. I look forward to hearing all about you when you were little." Laughter fills my voice. I'm sure Anne has plenty of stories.

A pang of sadness that my parents couldn't be here hits me, but I don't dwell on the feeling. I'm sure they'd be proud of me and how I've triumphed over difficulty. And they'd absolutely adore Jack, just like I do.

"I have to use the bathroom," Luke announces when he and Sarah stop by our table. "Aunt Sarah's taking me."

"Okay, sweetie. Are you having fun?" Luke and Cole are the only two kids here; I hope they're having a good time and staying out of trouble.

"They're keeping us on our toes," Sarah says, and they head into the Westin.

"She's here with Zeus," I whisper conspiratorially to Jack.

"Zeus? *My* Zeus? How did I miss that?"

"Yep. Turns out they hooked up at Suzanne's going-away party and exchanged numbers. They're not dating, she says, but I wonder."

"I see Suzanne is here with Mr. Suzanne," Jack says. We watch as Henry holds Suzanne's hand and whispers in her ear, making her laugh. "It looks like everything is happy in Suzanneland."

Well, happy for now.

Some of Jack's band friends set up by the pool. They were told to be on their best behavior. Absolutely no limbo contests!

"Dance with me." Jack stands and holds out his hand to either invite me to dance or help me out of my chair. I'm not sure which it is, but I take his strong hand and get to my feet. Now that I've been sitting for a while, adrenaline has stopped racing through my body and I'm feeling stiff. I make a fist and push it into the base of my spine, then lean back.

Instead of the crack I'm hoping for, I feel a pop low inside, and liquid gushes down my legs.

"Jack, I think my water just broke," I say quietly so I don't alarm anyone.

"We're having the baby? Now?"

"Looks like it. You're getting a wife and a new baby all in one day."

"I'm the luckiest man in the world!"

NOVEMBER *11*

THE RAIN HAS STARTED on the island, and sheets of water are blowing across the bay.

Zeus is making Jack work out in the rain like he's a Navy SEAL. The boys are at school, and I'm nursing BG on the sofa.

My new husband—it gives me such a thrill to say that—and I had our first fight about naming our daughter.

"It's been over a week, and you still haven't named her," Jack had said. "You can't keep calling our daughter BG." He finished changing our baby girl's diaper for the fifth time that day and handed her back to me for another meal.

"BG? What's wrong with BG? It's short for baby girl. Once the paternity test results are back, I'll feel better about giving her a name." I lifted up my shirt and opened the nursing bra. BG latched on to my nipple and started to suck. "I feel like I'm living in a Jerry Springer episode."

Jack had laughed. "I think Jerry might think this is a little over the top for his show."

"Isa?" Gabrielle calls now.

I raise a hand so she can see me where I'm lying. "I'm here!" She bustles over and hands me a big, brown envelope. "This just came for you."

"Thank you." I accept the envelope, then just stare at it. I know exactly what it is—the results of the paternity test. With a sigh, I drop the envelope on the floor and finish feeding BG.

Fed and burped, BG is a happy child. I set her down on her little bouncy chair and slide the door open to the deck where Zeus is yelling at Jack.

"How much longer?" I shout, hoping they can hear me over the noise of the rain.

"I'd give him about an hour, then he'll be on ice," Zeus says to me in a much more pleasant tone than the one he was using on Jack.

"Okay, I can wait." I smile at Zeus. I really feel bad for Jack, but he keeps doing this to himself. "I'll come back in an hour."

The next sixty minutes feel like fifteen hours.

Gabrielle watches BG while I take a quick shower. I let the warm water massage my head as I lean into the spray and think about what the contents of the envelope will mean.

If Ben is the biological father, my daughter will grow up knowing her bio dad died after attacking her mother. No mother wants that for her child.

But what are the chances that Jack is her bio dad? His surgeon had said the vasectomy reversal had failed, so Jack can't father children. We used condoms the first time we had sex, but condoms aren't entirely nonpermeable. Still, if this child turns out to be Jack's, her name's gotta be Miracle.

I'm startled when Jack opens the door to the shower and steps in.

"Hey you," he says as he puts his arms around me. "You've been in here for a while."

I rest my head on his hard chest while the water trickles between us. "I didn't realize the time. Is BG okay?"

"Gabrielle is sitting with her." Jack squeezes some shampoo onto my hair and begins to massage it into my hair. "Gabrielle said an envelope came for you. Did you open it?"

"No, I'm afraid to. I was waiting for you."

"Let's finish getting cleaned up and see what it says."

"You're always braver than me." I feel weak in my knees.

"But what if it's not what you think? Wouldn't you want to know?"

"I know it's what it says. If it can't be you, it has to be Ben." How could she be anyone else's but Ben's? I've only been with two people, Ben and Jack, and since my husband's out of the question, Ben must be the father.

"Either way, I'll love her like she's my own, just like I love the boys."

"Well, let's find out."

Jack rinses out my hair, shuts the water off, and wraps me in a towel before we step out of the glassed-in shower.

"Is it still raining outside?" I pull a dress on.

"Buckets," Jack says as he pulls on a T-shirt and some shorts. "This it?" He picks the envelope up that I left on the nightstand.

I nod as we sit on the edge of the bed.

"Ready?" Jack asks.

I take a deep breath as he slides his finger into the flap and tears it open, removing the paperwork inside.

He holds it so both of us can read it together. Jack seems impatient with all the literature at the beginning and flips through to the last page, labeled "DNA Paternity Report."

The sheet has four columns. The first is a bunch of numbers. The other columns are labeled "Mother," "Child," and "Alleged Father." The mother column is blank; we all know who she is. Me.

All the numbers in the "Child" and "Alleged Father" columns mean nothing, but at the bottom of the page is a blue box.

I start to cry. Jack is crying too.

In the blue box are two numbers. "Combined Direct Index" and "Probability of Paternity." Both numbers are ninety-nine. Jack is our daughter's father.

Jack throws his arms around me. "My mother said BG looks just me when I was born." He nuzzles my neck as he sniffles. "I didn't think much about it because I think all babies kinda look alike."

"Why didn't you tell me she said that you look like BG?"

"It just didn't mean anything at the time." He kisses my shoulder. "I thought she was just being nice in a weird way."

BG is Jack's baby. His revision must have worked, at least on one night.

"We can give her a name now." I don't let go of him. Jack needs the hugs now. "BG Kendall."

"Luke keeps calling her Charlotte after the spider." Mrs. Stackpole is reading *Charlotte's Web* to the class.

"Charlotte is my grandmother's name." Jack pulls back, his face a wreath of smiles. "It's a very nice name."

I nod. "I actually love it." I study his face. Despite the sun's weathering and the smile lines etched deeply into the corners of his eyes, Jack has a youthful air about him. He's strong and steady, traits he'll need as he raises three children with me. I love this man. "Avery. What about Avery for her middle name?"

"Avery?" Just when I thought he couldn't pull me any

closer or hug me any tighter, he does. "My middle name? Charlotte Avery?"

"Yes. Charlotte Avery Kendall." This is one of the happiest days of my life. "It's an honor to name her after her father."

"Thank you, Isa." Jack's voice is choked with emotion as he helps me to stand with him. "Let's introduce everyone to Charlotte. May she grow up to be strong and courageous, wise and perceptive, just like her mother."

I can live with that.

RECIPES

Mainer's Banana - bring the taste of the USVI to northern climates!

Combine into a cocktail shaker and shake:
- 2 oz. Banana Liquor
- 1 oz. Light Rum
- 4 oz. pineapple juice
- 1 oz. cream of coconut
- 1 oz. orange juice

Fill your favorite glass with ice and pour in rum concocktion.

- Splash of Grenadine on top (to look like a Maine sunset)

Garnish with your favorite fruits to nibble on.

Snorkling Waffles - Share often with someone who loves waffles as much as you do. (Bonus tip: use a heart shaped waffle iron)

Ingredients:
- 2 cups all-purpose flour
- 2 tablespoons sugar
- 1 tablespoon baking powder
- 1/2 teaspoon salt
- 2 large eggs
- 1 3/4 cups milk (whole or 2% for best texture)
- 1/2 cup unsalted butter, melted and cooled slightly
- 2 teaspoons vanilla extract (or more, for extra vanilla flavor)
- 1/2 teaspoon vanilla bean paste
- Cooking spray or extra melted butter for the waffle iron

The How to:

1 Preheat Your Waffle Iron: Preheat the waffle iron according to the manufacturer's instructions. (The hotter the better)

2 Mix the Dry Ingredients: In a large bowl, whisk together the flour, sugar, baking powder, and salt.

3 Combine All the Wet Ingredients: In a separate bowl, whisk together the eggs, milk, melted butter, vanilla extract, and vanilla bean paste (if using, but I recommend!).

4 Combine Wet and Dry Mixtures: Pour the wet ingredients into the dry ingredients and gently stir until just combined. Be careful not to overmix; a few lumps are okay.

5 Cook the Waffles: Lightly grease the waffle iron with cooking spray or a brush of melted butter. Pour the batter onto the hot waffle iron, using about 1/2 to 3/4 cup of batter per

waffle (depending on the size of your waffle iron). Spread the batter to the edges if needed.

6 Close and Cook: Close the waffle iron and cook according to the manufacturer's instructions, usually about 4-5 minutes, until the waffles are golden brown and crisp.

7 Carefully remove the waffles and serve immediately with your favorite Mango or real Maine maple syrup and/or extra butter!

8 Enjoy with your favorite pairing like a Mango Mimosa

**Mango Mimosa - ** Island Yum!

Ingredients:
- 1 cup or mango nectar (I use Goya in a carton)
- 1 bottle (750ml) of chilled Prosecco works well
- 1/2 cup fresh mango, diced (optional, for garnish)
- 1 tablespoon lime juice (for a citrusy twist!)
- Mango slices or mint leaves for garnish

How to:

1 Chill All Your Ingredients: Make sure both the mango juice and champagne are well chilled before making the mimosas.

2 Pour the Mango Juice: Fill each champagne flute about halfway with mango juice. If you're using lime juice, add a splash to each glass now.

3 Add Prosecco: Slowly top off each glass with champagne or sparkling wine. Pour gently to preserve the bubbles.

4 Garnish: For added flair, drop a few pieces of diced fresh mango into each glass. Garnish with a slice of mango on the rim or a sprig of mint.

5 Serve ts right away while they're still bubbly, cool and refreshing.

Mango Syrup - For your favorite retired swimmer to wipe gently off your lips.

Ingredients:
- 1 cup fresh mango, peeled and diced (about 1 large mango)
- 1 cup sugar
- 1 cup water
- 1 tablespoon lemon juice

How to:

1 Peel and dice the mango into small pieces. You should have about 1 cup of diced mango.

2 Combine All the Ingredients in a Saucepan: In a medium saucepan, combine the diced mango, sugar, and water. 3 Cook the Syrup: Over medium heat and bring the mixture to a boil, stirring occasionally to dissolve the sugar.

4 Simmer: Once it reaches a boil, reduce the heat to low and let the mixture simmer for about 10-15 minutes, The mango will become very soft and the syrup is thickened slightly.

5 Mash the Mango: Use a spoon or a potato masher to gently mash the mango pieces while they cook, This will release more flavor into the syrup.

6 Strain the Syrup: Remove the saucepan from heat and let it cool slightly. Strain the syrup through a fine-mesh sieve or cheesecloth into a bowl or jar, pressing the solids to extract as

much liquid as possible. Discard the mango pulp or save it for another use, like a smoothie.

7 Store the mango syrup in the refrigerator for up to 2 weeks.

A NOTE FROM BEATRIX

Dear Reader,

Thank you so much for going on this journey with me. I'm so grateful you took a chance on my debut novel.

Writing this novel was a labor of love, and knowing that it has found its way into your hands is a dream come true.

Your support, whether through reading, sharing, or simply holding this book, is a gift that I will never take for granted. I hope this story has touched you in some way, as you have touched my life by being a part of this adventure.

Currently, I'm working on Suzanne's story, and Sarah might have a story as well. Please keep a lookout for Isa and Jack's first Christmas together!

All my best,
Beatrix

ACKNOWLEDGMENTS

A huge thank you to my family,

Your love, support, and encouragement have been my greatest source of strength throughout this journey. Thank you for your endless patience, understanding, and for believing in me even on the days when I didn't believe in myself.

Joe, thank you for giving me the time , for cheering me on through every draft, and for always reminding me that I could do this.

To Mason, Noah and Abby. thank you for your hugs, laughter, and for being my constant reminders of what truly matters.

You have been my inspiration and my biggest fans, even though you aren't allowed to read this, this book is as much yours as it is mine. Thank you for standing by me every step of the way

I am incredibly grateful to my editor and book coach, Dayna M. Reidenouer, Your Publishing BFF, whose guidance, wisdom, and unwavering support have been instrumental in bringing this book to life. Your keen insights, meticulous attention to detail, and tireless dedication have transformed this story into something far greater than I could have ever achieved on my own.

Thank you for believing in this project from the very beginning, for challenging me to dig deeper, and for always knowing just the right words to inspire and encourage. Your expertise and passion for storytelling have not only shaped this book but have also made me a better writer.

I am truly fortunate to have had you by my side on this journey. This book would not be what it is without you, and I am forever grateful for your invaluable contributions.

A heartfelt thank you to my incredible helpers, Abby and Grace, whose sharp eyes helped polish this book into its best version. Thank you to Michael and Abby for all thier technical mumbo-jumbo. Thank you to Noah for helping with his amazing Adobe skills! And, thank you to Mason, for being a constant source of laughter throughout this journey.

And last but not least, a big thanks to my awesome Mom! Although you aren't allowed to read this book either, your endless encouragement, wisdom, and unconditional love means the world to me.

ABOUT THE AUTHOR

Beatrix Eaton is a sun-craving romance author whose debut novel, Cinnamon Bay, is dedicated to readers who love warm sea breezes, gentle waves, and female main characters who discover their inner strength when caught in quicksand on pink Caribbean beaches.

She grew up in Cambridge, Mass., then went to Maine for college and stayed. It's anyone's guess why Beatrix never moved away from the cold, but it might have had to do with the husband she met at a fraternity party. The couple has many kids and three dogs, but the dogs are the only ones who live at home full time.

Beatrix enjoys baking, U.S. history, romance, gardening, running, and lifting heavy things, not necessarily in that order. She's on Instagram @beatrixeatonwrites and shares her Wordle scores on X @thebeatrixeaton. For publication announcements and updates, follow her Amazon author page and sign up for her newsletter at https://www.BeatrixEaton.com.

NOTES

Made in the USA
Las Vegas, NV
07 January 2025

15999279R00184